SNOOSER

THE ADVENTURES OF LOGGER JED LASAL

DAN LAFRANCE

Tellwell Talent
www.tellwell.ca

ISBN
978-1-77302-023-5 (Paperback)
978-1-77302-024-2 (eBook)

TABLE OF CONTENTS

DEDICATION

This book is dedicated to my wife and soul partner, Cathie. It's hard to believe, it's been over fifty years since I first saw this skinny young girl in Duncan.

"May the adventure never end!"

PREFACE

This book will be the first in the Snooser series. Snooser is pronounced "sn-oo-ser(sir)," and is an old logging term for a logger. It is explained within the book how the loggers gained this most prestigious nickname.

I would like folks to know that this book is not just about logging. Although there is plenty of action-packed logging within these pages, there are many other "after work" things that happen in everyday life that most people will be able to relate to. Even though Snooser is a fictional book, I have loosely based all the material on actual events that have taken place in BC and Canada. The logging... is as real as it gets! I lived it and without a doubt, I understand logging as a logger. I will only drop one hint here, in Chapter Seven Long, I am the young fella that was badly hurt and almost died. The logger language I used is authentic and still used in the logging camps and communities on the BC coast. To not have written the book this way would only have been a disservice to all loggers and people within this most colourful forestry industry.

So please, enjoy these adventures and try and figure out who the characters are and where the events took place. The characters are well known, but as the old saying goes, all the names have been changed, except one.

Thank you,
Dan LaFrance
www.rambleology.com

ACKNOWLEDGEMENTS

I would first like to thank Kate Gilgan. Her guidance and knowledge during the final edit of this novel have not only been a great learning and valuable experience, but she also has a knack for making it fun. When I didn't want to make changes, in good'ol Kate fashion, she would explain the professional value most patiently and kindly that would ultimately convince me it was the right thing to do. However that being said, the most rewarding thing to come out of working with Kate, has been the development of a strong friendship that will inevitably last a lifetime. And that my good friends, is something that no price can be put on.

A big part of this novel has to do with aboriginal mystical legends, which have been handed down through oral history for many generations. I am very fortunate to be a part of Max Chickite's family. Our son Cody is married to Max's daughter, Jessica. They have given us two wonderful grandchildren. When I asked Max for permission to use his carving for the front cover of this novel, he graciously and without hesitation said yes. Both Max and Jess have over the years explained to me the legends of the Bakwus' and Tsonokwa, as they know them. It gave me great satisfaction to incorporat these mystical aboriginal beings throughout the story. Even though I am aboriginal, these creatures are not a part of my oral history. But after bringing these mystical creatures alive throughout the book, I now understand why Max and Jess are so passionate and protective about their ancestors and culture. Thanks Max. Thanks Jess. I love you both.

Cathie, Josh, and Cody. What can I say? None of this book and future books in this series would have been possible if you hadn't supported me in my rambling ways. To say it was an adventure is an understatement at best. You three rambled along with me no matter where or in what direction I went, in search of adventure. Not once did I hear a complaint when I uprooted you from where we were and off we went to another place, and adventure. So thank you, I couldn't ask for a better family. You are the reason my life is complete.

FOREWORD

It is a most exquisite quest - to write a book. For all the challenges and triumphs a writer experiences throughout each book's creation, it is often the final stages that present the greatest challenges and triumphs. And that moment when the writer meets with the satisfaction of knowing that the story has been fully revealed and . . . they must now turn their work over to someone else. Editors and publishers operate outside the realm of magnificent muse and inspired wordsmithing. They foist upon the writer phrases like change, correct and redo. They talk of uninspired elements like misplaced modifiers, verb tense and past participles. It is no small wonder that most writers cringe at the unavoidable act of inviting an editor into the sacred space of their writing.

I was half a world away when Dan emailed me to ask if I would take on the most important task to edit his manuscript. At the time, my husband and I and our two youngest children had departed Canada, where we had been living aboard a sailboat, and were now living in Bali, Indonesia. And it was there that I sat down to begin reading the adventures of Jed LaSal and was promptly and mightily transported from the humid tropical beaches of Indonesia to the majestic wilds of British Columbia's west coast. In Dan's story, I met the spirit of my grandfather and the rugged men of his time who worked in the woods alongside him. I met the spirit of my great-grandmother and the matriarchs of her Aboriginal sisters whose wisdom infuses the mystic souls of Elders in nations throughout this land. I met the spirit of every romantic fool - myself included, who stumbled upon the magic of love and dared to dance with the promise of hearts afire. And I met the spirit of adventure and intrigue that compels inquisitive wanderers who live a life beyond the limits of ordinary, of normal, of routine and expected. Dan and his wife Cathie are just two such people. They live life with adventurous artistry that inspires and compels others to investigate the joys awaiting the curious and the bold. Dan has captured this very spirit in the story you are about to discover.

Snooser is the best sort of book an editor can be invited to participate in - the sort whose story flows and unfurls to carry the reader from one page to the next, cheering and eager for each new chapter. Dan's work is an important and rewarding piece of British Columbia coastal historical fiction. The story before you will most certainly carry you forth into another time and place and your spirit will surely thank you for this enduring and endearing read.

CHAPTER 1

Root Wad

"Go a-head on the sonofawhore!" Roared the snarly old hooktender as he made his way down from the back end. "Stant! You're' not gettin enough goddamn logs to keep a fuckin' wood stove goin', so ya better get your ass in gear!" bellowed Larson, putting into lively logging words a riggin'-slingers worst nightmare."

"Come on, Jed LaSal, wake up!" I heard my wife say as she gently shook my shoulder.

"Just because you're retired doesn't mean you can snooze away the rest of your life," she added teasingly.

"Damn rights. I was dreaming about my first days at camp three – seems I can't leave logging behind, even in my sleep. Where the hell's Beav? He was going to be here over an hour ago," I ask. "Glad you bought this lazy chair when I hung up my caulk boots, dear. It feels good to have the odd afternoon siesta. It gets my motor revved up again," I mumble to my wife of forty-six years.

"Jed," She softly spoke. "It's an easy chair, not a lazy chair."

"Call it what you want hon, I'll still call it a lazy chair," I declared as I headed for the veranda and some fresh air.

I leaned on the railing and drank in the spectacular view looking down Cowichan Lake with the snow capped mountains in the background. I could not help but think to myself, I'm glad to be out of the woods, although I will miss it. It had been only a week since my retirement and I had to adjust to life on easy street, as once again, Gen and I will be off on other adventures.

The first time I met Genevieve Delorme, she was a skinny fourteen-year-old girl with the prettiest eyes and friendliest smile and lived in the community of Duncan in the Cowichan Valley. Me? Well I was not much older at seventeen and lived in Lake Cowichan or the Foot as most of us from there affectionately call it.

By the time I met Genevieve I had been working as a logger for two years and was damn proud of it. Being not interested in going to school, my parents said, "No school, it's the beads for you." Setting beads or chokers was the entry level job in the logging industry. I think in the back of their minds they were hoping that a taste of hard work on a side hill would cure me, sending me back to school. Little did they know, and for that matter, me either, that working out in the fresh air on a side hill would have the opposite effect. I was destined to live the rough and tumble life of a snooser. Loggers are notoriously famous for chewing, Copenhagen chewing tobacco. And over the years logger language evolved to include many terms that defined what they did on the job and who they were. Snooser is an old logging term for a logger.

Poking her head out the sliding glass door, Gen informed me, "Beav just drove up. He might need a hand."

I headed out to greet him. "Hey son, how's it goin'?"

"Not bad, how bout you? Has it hit home yet that you can toss your caulk boots away?"

"They're in too good of shape to toss son. Besides, I can use them on the trapline or getting firewood. What are we going to do with your gear?"

"Let's leave it in the truck, I don't want to pack it any more then I have to when we load the boat down at the dock."

With my arm draped across his back, I firmly squeezed his strong shoulder. "Okay son, let's go inside, your mother has got the coffee and snacks out for us. This is going to be a great trip over to the trapline, isn't it?"

"Sure is Dad. It's been a long time since we spent some time together, out on the line."

As usual, the coffee and snacks were going down great and it wasn't long before the conversation turned toward our next little adventure, the trip up to our trapline at the head of Knights Inlet. It promised to be a great place to start to put our life of adventurers down on paper. Our daughter-in-law, Beav's wife Jess, is a writer and is going to help me with my writing, assembling forty-six years of rambling.

There are only two ways to get to the head of Knights: you can fly or you can go by boat. We have gone both ways; however, with the downturn in the fishing industry, there has been an abundance of X-commercial fishing vessels for sale on the coast. Subsequently, it didn't take us long to find the right vessel that would be more than adequate for these excursions to our getaway.

The drive up Vancouver Island was uneventful. With the new highway it doesn't take very long to get to Port McNeill, where the boat is docked.

She's a forty-five foot wooden X-Troller, built in the late sixties, sound as a drum, seaworthy, and we renamed her "Voyageur." Having most of the latest and greatest navigational gadgets, we felt comfortable going anywhere on the coast. However, as with most waterways on the unpredictable west coast of British Columbia, you are better off to err on the side of caution. That way you'll maker'er back home to go out another day.

We finished loading the boat with our gear, untied her and headed out.

We had one more stop to make. It was a short but quick run to get fuel and running with the tide made short work of it. I eased Voyageur into the fuel dock at Alert Bay. Both Gen and Beav jumped to the dock with lines in hand, ready to tie up our vessel. We needed a full tank and the spare jugs filled before we headed up Knights Inlet. After all the years of boat travel up that Inlet there still is no place to buy fuel.

Alert Bay hasn't changed much over the years. If anything, it has gotten smaller. Mainly populated by the First Nations people and with not much for work on the Island to keep the young people there, most move on to brighter lights to make a living.

The upside of this is that it has retained its small west coast community feel to it – steeped in their culture.

"Hey Bill, how the hell are ya. I see you are still selling old watered down diesel that you got from some worn out beached boat!" I teased, opening the old rickety door into his dimly lit office.

"What-da-ya say, num-nuts?" Bill barks back. "You still trying to be a boat Captain? Watered down diesel? Hell!

How would an old broken down faller like you know the difference anyway!"

Bill Williams spent all of his life as a seine boat owner and captain. There's not a place on the coast of British Columbia that he has not piloted his boat or fished. Being First Nations, Bill was born and raised in Alert Bay. So, like most of the fellas from there, he was destined to fish from the day he was born. A man of about five foot seven, with a big barrel chest, and arms and hands the size of two normal men. I still tease him that, he, like his ancestors, was born to paddle a canoe not captain a seine boat. As long as I have known Bill, around thirty years, he has always been a man of few words. Soft spoken and gentle, he is forever the first to lend a hand when one is needed.

It still seems odd to see him at the fuel dock instead of up in the wheelhouse of his beloved seine boat.

"What's the weather and conditions like up Knights these days, Bill?"

"Well the winter southeast flow has changed and we are getting the usual summer outflows, late in the afternoon. So you should have calm motor 'in up the inlet most of the day. But remember, Knights can be unpredictable and there are not many places to run for shelter. With the heavy snow this winter, the mountains are still covered with deep snow, so the air cools faster, Jed, and that means more wind coming down the inlet earlier in the day. Keep your eyes on the mountaintops around Glacier Bay. If there are clouds covering the peaks, you can bet you will be in for an early wind. It might be a good idea to drop the anchor at The Bay and spend the night."

Even though we are anxious to get to our little piece of paradise, how could I not heed the advice coming from Bill? After all, he knows these waters better than anyone I know.

The air had an organic quality to it, seemingly untouched by the hand of man. The water, emerald in colour, glistened in the early morning sun as we were being guided into the mouth of Knights Inlet by the ever-present white-sided dolphins. Companions, entertainers, and comforters, one always feels safe for some reason when they are present. These acrobats of the sea dodged back and forth and up and down in front of the bow as they kept ahead of the boat with perceptible ease.

It never ceases to amaze me - the dexterity and uncanny ability these critters of the sea have as they effortlessly pilot us into the mouth of this wild fjord. When at the helm I almost become transfixed on them, wondering what it would be like to be that carefree.

But then I have experienced many things throughout my life, so in a small way, just maybe I've been like those critters, wandering with a purpose in search of new and carefree places to ramble.

"It's going to be a great day to head up the inlet, Gen. The weather looks fine and the water is calm. Would you make me a cup of tea, hon? Hey Beav, when's Jess scheduled to fly into our cabin?" I said while settling into the rhythm of the Voyager.

"I'm not sure what her plans are Dad, but she said she will call us on the marine radio by the end of the day."

I sipped on my mid-morning cup of tea and noticed the wildlife seemed to be quite active. The sea birds were busy feeding and soaring about. I couldn't help but wonder if a storm was on the way. The one thing about the west coast: if you wait five minutes the weather will change and paying attention to the wildlife will give you a good indication of what's going on. Planning to make Glacier Bay before lunch would make the rest of the trip up the inlet a lot shorter, and with the tide in our favour would be faster as well. If the weather turns foul we could at least spend the night on the hook within this pristine bay.

Rounding Protection Island, the wind seemed to pick up a bit from the northwest. Being an outflow wind they are unpredictable and cold. Indian legends say that Protection Island was where the First Nations people defended the Knight Inlet area. Worthy of the legend, some elders say that the uncharacteristic red sand on the beaches is from the blood of ancient invaders. The cave on the southeast side that affords the best view is knee deep with clam shells where sentinels stood guard. Every time I have been by this Island there is an inexplicable sensation that someone or something is watching me. So once passed the Island I always take a look back to see if a sentinel is standing guard. These oral aboriginal legends that have been passed down from generation to generation are quintessential within any aboriginal village and are an integral part of the rich and diverse culture on the coast.

"Hey dad, looks like we could be in for some wind," Said Beav as he came into the wheelhouse. "Ya, we could be in for a rough ride until we make it to the bay. Maybe you should go check the hatches and windows? I wouldn't want to make the same mistakes I made a couple of years back when a big storm hit us up on Granville Channel."

We were now steadfast on our way to Glacier Bay, but had at least a couple of hours of bucking the ever-increasing wind and waves. As blustery weather comes down the ninety-mile long narrow fjord it picks up extremely fast, building a sea that would rival any open water on the west side of Vancouver Island.

The black wall of wind, rain, and heavy seas that we now faced seemed unusually menacing. And it was coming down the Inlet fast. The Voyager is a very seaworthy vessel, however, with any boat there are limits.

The storm and seas were building rapidly. The rain and wind pounded our vessel. As the bow came down on the backside of these now huge waves the water came up and over the top as we smashed into the next wave, ready to climb up the face.

With every wave the momentum was building, sending more and more water over the bow as we sliced into every breaker. For now the Voyager was handling'er well if it doesn't get worse we'll make'er through!

The further we plunged up the inlet, the narrower it became. Precipitous rock walls and bluffs that stopped abruptly at the water's edge gave the giant waves a soundboard to rebound off, increasing the already and ever growing surf. The sea gained such power and ferocity, one would think that a force from the bowels of the earth were sending a signal. Wind, rain and fear were now constant companions, which added to our escalating anxieties.

"Gen, you and Beav get your survival suits and bring mine. Hopefully we won't need them, but it's better to be safe than sorry," I assiduously hollered. This was not the first time over the years I had given that order.

"Beav get your suit on then grab the helm. I've got to put this suit on."

While exploring the waters of the coast I have had my share of scary moments; nevertheless, I have never had to abandon any of the vessel's I have owned. However, like they say, there is a first time for everything.

While I struggled to put on my survival suit, Beav screamed, "Root wad."

CHAPTER 2

Close Call

Instinctively, and with the speed of an Olympic sprinter, I lunged towards the helm. Beav batted the sea and ever growing wind. I grabbed the helm and we both pulled hard to the right. Root wads and other floating debris are the curse of the sea for mariners. For the most part, keeping a watchful eye, you can spot drifting rubble easily. Some are waterlogged and half submerged. Those are the ones that create havoc for the unwary boater. With the combination of a vicious storm and a marauding root wad bearing down on us, things were taking a turn for the worse.

"Keep pulling son. We've got to miss that fuckin' root," I expressed as we tussled with the helm. We needed to desperately try and get around that ominous obstacle that had the potential to tear a hole in our vessel – sending it and possibly us to an untimely grave at the bottom of the ocean.

Climbing the face of an unusually large powerful wave, both Beav and I were straining against the pressure and force being exerted on our now, what seemed like, little boat. Suddenly and unexpectedly, with a crack, the helm broke free, sending us violently to the floor on the other side of the wheelhouse.

"Sonofabitch! The steering cable must have broke!" I hollered.

I grabbed the windowsill and pulled myself up and on my feet.

There was no time to dilly-dally around. We were now at the mercy of the sea, the storm, and powers beyond our universe. This scene has played out many times on the coast. Those powers of fate are, at times, in favour of some. Let's hope they shine on us today.

Without steering we are doomed. Somehow it had to be fixed!

"Beav, get on the radio and let anyone know our fixed position. I'm going down below to see what I can do to get our steering back."

As I was making my way through the wheelhouse I met Gen in the doorway. "Better stay here and brace yourself, we're going to hit a root and our steering is gone!" I said to her with a concerned look that she has seen a number of times. By the look on her face she knew what might lie ahead.

"Hang on! It's going to hit!" screeched Beav.

We braced for the impact and nobody spoke a word. Lost in our thoughts, I'm sure that my family wondered what was coming next and expected the worst. It's times like this that words are insignificant. I have to admit though some of my thoughts were with our eldest son Lloyd.

Lloyd would be at home with his family, probably watching a little TV. Following in my footsteps he is a good faller, farrier, and a great family man. Our daughter-in-law Hazel and two grandkids Lynn and Rick, are all that a man could ask for and then some.

It's interesting how a person's mind works at a time like this. Everything seemed surreal and moved in slow motion. I glanced over at Beav and noticed a faraway look on his lean strong face as he gritted his teeth. Quick with his feet and mind, and strong, not much rattles him. I'm glad he is here to help us get out of this predicament. Beav slowly turned his head and our eyes met. A smile came across his face reminding me of the first time I took my little boy hunting. He nodded his head without a word. I knew what he was thinking. My gaze now turned to Gen. Tears ran down her face.

She mouths, "I love you."

I gave her a wink and said, "Don't worry hon, we'll make'er."

It hit us with the force of a freight train. The root wad and vessel collided, which knocked all of us to the floor.

Next came the alarmingly gruesome sound of wood breaking and water crashing all around us. I thought this is it. We're going down! The boat now listed heavily and we were taking on water, fast. Dreamlike, the next few seconds seemed like an eternity with everything in slow motion. I felt as though I could not move, frozen in time, heading into a watery abyss. In this unmoving state I hollered at Gen and Beav, but my words were slow with no purpose. I tried desperately to reach out and grab a hold of them but my arms felt heavy and unmoving. So I lay there motionless, a victim of intense fear.

I was jolted out of my surreal trance by the second hit we took. Something was hung-up on the side of the boat and we were being dragged around in the other direction which righted the floundering vessel.

I lunged towards the hatch that lead to the engine room below. I cried out, "Keep trying to contact someone on the radio!"

Beaver stood there with his hands on the helm and throttle. He instinctively knew that I was going to try and fix the steering.

Gen regained her steadfast composure, was on the radio sending out maydays hoping that someone out in radio land would hear her pleas and send help.

We were not out of the woods yet but at least everyone had their wits about them which increased our chances of surviving this goddamn ordeal.

Floundering in the ominously angry and fearsome sea, there was no time for reflection as we were being pushed towards the abrupt rocks on shore. I had to react quickly and decisively for surely our beloved boat would be smashed to bits in the ever-increasing monstrous surf that pounded the shoreline.

I fought my way through the debris in the engine room, which took a little finesse. The junk laden floorboards were wet with sea water and diesel fuel. Shit, how do I get into these situations, I thought to myself as I squeezed in between the engine and the panel that housed the steering. With some luck I would locate the break promptly and in no time flat repair it before we had to take an unwanted and troublesome swim.

Without hesitation I punched a hole in the thin panel. I reached through the hole and started tearing the boards out like a mad man. There was no time to be fancy. Spotting the split cable I tried to tie the ends together, but no luck the ends won't reach! Worming my way back out I looked for anything that could couple the ends together. The jumper cables hung next to the engine and being made of heavy gauge wire might hold if I tied them properly. I had no choice as time was not on our side.

Splicing or joining metal cables is part of a logger's job and, without exception, I had learned the craft. At a time like this it served me well, however, working as a faller for years it had been a long time since I had worked with cables.

I crawled back behind the engine and positioned myself to fix the torn cable. With both ends in tatters, it took a little ingenuity. I started by tying an overhand loop in both ends that way to put in a cat's paw. Instinctively, I threaded one end of the jumper cable up and through the loop and circled it down around and back up – finishing the cat's paw by threading the end through and in between the loop and bite of the jumper cable. With one mighty tug I tightened and tied off the other broken end. We now had steering!

Gen stood over the hatch. When our eyes met, there was no need for words. She turned at once and hollered to Beav, "It's fixed!"

Impulsively, Beav pushed the throttle full on and cranked the wheel hard to starboard with not a minute to spare!

I stood there for a moment and made sure my handy work would hold. I couldn't help but think to myself, "I'm glad that old prick of a hooktender Larson showed me how to put in a cat's paw." Ollie Larson, long gone up to the big logging camp in the sky, must have been looking down at me today, smiling.

With the splice holding we now had some control of the vessel and, with that relief, I made my way back up to the wheelhouse.

I watched my son and knew he could handle piloting the boat across the inlet to a little cove that might afford some protection against this storm. We were now running with the wind, quartering the waves as we made our way to safety. I kept a watchful eye out for more floating debris in the water, as we could not afford to take another hit.

"Beav, head over to the other side of the cove, by that big spruce tree on the shore. There is a good anchorage in that corner of the cove and we can check out the damage to our boat," I said to my son.

"OK Dad, I'll nose her in as close to shore as I can," Beav said with a now relaxed look on his face.

"If I remember correctly, the beach drops off quickly here and I think it is about thirty to forty feet deep so we should have a solid anchor," I said as I headed for the door leading out to the bow for a closer look.

The anchor grabbed the bottom like a thirsty Frenchman grabs his beloved red wine. Only then did I really feel safe. We made it! What a relief!

"Gen, where's the bottle of whisky? I need a shot after that ordeal."

"It's under the cupboard where we keep our old charts," Gen reminded me.

Rummaging around I found what I was looking for.

I spun the top off the cheap Five Star whisky and took a long and well needed pull on the fiery amber liquid. Finished, I wiped my mouth with the sleeve of my shirt and looked over Gen and gestured to her if she wanted a sip.

"Not in your life, Jed. You know that I never touch that rot gut."

"Well I'm not that crazy about it either. But I forgot to bring some beer, and after what we have just been through, I really need a drink. Say, did you ever get out on the radio?"

"No, it must have been the storm. Someone may have heard the mayday, but if they were trying to contact us I couldn't hear them. Hopefully no one is on the way to look for us."

"Good point hon, why don't you go try and get out again? If someone is searching for us, it's best we let them know that we are OK and where we are anchored."

"If I can get through you might want to talk to someone about a steering cable. I guess we can't leave here until we get a new one put on. Maybe there is a fisherman in the area or close by? With any luck someone will have a cable on board. That would be a stroke of good luck Jed."

I inspected our vessel for damage and found weathered the hit well. Seems there was some minor damage, all superficial. What luck!

"Hey hon, I just had a thought. Let's see if we can get a hold of Jess. She is flying this way tomorrow so if we are lucky enough to reach her tonight she can bring the cable we need."

CHAPTER 3

Bakwus'

We were still in bed when the roar of the plane buzzed low over the boat and woke us up.

"Damn that Popeye! He does that every chance he gets," Beav groggily mumbled as he pulled on his pants. "Mom, I'll put the coffee on if you want to give Dad a hand, he's already out on the deck pacing back and forth."

Genevieve looked up at Beav with a pleasant grin. "Those two old buzzards are cut from the same cloth - one always trying to outdo the other. Ya, I'll go give him a hand. Say, while you're putting the coffee on, why don't you grab the bacon out of the fridge and start breakfast."

I stood on the deck at the bow and watched the floatplane make its final approach. The wind was now light and came from the east. The morning sun illuminated and reflected off the fixed-wing craft as it banked in and around the small cove. Like many times in the past, I watched Ray's approach for a landing. It was like watching a ballerina on stage. We watched the Cessna 185 and heard the constant drone of the engine which echoed through the mountains and off the water and scattered all the gulls and divers from their constant search for food. Reminiscent of a loon gliding in for a pinpointed landing, Ray defied gravity, gave the aircraft a little throttle which held the plane a few feet off the water as he pinpointed his spot to put her down. This old man of the sky taxied up to our boat. The long time bush pilot eased the 185 softly and straight onto the port side of our boat. Ray flung the door open and stepped onto the floats and smiled. The grey-haired grizzled pilot always wore monkey-face work gloves and a tattered blue-jean jacket that he wore with the sleeves rolled up, which revealed his tattoos. I am sure many clients were wary about flying with him. But rest assured there was no better pilot around!

"Popeye! You old piss-ant, how's she goin'?" I teased my friend for many years.

I thought back to when I first met Ray Burns. I was twenty-five years old and guided for big game animals up in northern B.C., for an Outfitter by the name of Ervin O'Dell. One of the hunting camps consisted of nothing more than an old trapper's cabin and a few wall-tents. Situated northwest and about an hours' flying time from the community of Telegraph Creek, the landing strip was the big meadow where we grazed the horses.

Halfway through the hunting season, Gen became sick one evening with a very high fever and excruciating pain in her back. By morning her condition was not improving, so I called the plane base in Telegraph Creek. My message was simple, we have a very sick woman at our camp that needs to see a doctor without delay.

Immediately, a voice came on the radio, "Highland ranch this is Popeye. I'm in the area looking for that wild man of the woods, The Bakwus'. The cops want to find him. I guess the old German trapper is missing. Some folks are wondering if that wild bastard killed him. I'll be there in ten minutes."

Popeye buzzed the cabin to let us know he was landing. I watched the 180 tail-dragger circle around to approach from the far end of the meadow. The plane skimmed the pine trees and dropped into the field abruptly and neatly. The 180 bounced wildly down this makeshift airstrip. The big balloon tires handled the roughness of the unlikely landing field easily. While the navigator spun the plane around under power to ready it for the takeoff, I noticed that the tail wheel had broken off during the landing. The plane had hardly come to a stop when out jumped the pilot, with a hammer and piece of pipe in hand.

"Lift on the fuselage, will ya. I've got to hammer in this pipe," said this very unordinary looking man of the skies.

With one mighty blow, the pipe was tightly put where the tail wheel once was.

The pilot immediately turned and trusted his hand out to greet me. "Hi. My name is Popeye. ome people call Ray."

"Nice to meet ya, Ray, I mean uh, Popeye. I'm Jed LaSal. Can you take off without a tail wheel?"

Ray stood there in a worn-out sleeveless blue-jean jacket, with pants that matched, and monkey-face gloves on his hands. Popeye reached up and adjusted his equally worn out greasy hat, as a smile beamed across his face. "Its' good for a couple of take-offs and landings in these parts, LaSal."

***

Ray balanced on the floats ready to buffer his beloved aircraft from hitting our boat and bantered back, "LaSal, ya never learn do ya. Good thing I live around these parts to save your ass. How many times is it now? When are you going to stay home in that new rocking chair Gen bought ya?"

I was glad to have my aged friend bring me both the parts I needed to fix our steering and to fly Jess here to our boat. Ray was ten or twelve years older than me and was in excellent shape for a man his age. Flying every day, he and his sons now own the charter service out of Kelsey Bay, of which he presides over like a cantankerous old emperor. One thing is for certain - you can always count on and trust them. There is no substitute for the kind of combined experience their family has in the skies.

"Hi, Dad," cuts in Jess. "Nice to see you. I hear you guys had quite a day yesterday?"

"Ya, it was a little nerve-racking for a while. I guess that demon was after us again. One of these days he just may get us," I tell our daughter-in-law as she reaches out to hug me.

Reg and Jess have been together since they were teenagers. Scarcely spending a day apart, they are partners in a very successful Eco Tour Company based out of Campbell River.

As well, Jess is a successful writer. Together, they have given Gen and me two wonderful grandkids. Toby and Melissa are a chip off the old block, always on the look for adventure. But then again, they were born into it.

Beav and Jess enjoyed a long hug. "Was it kind of scary?" asks Jess. "Naw, Dad and I have been through this kind of stuff before. You really don't have time to think about it much, Jess."

"Hey LaSal, you got the bacon and eggs on? I need to put the nose bag on," asks Ray.

"Popeye, you old coot, I've already had my breakfast," I said to my friend. "I had a contract faller's breakfast!"

Popeye frowned and asked, "What the hell kind of breakfast is that?"

I tried to keep a straight face and jokingly poked fun at him. "It's a piss and look around!"

Gen stuck her head out the window to let us know that breakfast was on the table. Bacon, eggs, hash browns, and stacks of buttered toast with Gen's homemade Saskatoon berry jam was the order of the day. Beaver slid his chair back from the table in the galley and reminded us, "It's going to be a long day, so let's fix the steering and get underway."

The Cessna 185 lifted off the water and circled around. It flew low and over us. Popeye was off to pick up some Americans for a flying trip into the Mt. Waddington area. I waved back at him as I watched the anchor seat into the winch. We were now on our way.

We set a course for the head of Knights Inlet and I settled into the comfortable captain's chair piloting the Voyager out of the cove when Jess came into the wheelhouse.

"Hey, Dad, why don't we start putting your early years of logging on tape? Let's start from when you first went to work at Nitinat," Jess said, putting the recorder down next to me.

"OK, let me get my notes. Over the last little while I have been putting a pencil to the paper, jotting down some of my early days living at the Foot and when I started logging.

"Hey hon, would you dig out the notes I brought? Jess wants to get started putting material together."

My wife slid in next to me and handed me the notes I have been working on. She had a witty look on her face. "Ya know Jed, I have been doing some thinking this morning. Maybe it's time for us to sell out here and head back up into the interior. We could get a good buck for our place, the trapline here and this boat. We could probably find a good trapline up north. Who knows, perhaps we could build a place on a nice secluded lake. Jed, I'm getting kind of tired of all this traveling back and forth to this trapline. Not to mention the incident we just went through, but you know we are not getting any younger. Wouldn't it be nice to live fulltime on a line somewhere up north?"

I sat and looked out and over the helm and kept my thoughts to myself. For that matter, none of us in the wheelhouse spoke a word. After a couple more sips of my coffee, I slowly looked over to my wife of many years and smiled.

"Gen, over the years you have not made many requests and you have followed me wherever I took a notion to go. Believe it or not, I was thinking along the same lines as you. I just didn't want to ask you to pick up and move again. I too think it may be a good idea to sell out and live on a line up north. So when we get back home let's put our house, trapline, and boat on the market. I'll bet we can find a good place around the Kamloops area. That way we would not be that far away. What do ya say?"

Without a word, Genevieve stood up and turned and put her arms around me. There was no need to say anything. I knew from her firm hug that she approved.

"OK, you guys, let's get this show on the road," piped in Jess. "If you want to start to put together a manuscript we had better begin rolling the tape."

The morning was calm, the air was crisp and clear, and there was a scurry of activity all around us on the water. Sea birds of every size and description scurried in every direction with the ever pursuit of a meal. The sea, now that the storm was over, was alive with activity.

I was in what I call the zone, trance-like, while I watched the goings-on and piloted my beloved Voyager up Knights Inlet. I liked being in this state as it was a way for me to center myself after what happened yesterday. I guess it goes without saying that we don't need any more mishaps like that for a while, if ever.

Jess tugged on my arm. "Dad, I know you were lost in your thoughts but let's put them thoughts on tape."

"Ya know guys, let's have a family meeting. I've been thinkin, maybe it's not such a good idea to head up the inlet right now. I understand that we are all looking forward to spending a couple of weeks on the trapline, but that storm yesterday was weird. It was almost as if something else from beyond was trying to take us into another world."

"Ah come on Dad, don't go giving' us that supernatural baloney again!" interrupts Beav, with a goofy look on his face.

"LaSal, you old fart, how come every time something like this happens to us, you blame it on the Bakwus'?" Genevieve wily asked.

"Ya, Jed?" Jess joins in. "Beav has told me that you are superstitious. The Elders have told us about these ancient Indian legends. They believe they are true. Do you?"

"Superstitious my ass. Beaver knows damn well what I am talking about. Don't ya son? He just won't come out and say it as I do. Are we all in favour of turning this boat around and heading home? If so, let's head back."

With a nod from everyone, I cranked the helm and pointed the Voyager back to the dock. The seas were calm and the tide in our favour, so in a matter of a few hours, we'd be at the dock in Port McNeill.

I spoke up. "I'll tell you something. The north is full of folklore, none more mysterious than the wild man of the woods. The aboriginal people call him Bakwus' and avoid him – fearing his crooked spirit. The Bakwus', they say, can take on many forms, good or bad. And when you least expect it, the Bakwus' will show up.

CHAPTER 4

Rogue Orca

We rounded Seagull Point and were now on the home stretch. Jess stood next to me. She enjoyed the view from the wheelhouse.

"Now that we're not going up to the trapline, Jed, Beav and I thought we might stop at Minstrel Island for the night. It would be nice to visit some of my relatives who I haven't seen in a while. In the morning we can catch a ride into McNeill."

"Okay, Gen and I would stopover as well but by the way she is talking about a move up to Kamloops area, we've got our work cut out for us for the next while."

We pulled up to the dock at Minstrel Island and we stopped briefly, to let Beav and Jess off.

"See ya in a day or two," Gen said with a big wave goodbye. "Jed let's head up through Blackfish Sound on our way to Port McNeill. There is always a chance to see the killer whales."

"Ya, that's a good idea, maybe we'll jig some cod off the end of Clam Island. It would be nice to have a feed of cod."

The one thing about Blackfish sound, one never knows what they'll see. It is teeming with all kinds of wildlife, some of which present themselves only at certain times of the year. With the salmon runs in full swing, the Orca's are usually on the hunt.

Gen sat out on the front deck and pointed to the starboard side, "Look, Jed, over by Red Cove, there's a pod of Killer Whales," she said as she comes into the wheelhouse.

I cut the engine and we marveled at these amazing creatures. This was a large pod. The dominant bull riding herd just off and to the side of the rest of the pod was magnificent.

"I was having a cup of tea, the other day, with Jess's old Auntie and she told me that in her culture when a Hereditary Chief dies he comes back as an orca. She said that depending on how he lived his life, how he treated his people, will dictate how he comes back. If he treated his people well, then he will be a part of a pod. If he didn't treat his people well, he was destined to spend his days as a rogue killer whale and destined to struggle to survive. I was told that rogue orcas are cunning and untrustworthy and keep their distance from pods. But they are never far away from the main pod."

I flashed up the Voyager and we are once again on our way. We savored a moment.

"Get me the binoculars, hon! I want to have a look at Dreary Inlet, it has a strange fog in it."

"Yes, and there is an orca towards the eastern shore. See it, Jed?"

"Yes, I see it. Must be one of them rogue bulls or maybe it's from the pod we just watched over at Red Cove."

"I don't think it is. I believe it is a rogue," my wife said as she looked through the binoculars. "It's coming this way Jed!" she exclaimed.

"Not to worry, we have a big enough boat. There won't be any problems. Besides, Have you ever heard of an orca sinking a boat?"

"I guess you're right, but all the same it makes me nervous."

"That sure is a strange fog. Does it seem a different color to you?" I said.

Gen nodded without taking the binoculars away from her eyes. "It has a greenish-blue tinge to it," she said.

This menacing fog was mysteriously on the move. It headed out of the inlet and straight towards our boat. The rogue killer whale was circling in front of us and flipped his broad tail against the water, which sent plumes of spray high up into the air. This orca, his slick body sliced through the sea with ease and hesitated close on our port side. One of his big eyes was fixed on us and gave us the chills. Silently and quick as he appeared, he disappeared into the dark foamy depths beneath us. Then like a ghost from the deep he pierced the surface and projected himself completely out of the water. The beast twisted in the air and hit the water with a mighty splash and sent water everywhere. This scoundrel orca was headed straight at us. His huge dorsal fin looked like a battering ram. Suddenly and without a second to spare he submerged under the boat, only to return and stop in front. The orca now stood straight up and down with his head and part of his body raised from the surface of the sea.

"Jed he is acting like he wants us to follow him. That's weird!" Gen said with a quivering voice.

I did not say a word. For the hell of it, I followed the orca towards the fog that was now very close. It was as if he was leading us into the creepy mist. The closer we got to the fog the more my skin began to crawl. Gen, now by my side with her arm draped over my shoulder, seemed very concerned.

"I don't know if we should follow him, Jed. This is disturbing," my wife warned me.

"Strangely I feel as though I have to follow him, Gen," I said.

Our vessel was now engulfed within this eerie, greenish-blue fog, quietly entombing us. The villain orca was gone and the silence was unnerving. Slowly we kept going. The dark hole up ahead was reminiscent of a vortex sucking us down into a chasm. And there were silent bolts of reddish-orange lightning which struck the water in front of our vessel, illuminating this ghostly fog. Everything seemed surreal - when we spoke our voices were distorted. What the hell's going on?

***

The aluminum crew boat broke through the fog-bank and skimmed along the calm water towards the government dock. Everyone was in a joyful mood. The logging crew had just spent twenty-one days in a gypo float camp up Dreary Inlet. With paychecks in their pockets and beer in their bellies, it was nice to be headed for town.

"Hey Frank, you old shit-head, grab me a beer will ya, and grab one for young Jed as well," the riggin'-slinger said, " Going to be nice to have some days off after all the bullshit we have had the last twenty-one days?"

"What the fuck do ya mean?" said a weathered old buzzard from the back of the crew boat.

Freddie Hanson was the hooker on the ninety-foot tower in camp and he was mean as they come.

"You fucker's got a problem? I'll take a round out of any of you right here, right now!" shouted this tough and seasoned logger.

Everyone was quiet and no one wanted to cause a disturbance on the crew boat. Except for Freddie Hanson. Whadda prick!

I was going to start work at Camp 3 next Monday. It was a Crown Z camp at Nitinat and boasted that it had some of the best loggers on the west coast of BC. I was nervous because I had heard that Freddie Hanson had hired on to hook on a tower at Camp 3. His reputation as a mean fucker was well earned and known all up and down the coast. Trouble seemed to follow him wherever he went.

CHAPTER 5

Camp 3

Goddamn'it was it ever going to quit this downpour, I thought as I stood and waited for the crummy? Oh well, my brand new rain gear seemed to be holding out this sodden deluge. I couldn't imagine what it was going to be like to work in this confining extra set of rubber. Better get used to it LaSal, I continued with my silent thoughts. We got a heap of rain in these parts and I was on my way to Camp three to set beads.

I was decked out in the finest brand new logging attire, consisting of red-strap loggers pants staged off short and four sizes too big, a checkered wool shirt, and logging suspenders which held this distinctive garb in place - set me unquestionably apart and let the world know that I'm a west coast logger. Damn I felt proud, even though the knot in the pit of my stomach made me quite off-colour. Rounding off my gear was my recently purchased caulk boots, lunch packsack and a borrowed tin hat.

The rain was constant as I watched the approaching set of headlights. Daybreak was half an hour or so away and the darkness added to the lacklustre of the day.

The big bus, or crummy as they are known in the world of a logger, came to an abrupt stop. The mechanical door squeaked as it was flung open. A big burly man with the sleeves of his shirt rolled part way up his sinewy arms, which showed his faded tattoos, sat in the driver's seat.

I hesitated a moment which triggered a response. "Get the hell in here out of the rain young fellow," said this intimidating man of the woods. "Find yourself a seat, LaSal. The Forman called and let me know you were starting today. Welcome aboard."

The front seat was empty and, feeling a little intimidated, I plunked my ass down in it promptly. Sensing that the crummy was full I could not see how many men were in the seats. However there was an unmistakable smell of the woods in the air, mixed with a smidgen of musty aroma. Damp cloths with a daily dose of wood sawdust, pitch, and sweat permeated my nose. This added to the anticipation I was feeling and the knot in my stomach.

Barrelling down the road it was not long before we stopped at the service station, the only one in our small town. Once again the driver opened the door, and in jumped a grizzled looking older man carrying a tin lunch bucket.

"How's it goin' Larson?" asked the driver as he slid open his side window and spit out a mouthful of snoose.

One of the hallmarks of being a logger was the constant and ever present container of Copenhagen chewing tobacco carried in his back pocket and a huge wad between his bottom lip and gum.

"Not bad. Looks like it is goin' to fuckin' rain all week!" grumbled this rough looking individual. "Shove over kid. I sit in the front seat cause them assholes in the back snore and it drives me nuts. Looks like you're a greenhorn. First day?"

Sliding over to give him more room I awkwardly mumbled, "Ya first day."

"Hey Ray. Looks like we got another pansy. Oh well. Won't take long to break him in."

Ray, keeping his eyes on the road, never gave the comment a second thought, but I could tell by the grin on his face that he had seen this play out before.

The paved road gave way to gravel and it was full of potholes as the bus whizzed along. I was nodding off a bit as I slouched in the bench seat. My thoughts were now on what lay ahead.

Jolting me out of a half trance I felt an elbow poke me in the side.

"Hey kid. Wake up. It's time to go get some logs," Larson smugly informed me.

Camp was abuzz. Loggers of every size and description were scurrying about in what seemed to be organized confusion. I looked for the office where I was to sign up with the company.

"Hey, are you LaSal?" asked this guy in a tin hat and green mackinaw jacket. "Head over to the office and get the paperwork done, then get your ass back here. I will find a side that is short handed."

"Don't worry about that guy, young fellow. It's only the woods foreman. You'll get used to him," spoke this friendly looking chap.

Glancing over at this person that spoke to me, I noticed a smile on his face. Immediately it put me somewhat at ease and the nausea in my stomach backed off a little.

"What building is the office in?" I nervously asked.

Putting out his hand he introduced himself, "I'm Slim. The office is the third on the left." He pointed over to a group of buildings. "Nice to have you in camp. Hope things go well for ya."

"Hey LaSal. Get the fuck over to the office. We've got wood to get!" bellowed the woods foreman.

Immediately I headed towards the office, not wanting to piss off the foreman. He could send me packing in a heartbeat. There is a saying in the woods: "Up the hill or down the channel." For the most part it means get your ass in gear or go home.

The ill feeling in the pit of my stomach returned. Woods foremen are not known to be the friendliest guys on a Monday morning while marshalling the crew. As a matter of fact, they are as miserable as the rainstorms that frequent the west coast. When it comes to logging, all, in those days, came up through the ranks. They were usually asked to do the job based on their ability to handle a variety of hard-nosed loggers that worked in these camps. It was a badge they wore in a time-honoured tradition.

"LaSal. Let's get you signed up and out of here," said a pleasant voice coming from behind a worn counter. "Or Custy will be in here pronto and give us all shit. The papers are filled out, you only have to sign where I marked them. By the way, my name is Bill Pratt. I'm the personnel-man around here. If you need anything from the company store just ask." Taking off my rain jacket, I picked up the pen and put my John-Henry on the dotted lines where Pratt had marked."

On the way out the door Pratt stopped me with a yell. "Catch! You will need these," tossing me a pair of gloves. "Hey LaSal, have a nice day."

Hurrying over to see the woods foreman, the yard was now filled with men coming and going in every direction. There seemed to be quite a few loggers coming from the direction of the bunkhouses. Small groups of men were chit chatting, paying no attention to the rain pelting down. Others, they made their way to the crummies as fast as they could, not wanting to get wet. It was all very confusing to me and made me nervous.

"LaSal!" hollered the same guy that told me to get my ass over to the office. "Let's find you a side to work on," Custy mumbled as he made his way over to a beat up old looking box crummy, with me in tow.

Opening the door the weathered man of the woods hollered out, "Hey Larson! Everyone show up? Here is a fuckin' chokerman for ya. Hope he works out. Try not to be so hard on this new guy, eh. How much longer before you can tower down and turn the yarder around?"

"Yaw-by-golly. We got half a dozen roads or so, then I have to drop the square guyline and diamond lead a couple of short roads," slurred Larson.

Tuning around without saying a word to the old hooktender, Custy mumbled as he walked away, "Rum-dumb old prick, don't know how he does it."

The dim dome light afforded just enough light to find a spot to sit. At a glance there must have been five or six men in the back of this crummy. Larson was stretched out on the bench seat. The rest were sitting up with their eyes trained on me - the new guy. One guy greeted me with a good morning, the others sat quiet in their own thoughts.

I sat down and the first thing that struck me was the blend of smells. Not unlike the big bus I rode into camp, only more intense. Probably because this box crummy is more confined and being a bush crummy they probably don't clean them out as often.

It was still dark as we pulled out of the marshalling yard and headed out to the woods. Everyone was quite - the only noise was the unrelenting whine of the heater going full blast. My only companion being my own thoughts and the thick smoke that was being exhaled into these close confines. I wondered how far we had to go.

Daylight comes to the mountains in strange waves. Tall timber shades the ground helping to guard the dark so as the light breaks over the precipitous peaks, night lets go in a slow and unyielding guise. It is even slower when ravaged by the incessant storms that have beleaguered the west coast since time immortal. Today was one of those days.

"Don't worry young fellow," piped up the guy in the seat right behind me. "We'll be at the machine soon."

Sticking out his hand he introduced himself, "My name is Ed Stant. I'm pullin' riggin'. That's Sam and Tom over in that corner seat, their settin' beads. That's Old Bud, he's chasin'. I will introduce you to the guy that runs the donkey and the loadin' engineer when we get to the side. They'll go and start up their machines then come and coffee up for ten or fifteen minutes before we head out on the side hill."

"Thanks." I said, feeling a little more at ease. "Kind of a wet looking day, hey Ed."

"Ya, it looks like it's going to be a wet one, better get use't to it kid, we get a lot of days like this."

The crummy came to an abrupt stop and out jumped the fellows running the machines.

With a growl and a puff of black smoke the big logging machines flashed up and were humming away – ready to gather and load logs.

The door opened and in jumped a crusty looking fellow wearing a rather beat up tin hat on his head and an old torn canvas jacket. A hand rolled cigarette hung from the corner of his mouth and he wore a steady grin on his weathered face.

"How's it goin' young fellow?" he said as he stuck out his hand to greet me. "My name is Buck."

"Nervously, I offered my hand and said, "My name is Jed."

"Looks like you got some new duds. Well it won't take long to break those in."

I sat there not knowing what to say and thought it may be better to say nothing. In jumps a jolly looking guy and right away introduces himself as Red and turns to talk to the old chap in the back of the crummy.

"Say Ollie, can you hold up a while, there's a truck coming and I won't be able to put a load on while you're logging? The landing's small and it wouldn't be safe for Buck to land the turns."

"No problem, I have to change roads after Ed cleans up a few chunks. I'll take the riggin' crew down to the back end and we will move the blocks and string some strawline."

"Had a good weekend Ollie? Looks like you are a bit hung-over?"

"Fuck, it was a piss-cutter. I was at the Riverside playing shuffleboard and we shut the place down both Friday and Saturday night. On Sunday I was over at Terry's for a little of the hair of the dog that bit ya. So, yaw-by-golly, I am hung over."

Buck piped up. "I will grease up the machine while you guys set things up."

The morning was in full light or should I say as light as it could be considering the grey skies. Into the landing came a pickup truck. Looking out the window I could see the woods foreman waking up to the crummy. There was another guy in with him.

Climbing in the crummy, Custy looked at Red and said, "Here is a landing bucker for you. You'll need him with all the long logs coming in off of that steep fuckin' side hill. Say, Larson, you gonin' to change roads this morning? How many roads do you think you have left before you will tower down?"

"We got about a half a dozen roads, but on the last one we are going to have to tag a few logs that I know we'll not reach. Because it's so fuckin' steep it's slow going. We'll be most of the day." Larson groggily says as he sits up to talk to the woods boss.

"Good. Your next show is a little better. Lots of full-length logs, those goddamn fallers never bucked much," Custy grouchily mumbles as he exits the crummy.

Standing there looking around with the rain pelting down on him, I could not help but wonder how many interesting stories this woods boss could tell. He had the look of a chap that had scores of years behind him. Tall with a craggy face and eyes that are wise, Custy seemed not to mince his words. He let everyone know who was in charge around this place.

Stepping out of the crummy the side boss hollered at the crew, "Let's get at her boys. We'll head to the back end to set up a road change. Ed, you stay in the landing and when Buck is ready drop the square guy."

Hesitating at the edge of the road, the hooktender turned to the crew.

"For chrissake be careful!" warned Larson. "With all the weird shit that happened last week I don't want anyone to get hurt! Sam, no more of that Indian hokey-pokey stuff. It scares the hell out of me."

Sam smiled and looked over his shoulder at me. I wonder what Larson is talking about? By the look on Sam's face I knew I would probably find out.

CHAPTER 6

Indian legends

By the wry look on his face, Sam was never going to heed what Larson had said.

The hooktender is the side boss of the crew and the most experienced. Inherently gruff and mean as hell, they march to their own drum. I was warned: piss off the hooktender and you'll pay for it one way or another.

To say the least, I had to trust this group of sidehill gougers because it is their experience that will keep me alive.

Awkwardly, I stumbled along and followed the crew down and into the logging slash. The logging slash was covered with all sorts of debris left over after the logs were removed and was dreadful to navigate. It will take time to get my bush legs and make walking through the slash easier.

By the time we reached the back-end the sweat rolled down my face and my legs felt like rubber. I thought to myself, I don't know if I am going to be able to cut'er out here? I no sooner sat down on a stump to get my wind when the hooktender nimbly walked down a large fir peeler in the fell and bucked timber with an axe in his hand.

"Fella's, let's set up for our next road change. LaSal, follow me. We are going to move a block and strap. I coiled a couple of extensions of straw-line over behind that hemlock stomp. You other two can string them over to that big o'll fir stump at the back end. I'm going to hang the block and strap on it. Make fuckin' sure you string the lines straight. I don't want any si-washes," orders Larson.

Those words set in motion a scurry of activity. The other two chockerman knew exactly what to do and wasted no time. I could tell by the way they moved with ease through the slash and over and along the logs that they have been doing this a while.

"OK punk, grab that block and follow me," Larson ordered.

The hooktender, with an axe in one hand and a long steel strap in the other, took off through the fell and bucked timber and left me on my own. I looked at this contraption he called a block and was not sure how to pack it properly. This piece of equipment that looked like a giant pulley was made of steel and must weigh over a hundred pounds! I weighed in at one hundred and forty pounds so the damn thing weighed almost as much as I did.

I stood, paused and looked down at the ugly backbreaker. I didn't know how or if I could even lift it, let alone carry it through the slash or fell and bucked logs. I bent over and grabbed the thing and started to drag it towards the fell and bucked logs. After a very short distance, and great difficulty, I realized that this was not the way you do this. Larson was already on his way back to meet me.

"I'll show you how to pack this block, young fellow. See this part here, it's called the gooseneck, have it facing you. Watch how I grab the damn thing by the shell with both hands and lift it up and onto my shoulder," the hooktender said calmly. "Once you have it up on your shoulder, grab aholt of the gooseneck and away you go. Now you try," Larson said and threw the block back onto the ground.

I knew enough to stand on the low side so I swung the block around and took hold of this massive hunk of metal. With one mighty heave, I lifted the block and tried to place it on my shoulder, just the way Larson did. I got this thing up close to my shoulder when I felt myself going over backwards – and I could not stop myself!

I hit the ground and rolled down the hill about five or six feet. I sensed I was being watched. And Larson chuckled. He must have seen this a few times.

Instinctively, and I might add with a little bit of anger, I grabbed the block and flung it up and onto my shoulder. I did not want these seasoned men of the woods to think I was not capable of this task.

I staggered under the immense weight of this apparatus but followed him as he made his way over to the next tail hold. What a nightmare. The ground was strewn with rubble of every description. Chunks of broken wood, limbs from trees the fallers had cut off, rocks, mud, and steep goddamn ground. What the hell! Maybe my mom and dad were right; I should have stayed in school, I thought.

Finally, I made it to the stump and flung the block down. I don't think I could have gone a step further. The sweat ran down my face and dripped off my jaw. My legs felt weak and shook slightly and my lungs burned from the physical exertion. I fell to my knees and sat back on my heels to try and compose myself. This was not going to be easy work!

Larson paid no attention to me and swung the axe with ease, which effortlessly knocked the bark off the stump and cut out a large notch that went completely around the fir stump. He wrapped the heavy gauge wire strap around the stump and then hung the block in the eyes of the strap to complete the job.

"Yaw by-golly, where the fuck are you guys?" Larson yelled at the choker men. "String that goddamn straw-line on an angle over to me. And make damn sure you don't get any fuckin' si-washes in it!" he continued.

Sam and Tom knew their job. They scurried over the maze of logs and debris and moved nimbly and didn't miss a step. Not once did they hesitate in their chore of stringing this steel line. Not once did they stumble or shilly-shally as they strung the straw-line over to us.

Olie Larson wore a bug around his waist, much like a belt. It is an electronic device that when one pressed a button on it, activated a whistle on the tower. A bug is what loggers used to signal the yarding engineer with a variety of whistle signals to do different things about logging.

The hooktender blew for the straw-line. Three short and a long whistles: the chaser up in the landing unhooked the haulback off of the butt-rigging and hooked it to the straw-line and Buck sent it down the hill. Larson spotted the eye of the haulback and blew one short to stop it where he wanted it.

Once the straw-line extensions had been strung through the block and hooked up to the eye of the haulback, Larson gave the signal to go ahead on the straw-line. Three short and a short: beep, beep, beep - beep. With that signal, Buck went ahead on the straw-line and the haulback was pulled up the hill and back to the landing.

"You guys head up to the front-end. Let's see if we can get a couple of loads before lunch," said Larson as he stood there in his sweat-soaked Stansfield sweater. He tipped his tin hat slightly back on his head and went on to say, "Show Jed the ropes, will ya?"

I followed the chokerman as we climbed up the hill to meet Ed, our rigging-slinger. He sat on a stump with a smoke in his hand. Ed Stant was a cool looking fellow and sat with one leg crossed over the other and hard-hat worn low on his eyebrows. A young, well-built man of twenty-nine, he had a self-confident look that only came from many years spent in the woods.

"How's' it goin'?" asked Ed, pleasantly, when we arrived at the place where we would start to log.

I looked him directly in the eye and smiled and nodded my head. "Not bad I guess. I'm a little shaky. Never done this kind of work before."

"You'll get use't to it. It takes time to get your legs under you. These side-hills are hard on all of us, in more ways than you know."

With a grin and a nod, I didn't say a word.

We were close to the landing so I had a bird's eye view of what was going on. I watched Old Bud, the chaser, as he hooked up the haulback to the butt-riggin'.

"Phssss," went the air exhaust as Buck pulled on the levers which engaged the drums that held all the line. He tight-lininged the riggin' out of the coal deck pile of logs and was ready to skinner back. Buck slid the window open and hawked out a wad of snoose.

"Hang on a minute Stant, I need to grab a fresh chew." Buck reached into his shirt pocket to grab the can of snoose. He gave the lid a gentle wrap with his knuckles then cradled the can of snoose in the palm of his hand and took off the tin lid. Buck reached in with his thumb and first two fingers and pinched out a sizable chew and replaced the snoose he had spit out. He seemed to pause and savour the whole process. Satisfied, he looked our way and gave us a nod. He was ready.

Beep, beep, pause, beep, beep. Ed blew the signal to skinner back. "Phssssh," went the air exhaust and a roar from the diesel sent the rigging jingling back to us. With his hand on the bug, Ed kept a watchful eye on the chokers flying down the hill.

"Beep." Ed stopped the riggin' right over the logs we were going to hook up and send in. Without a word Tom, Sam, Ed and I walked towards the rigging. As we approached the butt-riggin', Ed pointed to the logs he wanted the other guys to get. He motioned for me to come with him.

"Give me a hand for a turn or two. That way you will get the hang of it," Ed said as he reached for the front chocker on the butt-riggin'.

With the choker in one hand and the bug in the other, Ed blew a series of short whistles to slack the mainline – and down came the butt-riggin'. This gave everyone enough slack in the chokers to wrap them around the logs. "Clink" went Tom's choker bell as he inserted the knob into the bell, completing the process of choking the log. Sam did the same and they both turned around and immediately hustled out of the turn. I helped Ed set the other two beads. We doubled up two logs on the lead choker and hooked up a single on the other. All were on nice fir. When we were in the clear, Ed blew go ahead on'er.

The butt-riggin' moved forward, tightening the cables, which put a strain on the wire ropes. Bang, clang, boom, thump and cras - the noise was frightening! I watched these massive logs being dragged up the steep hill and was amazed how with ease the yarder pulled the turn of logs in. Like a giant clothesline with logs dangling from it, these fir peelers were being hauled up to the landing. Along the way they bounced off stumps and dug long furrows in the earth. The air smelled of fresh dirt, fir bows, bark, and newly cut logs – oddly, it was a pleasant aroma.

Over the next couple of hours I slowly got the hang of my new job. It was hard physical work. My lungs burned and my arms were getting weak from handling the large wire rope.

"Getting tired young fellow? You'll get use't to 'er. We've all been there kid," the seasoned riggin' puller reassuringly but bluntly told me. "Sit this next turn out. We are going to send that oversized peeler as a single."

Gladly I sat down on a stump and rested my aching and fatigued muscles. After the log was hooked up Ed blew go ahead on er and the giant log started to move.

"Quick! Quick! Look over on that rock bluff?" Sam excitedly pointed. "Did you see it?"

"Sam! Quit that goddamn bullshit!" retorted Ed. "You scared away the last two chokermen and they were good men."

Sam looked at me with a smile on his face, but it was the look in his eyes that sent a shiver up my back!

The display of this ancient monarch of the forest reluctantly being forced up the hill was a sight to behold. The diesel engine was full steam ahead on the mainline winch which spooled the inch and a quarter mainline on the huge drum as it reeled in its quarry. The roar of the engine and the steady growl of the winch was an indication of how much weight was contained in this single log.

Everything was going smooth as Ed watched with his hand instinctively resting on the bug at the ready. This peeler would soon be corralled in the landing.

About fifty feet from the landing the big log nudged up against a fairly large stump and came to a halt. Ed quickly blew stop.

"Fuck! That's not what I need so close to the landing, a goddamn hang-up," mumbled Ed. "I'll try to skinner back and see if I can get er'"

The log started to move a little back down the hill when Ed blew to go ahead on the riggin'. Quickly the yarding engineer had the butt-riggin' going ahead and once again this outstanding log was heading up the hill towards the landing.

Again the log came to rest at the base of the stump. Suddenly, with a loud crack, the choker broke and the riggin' flew up into the air and, on the rebound, crashed to the ground in a pile of tangled metal. The gigantic peeler hesitated with nothing to hold it and then started to slide back down the side hill. Slowly at first, then it gained momentum and speed - this old-growth stem looked like a runaway locomotive.

Instinctively and instantly the crew ran for cover, each taking refuge behind the closest stump possible as this looming run-away menace of a log had its sights on us. I dove behind a large stump. I did not have to be told to take cover as human self-preservation is a strong innate quality.

Within seconds this enormous projectile whizzed passed all of us and continued on its path. This destructive run-a-way created an amazing amount of destruction along its path and finally came to rest at the timberline. But not before hitting a good size hemlock tree. It hit with such a force that the tree broke in half, about sixty feet up, and sent the top like a javelin into the hard-packed ground.

Everything was quiet. I looked up towards the landing and could see Old Bud. He looked down the hill and saw that we were all OK. Bud gave us a wave of acknowledgement and stepped back from the edge of the hill.

We looked at each other. Tom spoke first, "That was close Ed. Lucky for us that sonafabitch was not on this side of the hump or it would have gone right through the middle of us."

"Ya, hate to think what might have happened," replied Ed nonchalantly. There was no doubt, from his complacent manner he had seen many a run-a-way during his time working in the woods.

Ollie made his way through the slash towards us to see if everyone was all right. With a nod from the crew, he knew that everything was fine.

"Well. I just about shit my pants," Sam sarcastically embellished. "Those run-a-ways are the curse of us sidehill gougers. I'll never get use't to those big bastards barrelling down the hill towards us! I know it was Bakwus', letting us know he is not happy!"

"I agree, Sam. Many a logger has been killed by a rogue log," solemnly responded Ed as he rolled and lit a cigarette.

"Ed, you and Tom head to the back end and clean up the mess from that run-a-way," Larson instructed. "When you're done head up to the landing for lunch. Sam, you and Jed stay put till those guys are done, then come up with them. I'm going up to check the guy-line stumps, after a hard pull like that I want to make sure everything is solid."

With the riggin' puller on his way to clean up, Sam and I were alone and it was a welcome rest.

"Say, Jed, anyone ever explain to you about the wild man of the woods?"

"Can't say I've heard about that one before."

"How about the Tsonokwa?"

"Nope."

"See those ravens that are playing in the breeze? They are tricksters, always trying to fool or confuse you. Notice how they spin over on to their back while swooping down and call out, caw, caw? They are warning us that something else is around. Something most people don't understand."

"Whaddya mean?"

Sam seemed to change, he spoke in soft tones yet very clear. His eyes had a faraway look, a bizarre gaze that seemed to put him in a different place and dimension.

"The wild man of the woods, Bakwus', is real ya know. He is out there protecting our earth. Sometimes he's good and sometimes he's evil. I've been told by the Elders that Bakwus' can invade a person's spirit, summoning them to follow him on his quest. At times he will take on a different form. Bakwus' can be what he wants to be."

I was spellbound by this ramble of Indian myth. For some strange reason I sat transfixed, unable to move, only to listen. Sam stood up, stretched his arms out and reached for the sky and started to chant in his mother tongue. After a long pause and without a word he started to move towards the timber. I watched Sam disappear into a gully, with an undistinguishable and faint but brightly coloured fog that followed him. Was I seeing things? I rubbed my eyes and shook my head and took another look. Yes. There seemed to be this strange looking fog that followed Sam into the standing timber. I was mesmerized and stood there and gazed to where Sam disappeared into the woods.

"Hey, LaSal! Where the fuck did that little snog-arse go?" hollered Ollie inquisitively.

Ollie's words jolted me out of this trance and I just shook my head and held up my hands in a gesture that indicated I didn't know.

Tom laughed as Ed cut in, "Don't let his Indian stories get to ya, Jed. He does this every once in a while. None of us guys understand him when he gets like this."

"Where the hell did he go?" I asked.

"Don't know, don't care," said Ed sarcastically, with a "and I dont give a shit look" on his face.

Tom piped up, "He'll be gone a few days or so, but he'll be back. I bet he goes over to the Nitinat Indian Reserve. It's not far from here. Probably got some relatives to stay with."

"For chrissake! Enough of the bullshit, let's head up for lunch," said Ed in his usual and straightforward manner.

The rest of the day was uneventful, but I had to step up to the plate with Sam gone. I was getting the hang of my new job. Eating lunch seemed to give me renewed strength and I was able to finish my first day on a sidehill.

Wearily, I climbed into the crummy at the end of the shift. I was glad to be heading home. Tired, I sat and gazed out the window and fought off the urge to sleep. My head gently bobbed up and down as I waited for the rest of the crew to climb in the crummy when something caught my eye. At the edge of the older logging slash and partially concealed from a shadow being cast because of the late afternoon, was something strange. I strained my eyes to have a better look. Somewhat covered by the salal brush was what seems to be a face that glared back.

This phizog appeared to be a blend of green and black with long coarse brownish-black hair – reminiscent of a horse's tail. The nose and lips were a brilliant red. The eyes were white with a tinge of red surrounding the center, which made it appear supernatural. This creature looked like it was draped in some type of a bark blanket to cloth it. It couldn't be Sam, I contemplated. Am I tired and just seeing things? Is it possible that this was the Indian legend Bakwus'?

As quickly as it emerged, this thing disappeared. And it, too, was followed by an eerie coloured fog that seemed to vanish into thin air. I sat dumbfounded and stared out the window on the ride home and never mentioned this sighting to anyone in the crummy for fear of being scoffed at!

CHAPTER 7

Tsonokwa

Eerily, my words were distorted, "Help! Help! I'm being chased! Goddamnit someone help!" I hysterically hollered. In a panic, I desperately ran from this mysterious creature that chased me through the woods. I staggered, stumbled, and zigzagged, within this out-of-body experience as I fought my way through dense underbrush. I sweated profusely and my eyes stung, which obscured my vision. My frantic calls for help fell on deaf ears. Thus, I was contained by this nightmarish hallucination.

I hesitated for a moment and caught a glimpse of this frightening anomaly. Its face was extraordinarily black with brilliant orange striping cast upon it. I couldn't see its eyes. But its hair was very long and seemingly dirty brown and there was a dissimilar yet pungent odour which filtered into my nose – almost begging me to stop in my tracks and gag! This life form appeared to be ghost-like, yet real. It moved with uncanny ease and purpose followed by an outlandish and weirdly coloured fog in its wake. Tsonokwa! My thoughts kept repeating over and over. In a desperate effort to be rid of this mystifying attacker, I ran blindly through the woods, but my legs failed me – or so it seemed?

I wrestled my way through the thick underbrush like a madman, when suddenly and without warning, I found myself on the edge of a dangerously narrow rock bluff. Abruptly I stopped, but alas my momentum carried me over the edge! With a dreadful plummeting feeling, I fell, spun and sank out of control into a very dark chasm. In this out of world state I had visions imprinted in my mind of the Tsonokaw. I waited for the end. Desperately scared, I closed my eyes.

Stangely, I had a sensation that I was being guided. I opened my eyes. The Tsonokaw was over top of me and gazed into my eyes. With a hand under me we floated within a time-warp and endured this never-ending and freakish free-fall. It felt as if the life was being drained out of me. Instantaneously I was jolted out of this trance-like vortex – by my alarm clock! My eyes were fixed on the ceiling and I could not budge. I was saturated in sweat and trembled violently! As I regained my composure I thought to myself that I am going to find out more about these Indian myths – damn that Sam!

"Hit the floor, Jed," called out my Dad. "It's time to go to work and if you want to eat breakfast ya had better get up son."

"Frank, breakfast is on the table. Is Jed up?" asked my mother Lorraine, who stood at the bottom of the stairs.

"I let him know. I'll be down in a sec."

"Well, the crummy will be here shortly. I wouldn't want him to be late on his second day. I guess he must be tired," said my mother.

My dad, Frank LaSal, met my mother while he was doing a stretch in the Canadian Navy. He was stationed in Victoria and was visiting relatives in the Lake Cowichan area. If I recall there was a barbeque or a get together at his uncle's farm. My mom was a single mother of three trying to make ends meet and did housekeeping for dad's aunt and uncle. They dated for quite some time before they finally tied the knot and settled down at Lake Cowichan or as the locals call it The Foot. They had a couple of kids. Both were boys, which brought the total to five kids. Along with my two sisters, it was kind of nice to have a couple of little brothers. Dad finished his stint in the navy and went to work in the woods. He tried working in one of the numerous mills around the Foot but didn't take to it. He was a road builder and enjoyed running the big machines pushing dirt around all day. It may have been a throwback to his days spent on the farm in Manitoba – where he was raised.

Life was pretty much normal in our household or as normal as it could be raising five active kids. Dad took me hunting and fishing. My brothers were too young to tag along. Mom taught the girls how to cook and do regular girly stuff and we all had our usual chores to do – but not without some prompting at times. Dad's work was seasonal, dependent on the weather, so there were times when money was lean. But that was the same for all logging families. It wasn't until I was out on my own that I discovered how hard it must have been raising a family during those days.

I grabbed my lunch and headed for the door. "See ya Mom," I pleasantly said.

"Have a nice day son, and stay safe."

"OK Mom, see ya after work."

Dad's ride was already waiting for him. He worked for a contractor and they had their own crummies. Dad kissed mom goodbye, he gave me a wave and hollered, "Keep your head up, son. I'll see you tonight after work."

"OK dad, maybe we'll go fishing this weekend eh?"

"That's a good idea. I hear the rainbows are biting at the mouth of Cottonwood Creek."

The crummy stopped out front so I waved goodbye to Mom and hustled down to the road to catch my ride to work.

The ride to camp seemed short because I slept all the way. Refreshed and ready to giver hell, I looked for my bush crummy in the marshalling yard and headed straight for it. Tom and Ed were already inside.

Cheerfully I greeted them. "Good mornin' fella's," I said as I found my seat.

With a cig hanging out of the corner of his mouth, Ed inquired, "How ya feelin' Jed?"

"Great! I'm ready to fly at it."

Ed smiled knowing that today would be harder. We were going to tower down and that meant a lot more physical work for us.

"Sam not here?" I inquisitively asked.

"No, the fucker's not here. That means we'll have to work short-handed," Ed dryly muttered. "Probably won't see him for a while either. That's going to piss off the woods foreman."

With a scornful look, Tom jumped into the conversation. "I don't know why Custy doesn't fire the sonofawhore."

"He's a good worker, Tom, besides, not many guys now days want to work in the goddamn woods," said Ed insolently.

"If you say so. But I'm getting tired of working short-handed, Ed. Sure puts more work on our shoulders."

When we arrived at the tower Larson wasted no time. "OK boys let's get at er'. I want to finish this bloody setting," he said as he was leaving the crummy. The cantankerous old buzzard meant business. "Come on, get your asses in gear! Or I'll fire the whole damn works of ya!"

We wasted no time getting out into the fell and bucked. Turn after turn we sent in all sizes of logs and chunks as we cleared our way down the hill to the back end. The time flew. It wasn't long before we had logged our way to where the big back end blocks were hung. Again we changed roads and began the process all over again – sending in logs! Things went smoothly.

In between turns, Tom pulled out a can of snoose from his back pocket. "Jed, want a chew," he offered. With a light tap on the top, he removed the lid and dipped in to replace the spent wad in his mouth.

"Sure why not, I'll giver a try," I shyly said and reached for his snoose tin.

"Take er easy Jed. This stuff is not for the faint of heart, it will bite ya in the ass if you're not careful. Don't tell your old man that I gave you some. He wouldn't appreciate it."

I carefully placed my first chew into position. Copenhagen chewing tobacco is the choice preferred by loggers. A telltale sign that a man chewed was the bulge in his lower lip. He would pull the small round can from his shirt pocket and give it a rap with his knuckle. He then opened the lid and with his thumb and first two fingers dipped into his favourite indulgence. The logger would then squeeze this pinch of brown heaven in between his lower lip and gum. Most would spit the brown juice out while they kept the wad in place. Others never spit. They considered spitting as a sign of weakness and called the ones that did spit sissies or pansies. The hardcore snoose chewers even ate their lunch with a chew still in the lower lip. Most chewed at home, in town, or at the pub. Over the years chewing snoose evolved into a hall-mark for loggers and among the many names used to describe these men of the woods, "Snooser" seemed to stick.

"Be careful, Ed. My haulback stump is a little shaky. Wouldn't want to pull er' with a heavy turn," mentioned Ollie as he stopped and rested on a stump a few feet from us. He was on his way up to the landing after changing roads.

"OK, Ollie. By the time we finish up this road it'll be lunch," Ed informed the hootender.

"There's no other tail-holts, Ed, so taker goddamn easy. I'll let Buck know, so that fucker doesn't runner tight. That old skin-flint has a habit of being heavy on the haulback brake!" Ollie sarcastically said.

We got down to the business of finishing the road we were on. Once we had finished we all headed up to the landing to eat lunch and have a well-deserved rest.

With a sly grin, Tom asked, "Hey Ollie, how was the Riverside Inn last weekend?"

"Yaw by-golly, it was full to the brim Friday and Saturday. Drank lots of beer and played shuffle-board. Seemed to be lots of old babes around. Tried to pick up that old blond broad, you know the one that works over at Barry's Café? She's got a nice set of knockers."

Buck cuts in, "Ollie, you're gettin' too old and worn out for that kind of monkey business. Besides those ladies are looking for a man as their keeper. You don't want that do ya?"

"Nah, I just need to get my oil changed once in a while and when you are as old and ugly as me, you take what you can get. Besides, after a night at the Riverside swilling beer, I never took home an ugly one, woke up with a few, but never took one home."

The crew chuckled as they listened intently to the banter. Everyone knew Ollie Larsen well. He had a long reputation as an old-time logger who worked hard and played harder.

Red, the loader operator, stood in the doorway and looked over at Buck. "You and your wife goin' to the dance this weekend? Hear there is going to be a dance contest?" Asked the loader operator.

"Oh, more then likely, Betty loves to dance. I heard there will be a 50's rock in roll band playing. Have you heard who's playing?"

"Sure did. Dave and the Dukes are coming from Victoria. Should be good, my neighbour claims they're the best. A bunch of them went to the Red Lion Inn in Vic to see the Dukes and had a blast. They play great dance tunes."

Ed put down his sandwich, poured a cup of tea and spoke up. "Custy told me that Freddie Hanson, that tough prick of a hooktender from up at Dreary Inlet, is in town. I guess he's going to hook on the slack-line here in camp. Any bets he shows up at the dance? That cocksucker is known to cause trouble and he loves to start a fight," said Ed. "I'll take the fucker on," he informed the crew, shaking his fist.

The loader operator headed for his machine to put a load on while we finished our lunch. Although I was dog tired I managed to eat, which gave me the much-needed energy for the afternoon.

Red was almost finished loading the truck but had to wait for the landing bucker to buck up a couple of full-length logs he had laid out. Lyle Nielson was an older fellow. He used to be a faller, but decided he had had enough of the steep sidehills and was going to finish his days logging as a landing bucker. His mastery with handling the power saw was evident, with not one wasted move. Lyle handled the saw with ease as he measured and bucked the remaining full-length trees in no time flat. His fluid motions were a testament to the years dedicated to this type of work and sparked an interest within me. Maybe I could become a faller someday?

Like a lot of Indian fellows, Lyle Nielson took to the woods to make a living. This type of work came naturally for these guys. Most spend a lot of time out in the woods hunting and fishing, so working outdoors was a good fit. Lyle always had a nice smile for anyone he greeted. He was a short and stocky chap and appeared to be in his mid-fifties. The weathered lines on his face and his callused hands are an indication of the hard work he has done over the years. Even his complexion appeared darker and had a healthy radiance. Lyle looked as if he enjoyed his job immensely.

I stood from a distance and watched him buck up the logs. When he was finished Lyle came my way. "How's it goin' young fella? Are you likin' your job?"

"Yes, I am," I said with a grin. "Kinda gettin' the hang of it and the guys are patient with me – showed me lots of stuff."

"That's nice Jed. Hope it all works out for ya. How are the new boots?"

"They're hurtin' my feet."

"Ya, I thought so by the way you were walking. Un-tie your boots, I'll show you what will help."

Lyle explained to me to leave out several lace holes in the middle – allowing the boots extra room and give. It worked! Maybe I'll have an easier time breaking in these heavy logging boots now.

The afternoon went smooth, we finished logging the last of the fell and bucked logs. Then sent in the blocks and straps on the eye of the haul-back. It wasn't long before Buck was in the process of towering down the big logging machine.

I was nervous because there was lots going on at the same time. And watched with my eyes wide open as this massive pipe was being lowered. Once the pipe rested on the bull-prick, all the guy lines were slacked and cut loose for the stumps. Buck then went ahead on the guy-line winches one by one and reeled in these stabilizing lines. As the slack was spooled on the drums, we would hook the eye on the end of the guy line to the side of the tower. Buck, stood on the running boards and lifted the jacks. He then went back up into the cab and pulled up the pad with the strawline. It was a neat package ready to be moved to the next setting!

With a job well done the mood was light and jovial. It was friday afternoon and the weekend was here – everybody was ready to go home. Custy showed up and asked Lyle if he would stay longer and finish bucking up the long logs. He readily accepted.

"I'll leave you my crummy, Lyle. Say, Jed, do you mind staying with him? Shouldn't take you guys long to finish bucking up."

"No problem, I don't mind staying," I willingly offered.

The logs were all laid out side by side and the rest of the crew, including the woods boss, were on their way to camp. "Jed we'll measure all the logs, first, then buck'em up. Here, take the end of the tape and hold it down on the butt." Lyle measured off a forty footer and we repeated this until all the logs were measured. He then took his saw and began to cut them into the lengths and trim the ends. What a pleasure it was to watch someone with his skills. Lyle made it look easy. It only took him a short while and we were done and on our way to camp.

The gravel road snaked its way through the immense valley. It wouldn't take long and we'd be in camp. We were alone in the crummy and I thought this would be a good opportunity to ask him about some of the things Sam had told me. "Say, Lyle, Sam told me about some weird stuff. He asked me if I had ever seen or heard about the Bakwus' or the Tsonokwa. He told me that these things do exist. Then all of a sudden he buggered off and disappeared into the woods – with what seemed to be a strange fog that followed him. Scared the shit out of me! Then, last night I had a frightening dream that I was being chased by a Tsonokwa. I woke up in a sweat and very agitated. Do you know about these things?" I apprehensively asked.

Lyle looked at me with a noticeably serious look on his face. His eyes were cold yet reassuring. "Sam is a dancer. He's on a journey. The things he told you, in our culture and traditions are real. Most will never gain this awareness and only a chosen few will be allowed to walk through life's journey with this knowledge. The bad dream you had - that was a vision. Embrace it, Jed, it's nothing to be scared of. We are having a ceremony at the Longhouse this weekend, so why don't you come? There will be drumming, dancing, and feasting. It will help you understand your journey."

Lyle's words scared me. But there was a certain comforting tone in his mannerism and what he said to me. Something unexplainable!

CHAPTER 8

The Dance

"Fish on!" I eagerly hollered over to my dad. "Bring the net. It's a keeper."

Dad wasted no time. He quickly hot footed over to where I was fishing at the mouth of Cottonwood Creek.

"Geez, looks like a good one, Jed. Don't horse him!"

The frisky lunker leapt high into the air and then came down on its side, hitting the water with such a slap that the noise echoed beyond the shore. Water sprayed into the air as the feisty rainbow trout fought for its life. I had to be on the ball or I wouldn't land this beauty.

"That's it, Jed. Nice and easy, take it slow. This one's almost in the frying pan. Oh ya!" dad eagerly coached me. "Hold the tip up and move away from that windfall. Looks like he's trying to work his way over to that sweeper and shake you off!"

'"OK!" I said as I gingerly moved away and forced the fish to stay in open water. "Damn, he's a strong fish. Bet he'll go six or eight pounds?" I reassuringly assumed.

Dad stood with the net in his hand, ready to scoop up our prize. He was so focused on this potential meal that he never noticed he was in the water up to his knees with both boots full – a soaker!

The fish crisscrossed, wriggled and jumped out of the water in front of me, in an effort to free itself. But with each pass it became weaker and resisted less. I backed up and held the rod tip up high. "Alright dad, scoop him up," I quickly said as the fish came close to the shore.

"Got him, Jed," said dad as he swooped our supper up into the net. "It's a dandy! You're right. It'll go five and a half to six pounds. Wow!"

Cowichan Lake, within the Cowichan Valley, is well known for its recreation opportunities. Cowichan is an Indian word that means warm land and has been inhabited for thousands of years by seven distinct tribes of First Nation peoples. From the shores of the Pacific Ocean to the far reaches of this wide and fertile valley, the Cowichan Tribes have hunted, fished and gathered life sustaining food and materials. The focal point within the valley is the Cowichan River, which starts at the foot of Cowichan Lake and winds its way to an immense estuary before emptying into the ocean. The Cowichan Tribes claim there are sacred burial grounds at the far end of the valley. The local scuttle-butt is that these sacred grounds are protected by some sort of strange supernatural beings – however most folks brush this off as simply Indian myths. Are they right? I guess time will tell.

"Hi Jed! How's it goin'?" said my long time friend, Drew Harvey, as he pulled up and got out of his car. "You goin' to the dance tonight? Should be a piss-cutter!"

"Ya, I'm going to go. Remember Genevieve? She's the girl from Duncan I met at my cousin's place. She's coming to the dance and I heard she is bringing some friends as well. So you may want to hang out with me," I jokingly poked fun at my friend.

Later, Drew and I sipped a glass of pop at the local hang out, Walt's Drive-In - a tiny drive-in restaurant in the middle of town in Lake Cowichan. I didn't see him much during the week as he worked in the mill at Youbou. We were having a good bullshit to get caught up on what had happened around our community.

I went up to the counter and ordered another coke when a familiar but unfriendly voice behind me blurted out. "LaSal! You little fucker! Can't wait to have you settin' beads for me."

Uneasily, I turned to find that prick of a hooktender, Freddie Hanson. There he was, right behind me. What the hell was he doing here, I thought? I guess the rumor was true: the logging company had brought him down from Dreary Inlet to work at our camp. Damn, I thought,

"Hurry up! Grab your pop and get the hell out of my way, LaSal. I want to order some lunch," he said mockingly.

Drew watched this encounter and I didn't want him to think I was a push over. "Hello Freddie. What makes you think I'll be working on your side?" I said with a noticeable unsteady voice.

"Because I said so!" he bolstered. "Those sons-a-whores at Nitinat do as I say. If they don't, I won't work for those pricks. And if they want to have some of you dumb ass-holes trained to high-rig, it's my way or the high-way. So get ready ya little fucker, I'm going to work your sorry ass into the ground!"

Taken aback, I stood staring at Freddie Hanson. I was surprised by his pointed verbal attack and my knees shook a little. I'm sure everyone in the place could see how terrified I was. Drew sat and looked out the window and didn't want to draw attention to himself. Fact is everyone at Walt's was worried they would be the next target. Hanson had a reputation for fighting at the drop of a hat. And it's said that he is one tough cookie!

Drew slid his chair back and looked my way. "Let's get out of here, Jed. We've got to go get ready for the dance tonight," he said, and wasted no time as he headed for the door.

Freddie, with a mean grin on his face, stepped in front of Drew and temporarily blocked his way. "Good, I'm glad to hear you idiots are going to the dance. I'll see ya there," he said and then laughed a hardy laugh. No one in the joint was amused. Except, Freddie Hanson!

The town of Lake Cowichan is nestled between tall timber carpeted mountains at the foot of the lake. It's the gathering place and the main hub of activity at the upper reaches of the Cowichan Valley. With the town of Youbou on the eastern shore and the towns of Mesachie, Honeymoon Bay, and Caycuse spread out along the western shore – Nitinat lies just past the head of the lake. All these communities are populated with families that make a living from the rich and seeming endless supply of timber. Most worked in the numerous mills or logging camps that dotted the landscape. These same families that worked together also played together.

The parking lot at the community hall that night was full. "Come on LaSal, let's get inside or we won't find a seat!" insisted Drew. "Remember the last time we were at a dance? We huddled in the corner with all the nerds!" he reminded me and laughed one of those belly laughs that got me laughing too.

"Good thing we bought our tickets early, Drew, or we'd never got in. Looks like a sellout."

The dance hall was packed and Dave and The Dukes were already playing when we walked in the dance hall. Although it was the early seventies, they covered tunes from the fifties like Rock Around The Clock, Meybellene, and Long Tall Sally. The dance floor was busy. Most of the men dressed in their old and ill fitting suits and the ladies, as always, were clad in their finest and usually homemade dresses.

We made our way to a table that had some space and Drew threw his coat on a chair. "I'm going to find someone to dance with, Jed." And he disappeared into the crowd.

I sat down and surveyed the hall to see who was around. To my liking, I noticed a few people at a table that were from Duncan and strained through the dim lighting to see if Genevieve was among the group. Her friend Carol was there but I didn't see Genevieve.

"Hello, Jed! Got your dancin' shoes on?" boomed a friendly familiar voice.

At the table behind me was a work mate. "Sure do," I said, as I turned in my chair. "Nice to see ya, Buck."

"How does it feel to be out in the working world, Jed?" asked his wife Betty.

"It's great," I said, "But I'm still getting used to it." Betty gave me a pleasant smile.

With a light tap on my shoulder I turned and found Genevieve standing there with her hand out. "Come on, Jed, let's have a dance," she asked, with a nice smile and an outstretched hand.

The dance floor was packed. People were upbeat and doing their best to keep time with the rhythm. Genevieve was a good dancer. I on the other hand was clumsy, but did my best to show her that at the very least I was not shy about being on the dance floor. I made it through the first couple of tunes and while we waited for the next song I noticed that Drew was still out on the floor. He nodded and gave me a wink. He knew that I had feelings for this gal and wanted to strike up a relationship with Genevieve.

The band started to play Can't Help Falling in Love, by Elvis Presley. Genevieve's long eye-lashes framed her green eyes that looked into my being. She took my hand and brought me close to her and held me firm yet gentle. Her soft long dark hair fell gently onto my shoulder and our embrace was euphoric as I nervously pulled her closer. I felt her breasts press against my chest and her warm hands held me with purpose. She laid her head tenderly on my shoulder and her perfume seduced me into a trance-like state. I didn't want this moment to end. I'm sure she felt my heart as it pounded in my chest! We waltzed slowly and by the vibe between us, we both knew that we were destined to be a couple.

The music finished and we held our bodies close for a short time afterwards. "I need to rest my feet, Jed," Genevieve spoke softly.

"I'm going to see how Drew is doing," I said, not wanting to let go of her hand.

"Hey LaSal!" hollered Ed Stant. "Glad to see ya made it to the dance. Who's the broad? She's a good looker, Jed. Too good for you eh!" teased my work mate.

Ed waved for me to come with him. "Let's go out back. I've got a sack of beer in the car."

Even though there was a bar setup inside the dance hall quite a number of men, and a few ladies, were always out in the parking lot to quench their thirst with a drink from their own stash. Ed handed me a beer and we joined the others. Like always, the conversation was shop talk.

"I heard you guys are going to log that untouched mountain up the Nitinat? Talk is that it's chocked-full of nice fir," asked a fellow that worked at Port Renfrew.

"That's right," said Lucky Larue. "The company has right-of-way fallers in there right now. Won't be long and the roads will be in. They said it's the best stand of fir in the Nitinat," he continued.

"Ya!" added Harry Bodine, Lucky's side-kick. "Their excuse is that they're running out of timber to log in the main valley, so they need to log it. I am told that it's against the wishes of the Indians. They call the mountain Sleeping Beauty and say that it's sacred ground and is where their ancestors buried their dead."

"No shit!" Ed joined in the conversation. "The Indians won't be happy. But with all the wood on that mountain there is no way the company will leave it. There is too much money at stake."

"Maybe so, but the Indians said unpleasant things will happen if the company logs it," said Bernie Walters, an old cat-skinner from Caycuse. "Before Lake Log sold out to Crown Z, they promised the Indian Band that they would never log that mountain. These silly bastards have no respect and are only interested in profits – no matter what!"

"I'll tell you what," said Frenchy Belcourt, a faller working at Nitinat. "When the engineers laid out the right-of-way, they said they were spooked. They could not explain it but they just felt that they were being watched or something."

"That's a crock a shit!" abruptly spoke an unwanted voice from the shadow – Freddie Hanson. "Look. The company told me that they are going to log it, burn it and pave it!" he mockingly poked fun at everyone in the crowd as he made his way past us, with a nice looking brunette on his arm.

"Never mind that trouble maker," said Bernie. And then he tipped up his beer and guzzled it down.

"Come on Harry, let's finish our beer and go inside. Enough of this shop talk. I'm here to have some fun and dance with the ladies," Lucky Larue said.

Most of the crowd outside followed. The band played old favorites which packed the dance floor. I made my way through the crowded hall over to where Genevieve sat.

I held out my hand and asked, "Wanna dance?" She smiled, got up and we headed for the dance floor.

The dance floor was filled to the brim with young and old alike. The older crowd danced with classic dance moves like the bop, hand jive, and the swing. The younger people preferred the modern dance moves. No matter how good a dancer you were, everyone enjoyed themselves. The band started to play a lively version of At the Hop. In an instant the crowd moved out of the way of a few couples on the dance floor.

Freddie Hanson and his date were one of the couples and could they ever dance. Dressed in a flashy, expensive suit, Freddie had all the moves. And his date for the night was just as good. Everyone watched and tapped their feet and swayed to the beat as the couple blended a number of the classic dances into one!

The other couples on the floor were damn good as well. Buck and his wife Betty were experienced dancers and did moves from the fifties that were a pleasure to watch as they sashayed around the dance floor. Harry Bodine and his partner kept time to the music with a solid Jive. Much to my surprise, Patty Henderson, the lady that ran Walt's Drive Inn was an excellent dancer. She and her husband could rival Freddie and his date with a variety of moves that entertained the crowd. Each couple on the dance floor was determined to try and outdo each other, which added to the excitement.

All was going well when Harry swung his partner around and missed his catch. The momentum carried her right into Freddie's side. It pushed him off balance which forced him to trip over his own feet and he hit the floor. Freddie Hanson leapt up off the floor in a New York minute. By this time Patty was the only one in view, right in front of him. Freddie must have thought it was her that slammed into him.

"You fuckin' bitch! I'll teach you to crash into me while I'm dancin'," he snarled.

Before Patty knew it, Hanson had pushed her hard. She hit the floor and sprawled out. Patty's husband, Bob, immediately attacked Hanson. But this was short lived as Hanson was a good fighter and decked him. Lucky Larue, who was on the sideline, with beer in his belly for added confidence, went after Hanson. Lucky was a good fighter in his own right and the two men squared off.

The band kept playing and the fight was on. Both men were nimble and moved quickly. They threw straight jabs and wild hay-makers. Both men landed solid punches but it was hard to tell who had the upper hand. Everyone in the hall watched and waited to see what the outcome would be. Some cheered on Lucky Larue. Others rooted for Freddie Hanson. Both men were liquored up so they tired out fast. They grappled and fell to the floor and rolled around and tried to get the best of each other. Finally they stood up and squared off again. Someone in the crowd hollered at Lucky and he momentarily turned his head. Hanson sucker punched him and down Lucky Larue went – out cold!

Freddie sensed that it was time to leave the dance so he collected his date and made his way to the door. "Get the hell out of here Hanson. We don't need your kind around here!" yelled Bob angrily. "And take that flat-chested bimbo with ya!"

Freddie hesitated, then turned around and glared at Bob. "Well ya know ass-hole, my date may be flat-chested, but your old lady's tit's, they look like two old work-socks with oranges in them!" he retorted back and then laughed all the way to and out the door. Those within ear-shot laughed a hearty laugh, too.

The dance continued on without a hitch. I danced the night away with Genevieve. It was a lot of fun and we got to know each other a little better. It was around five in the morning when the hall finally cleared out. Genevieve had put on her coat and was ready to head back to Duncan. She walked over to me and unexpectedly reached out and took hold of me. Gen then gave me a nice hug and a passionate kiss. We said our goodbyes and away she went.

Drew and I left too. I needed to hit the sack and get some rest. I was going to the Longhouse that afternoon.

CHAPTER 9

The Longhouse

My old beater of a car made it to Cowichan Bay without a breakdown. Apprehensively, I pulled into the gravel parking lot, which was full of vehicles, in front of the Longhouse. A fine stream of blue smoke filtered its way out of the top of this rustic building made of cedar. The Longhouse was built in a traditional manner, with a frame of cedar logs and covered with hand split cedar planks attached vertically. The structure had no windows, but there was a large entrance, on the side, that was framed by welcome figure totems with outstretched arms. On the corners of the building were protection totems with war-like figures, to fend off evil spirits and unfriendly intruders. Finishing the very simple outside décor was a large painting of a traditional killer whale, painted in Coast Salish style.

A young Indian fellow met me at the entrance. "Welcome. We've been expecting you, Jed. Lyle's sitting over in the far corner. Follow me," this friendly young man said.

The Longhouse was crowded, even in the very dim natural light I could see that on all four sides of the building there were bleachers full of people. And there was a large fire-pit in the middle of a big dirt dance floor that took up most of the interior of the building. The walls were laden with mask carvings and tall totems and the air was pungent from the smoke of the open fire. Fortunately my eyes started to adjust as we made our way over to Lyle. This place had a magical and comforting feel to it, which put me at ease with the surroundings. We paused at a section of aging people and the young fellow greeted them.

He then turned to me. "Jed, it is customary to greet the Elders first."

Without hesitation, I turned and spoke to the Elders, "Thank you for the invitation to your Longhouse and your territory," I spoke sincerely.

A very old and pleasant looking lady in the front row held out her hand towards me. "Young man, I would like to speak with you after the dancing and feast," she said as she gently touched my outreached hand.

I acknowledged with a smile and a nod. We continued on to where Lyle was seated.

"Hello, Jed. Please, sit down, I've saved a seat for you," said Lyle "Glad to see you made it. The dancing and festivities are going to start shortly."

"Thanks, Lyle. I'm looking forward to watching the dancers. I have never seen this type of thing before," I greeted my friend from work.

"When they're done, we're going to have a bite to eat. Ever have gow?" he asked?

"Can't say I have. What is it?" I inquisitively asked.

"It's one of our traditional foods, roe on kelp. The cooks are going to serve it along with other traditional food. You may like it. I caught a nice fresh halibut the other day and brought it to the cook to prepare for this feast. I remember you said the other day that it was one of your favorite fish to eat."

"Can't wait. I love seafood and we don't get that much of it at home. When I get my own place I will definitely be eating more seafood," I said enthusiastically.

The drumming started. The rhythm was spellbinding and the deep tones reverberated right through my body. All eyes were on the traditional button blanketed doorway at the far end of the hall, entrance to the dance floor. The people, who sat in the bleachers, bobbed their heads to the cadence. And the Elders turned in their chairs and watched with pride.

The first dancer through the doorway crouched low and twirled and moved up and down to the beat. His pace and foot pattern was a measure of the dancer's experience. Shrouded in a wrap of cedar boughs to the waist and a cedar bark loin-cloth, he was barefoot. I didn't know what kind of mask he wore, but it was awesome! It was made of yellow cedar and the features were painted bright red, black and green. The coarse hair on this supernatural being hung down to the dancer's waist, which added to the mystical look.

Leaning over to Lyle, I whispered, "I've never seen a mask like that one. What is it?"

"It's a transition mask. The long curved beak represents a supernatural Thunderbird and the eyes on the sides of the face, along with the long hair, symbolize ancient man. Just watch and see what will happen," Lyle intently and proudly informed me.

"What's that he's holding in his hand, Lyle?"

"It's an eagle wing. Eagle's are protectors of the sky and connect us to the Great Spirit. The lead dancer always carries an eagle wing into the Longhouse. It bonds and guards everyone in here."

Behind the lead dancer were four drummers, all kept time with each other and all danced in unison. Next in the procession were three other dancers, all with different masks and traditional dress.

Lyle leaned over towards me. "The first one is a Bakwus, the second is a Raven, and the last one is the Tsonokwa."

"That last dancer and mask, what did you call it, the Tsonokwa, is identical to the thing that chased me in that bad dream I told you about."

"That dream happened for a reason, Jed. You have been chosen," Lyle said.

"Whaddya mean?" I anxiously asked?

"Don't worry, Jed. You'll find out."

I didn't like the sound of what Lyle had said to me and in a strange way I wasn't bothered by his comment. I will wait, patiently.

The dancers moved with ease to the beat of the drums. Creatively and traditionally they all had their own distinct movements as they made their way in a giant circle around the dance floor. These ancestral dance steps had been handed down from generation to generation, preserving this primeval but rich custom and culture. With each song, the drummers sang out in guttural tones that kept the onlookers fixated on this special moment.

I was mesmerized by the beat of the drums and by the way the dancers instinctively moved. They had made their way over closed to where I sat, when the lead dancer broke away from the group. He danced in a tight circle in front of us and then he pointed the eagle feather at me and twirled on one foot. Then to my surprise he looked directly at me and the front of the mask open up and exposed another inner mask, a supernatural wolf. Wow! I was awestruck! Two masks in one. He seemed to be giving me a signal to follow?

"Go ahead, Jed." Lyle encouraged me with a nudge. "They want you to dance with them."

In an instant my mouth was dry and I was very nervous. I looked over at Lyle. "Do I have to?"

"You might not have a choice," he said with a grin. Lyle then stood up to coax me to follow the dancer.

Self-conscious, I was aware that all eyes in the Longhouse were on me. Now committed, I followed the dancer and joined in with the rest of the procession. Damn I was nervous and felt very clumsy. I was not a good dancer at the best of times, with two left feet. So at this point I didn't know what I was going to do. I decided I would just follow along. Little by little I moved to the beat and with every step I tried my best to move to the rhythm of the drums and mimic to some extent the others.

The pace and intensity increased and everyone seemed to be in a trancelike yet very aware state. We moved in unison in a giant circle around the open fire centerpiece while the flames licked out at us. I noticed a group of young men who sat together. All held elaborately painted traditional paddles. As we moved toward them, one of the paddlers stood up and approached me with something in his hand and he motioned me to stop. He then placed a woven cedar headband on my head. At the same time a middle aged man got up from his chair and approached me. He handed me a paddle. Humbly I took it and then kept on dancing to the beat.

The dance went on for quite some time and I felt a little less intimidated. We moved around the dance floor until we were in front of the Elders and then stopped abruptly.

The people in the Longhouse erupted into a vigorous applause and some whooped while others cheered in the Salish language. The paddlers, in unity, with their paddles upright banged them on the floor and made guttural war-like noises. I was overwhelmed and didn't know what was going on but I felt elated!

One of the Elder ladies stood and approached me. "Young man, I have something for you," she said as she extended her hand. "This is a feather from the Northern Flicker. I am gifting this to you because you have had a vision of the Tsonokaw. You have been chosen, young man. Keep it close to you and it will help protect you on your life's journey."

"Thank you," I said politely, and took the feather from her. "I don't understand?" I asked.

"In time you will find out what the meaning of all this is, Jed. Do not be afraid, you are a lucky person to have had a vision, especially of the Tsonokaw. Very few people are guided by dream visions. Your life will be full of adventure and journey and you will walk in the spirit of your ancestors. You come from a distant Nation, one that is a mix of different cultures – the Métis. They were the people of the buffalo and used to travel great distances to gather food and were know as nomadic people. The Métis are a friendly Nation that mixed with other aboriginal people in harmony," Elsie said, and then turned to sit down but hesitated. "One day you will be given an Indian name," she said convincingly.

I was dumbfounded at what had just been said to me, and my mind was awash in thoughts. Métis, who are the Métis and what does Elsie mean I come from these people? How does she know this? And she sure seemed to know a fair bit about these other aboriginal people. I'm going to have to find out.

My surreal spell was broken by a tap on my shoulder, it was the dancer dressed in the Thunderbird mask. "Hello," spoke the man as he pulled off his mask. It was Sam, my fellow workmate that ran off the side-hill that weird afternoon at work. "How's it going? Guess you thought I was never coming back to work. Well I had some things to take care of for a few days but I'll be back setting beads this week," he informed me.

"Nice to see ya, Sam. The guys said you'd be back sooner or later."

"Whatcha think of the gifts you were presented with? Do ya know what they represent?"

"No, can't say I do."

"Well, the paddle is a winter moon paddle. It is said that people that are presented with one will live a long time. In aboriginal culture, our life cycle is measured by the four seasons. The winter is the last of the life cycles and the winter moon means very old and wise."

We stood in silence for a moment. "What do you think of Elsie?" Sam asked.

"I like her. I have never met anyone like her before. She was kind and passionate to me, Sam," I sincerely pointed out.

"Elsie came to our people as a little girl, a very long time ago. Other Elders say she came from the plains people in the Manitoba area. Apparently her parents were killed in a boating accident and she was adopted by one of our families that lost a girl.

Elsie is very a special and wise Elder. When she talks, everyone pays attention to what she has to say," Sam said passionately about this lady.

"Elsie gave me a very pretty feather. -She said it came from a Northern Flicker. Have you ever seen a feather like this before?" I said to Sam, and pulled out the gift to show him.

A fellow sitting close to us overheard what I had said, "The Flicker is the only bird in North America that has distinct orange colored feathers on the underside. See the stem, its bright orange and the feather part has an orangey hew to it, and then fades to almost a pinky orange. Beautiful ain't it?" This fellow enlightened us.

Sam got up and headed for the dining room. "Come-on let's eat, I see they are serving up the feast."

I sat and ate in silence. I was beleaguered by the events that took place in the Longhouse and didn't understand why I was given the gifts and why Elsie spoke to me about the things she did. It scared me, but I had a warm feeling in my stomach and I felt comfortable around these generous people. What was all this about? Was I going to embark on a journey, guided by some supernatural force?

CHAPTER 10

Seven Long

The days, weeks, and months flew by and I was proud to call myself a west coast logger! Logging seemed to fit my adventuresome personality and lifestyle. Every time someone asked me where I was working, my chest would puff up and I'd reply, "I'm loggin'" with a degree of self-importance. For me, there was no better way to make a living. Experience at work was now my companion and I felt invincible.

"Ollie, how's Jed doing these days?" Custy asked. "Is he ready to pull riggin' full time yet?" the hardened woods boss inquired.

"Yaw, by golly, the little fucker's doin' alright. Stant's bin lets him pull rigging quite a bit and he seems to be doing alright. Why?"

"We're starting up the Tension-Skidder and we need a riggin puller to pull hook on it. Slim's going to run the machine and..."

"Ya mean Slim Johnson from Nanaimo?" interrupted Ollie. "Who the hell is going to hook on it?" Ollie asked, with his nose a little out of joint. The company never asked him if he was interested in the more prestigious job.

"Clint Swenson is going to take on the job. We offered it to his brother, Ivan, but he turned it down."

"He's not going to run the Slack-Line anymore? Dumb fucker!" Ollie sarcastically said as he fidgeted with his hardhat. "Where's it going to be setup?"

"We've got a cream show up Branch 20. The fallers are finished and the company wants to get the wood out of there before the snow flies. Here comes the town crummy, I'll grab LaSal and let him know that I'm moving him to another machine and a riggin' pullin' job," Custy said.

"Say, ain't that the mountain the Indians don't want the company to log?" the old hooktender probed. "I hear there is an old burial site somewhere up on the mountain. I thought the company changed its mind about logging up there because of all the protests these last few months. Dumb fuckers," said Ollie.

"Don't get your ass in a knot, Larson! It's all taken care of," Custy snapped back and went to meet the bus that just pulled into the marshalling yard.

Custy met me as I jumped off the crummy. "I'm moving you to another machine, Jed. Gonna give you a promotion. You'll be pullin' hook on the Tension-Skidder. Clint's going to hook on it, so he'll show you the ropes. Keep your head up and your wits about you and you'll make out just fine," the seasoned woods foreman informed me.

"OK!" I eagerly replied and followed him over to a big crummy filled with men. This was going to be a great opportunity to prove that I was capable of pulling riggin' full time.

Clint met us at the door. "Hello. Jump in, Jed. We're waitin' on the landing bucker. He's getting some parts from the power saw shop and then we're gettin' the hell out of here and goin' logging." It's a dog's breakfast in the mornings to try and get parts or anything for that matter because it's that hectic! "Hey Joe, where the fuck is Slim?" Clint hollered over to the head woods boss who was overseeing all the goings on in the marshalling yard in the morning – insuring that the company's interests were well looked after.

Joe spat out a mouthful of snoose juice and walked over towards Clint. "He's in the shop, I think he's picking up the bugs."

"I'll swing by the shop and pick'im up, he's probably in there bull-shittin' with the master mechanic. I'll also stop at the line-shack and let Shaky know where to bring the new haulback. It shouldn't take us long to put it on. It's a good thing we rigged up last week, Joe, if everything goes right we'll be loggin' before lunch."

"OK, fly at it!" The woods boss said with a thumbs up and tipped his hardhat slightly back on his head.

The trip out to the machine was quiet. The new chokerman in the crummy was apprehensive because Clint Swenson's reputation was larger than life. Clint's family is well known in the valley. They all are loggers - damn good loggers! Known as a fair yet demanding person to work with, Clint knew his stuff. He was an all-round logger who could do most jobs in the woods and do them well and expected everyone else to do the same.

We sipped on our coffees and put on our caulk boots. Shaky had pulled into the landing driving the line-horse with the new haul-back. Slim was already in the cab and had the machine running. Clint waved at him to come out onto the deck. "Once we put the haul-back on we're going to high-lead the first few roads before we put the carriage on, Slim. It'll give me time to finish rigging the back-spar," he ordered.

It didn't take long and the new line was on the haul-back drum. With an extra couple of guys on the crew we strung the lines and hung the blocks, ready to start logging. Clint took two of the chokerman with him to the back-end to give him a hand rigging the back-spar. I gave the chaser help with hooking up the butt-rigging.

"How many beads do you want to fly?" Emile asked, in his colourful French Canadian accent.

"Fill all four bull-hooks, we're gonna wood'er down," I replied. "OK fellas let's head up the hill," I said to the remaining two chokerman.

We were close to the landing and logging the uphill side of the setting so Slim could see us and, for the first few turns, I would use hand signals. I signaled the engineer to skinner-back and he smoothly tight-line the butt-riggingup and sent it back to us.

I untangled the chokers. "I want you guys to double up on the logs and make sure you get short ends. Tim, you'll have enough slack for those two firs on the low side. Jimmy, grab that bigger cedar and hemlock and for chrisske make damn sure you do it right. We don't want to fuck up the chokers on the first turn."

With the chokers set we hustled out of the turn. I raised my arm and signaled to Slim to go ahead on'er. He expertly guided the nice turn of logs into the landing and settled them on the ground for the chaser to unhook. Quickly, Emile unfastened the beads and the rigging was on its way back to us. The loader operator, Alf, swung his machine around and flung open his window. "Emile! Grab the saw and trim up those ends, will ya. I'm gonna lay those log out so I can coal-deck the turns as they come in. Looks like we have a high-ball riggin' crew. I'll need all the room I can get in this small landing," he said.

We already had our next turn set and I wooded it down. Slim pulled on the throttle and the machine easily handled the heavy turn of logs as the logs danced their way to the landing. Because we were close to the landing the logging went fast. We hustled in and out of the riggin' with not much rest in between. In no time flat there was an impressive stack of logs ready to send to the log dump at the beach.

We worked hard and fast so the morning went by quickly. We had logged our way up to the tail-holds and had time to change roads before lunch. With Clint at the back-end riggin' a back-spar I handled the change easily and saved him and the fellows from coming all the way down through the fell and bucked timber to change roads.

"Goddamn, am I ever hungry," Tim said. "Can't wait till I dig into my nose-bag!"

"Ya, LaSal worked the piss out of us. The prick never gave us a break," Jimmy jokingly poked fun at me.

"Ah, you guys are tough bastards," I said. "But come to think of it, you are from Duncan," I wittily dropped a sarcastic hint, and chuckled. Jimmy looked my way and gave me the finger, but he did so with a smile.

We arrived at the crummy and Custy was waiting for us. "How long till you can jump onto the spartree, Jed?" He asked.

"If everything goes right, we'll change over in the late afternoon. Clint already said that if it was close to quitin' time we'll stay and make the change before we head for camp," I told the woods boss.

"Great! That way you'll have a fresh start in the mornin'. Maybe we'll get enough loads to meet our weekly quota? The manager has been on my ass all week. The fuckin ass-hole is never satisfied. All he wants to do is clean out this new valley before all hell breaks loose," he grouchily said before he got into his truck and took off.

"Man that guy is always in a pissed off mood," Slim said. "Wish he would lighten up with the production bull-shit. No matter what, the company will never be happy with production. Say, have you guys heard about all the protest over logging this mountain – Sleeping Beauty?"

"Well, Slim. There are a number of us working here that figure we shouldn't be logging here," Alf nicely mentioned.

"Custy's back. Wonder what he wants," I said. "Looks as though he's got another man with him."

Slim had a serious look on his face. "It's Hunky Bill! He's Freddie Hanson's best friend so as you can imagine, he's just as big of a prick! Custy's probably brought him here to push us guys for more production. He's known on the coast as a high-ballin' mean sonofabitch," Slim let us know.

"LaSal, Hunky is going to give you a hand out on the riggin'. You're still the rigging puller, but he has a lot of experience and can show you a thing or two," Custy ordered.

Hunky Bill was quiet while we ate. But by the look on his face we all knew that he's itching to cause some trouble.

"Have there been many people at those protests?" I casually asked Slim?

"Mostly Indian folks, a few Hippies and the odd politician looking for votes. From what I hear they are planning a big rally down at the Parliament Buildings. There are going to be people from all..." Slim was cut off speaking.

Abruptly, Hunky Bill butts in. "Fuck'em, those goddamn lazy ass-holes are always protesting against logging their so called land! They think they own it all. Well they don't. Us white people own it, lock, stock and barrel. And we'll log all of it if we want. Fuck'em! Don't be surprised if me and some of my buddies show up at the protest in Vic and kick some ass," he continued and shook his fist. Hunky had a look on his face that could kill.

We all were stunned by this off the cuff comment and it was the first time I had heard someone meanly show aggression towards Indian people. I knew that there was discrimination against these people, but I had never experienced it before now.

Hunky put a chew in his mouth and said, "Come 'on you ass-holes let's go get some logs." as he pushed his way out of the crummy and headed for the side-hill. I wasn't looking forward to this afternoon.

Once we started to log after lunch I was nervous. Hunky Bill was an experienced logger and knew the ropes. He moved like a cat thought the slash and knew exactly what logs to grab and he didn't say a word.

His silence had an effect on the rest of the rigging crew and everyone seemed to be edgy and didn't have their mind on the job. This was not a good situation and could be dangerous, so I was going to try and break the ice with some light conversation in between turns.

"Helluva hockey game the other night eh?" I said.

"Ya I thought the Leafs were going to win, but the Canadians came through in the last period," Jimmy said.

"They got lucky," spoke up Tim. "The Canadians are in last place and will really have to pull up their socks if they want to make the play-offs."

"They are only getting warmed up, remember last year? They played their best towards the end of the season. Besides, they…" I was going to continue.

Rudely, Hunky Bill spoke up. "Look you fuckin' idiots we're hear to get logs, not play hockey. Custy wants eight loads a day from this setting, so keep your goddamn minds on the job and not hockey! We want to finish logging this valley before those drunken Indians whine and cry about it," he mocked us.

Everyone went silent and kept their thoughts to themselves and looked a little scared. I was pissed off but didn't say a word for fear of a fight breaking out. That bugger is one hell of an ornery bastard and kept the whole crew on edge. Sure wish Clint would hurry up and finish rigging that back-spar and get down here – he would be able to control this idiot.

We worked our way back to the blocks and there were only a few more logs to get and then we would change roads.

When we finished logging that road, I blew for the straw-line which the chaser sent out on the eye of the haul-back. I unhooked it and Hunky Bill pulled it back and with Jimmy's help they were going to re-string it over to the next block and back down to the haul-back eye.

"Come-on you little fucker, get your ass in gear!" Hunky Bill hollered. We watched as Jimmy hustled back down the hill towards us. I could tell he was intimidated by Hunky Bill's persistent taunts by the way he moved through the fell-and-bucked logs. We hoped he is stringing the straw-line straight because we don't want any si-washes in it.

With everything hooked back up I gave the go-a-head on the straw-line and sent it back to the landing. "I don't like that guy," Jimmy said. "He gives me the willies. All he talked about was how much he hated the Indians and that they had no right to any land."

"Never mind, I'll let Clint know and he'll deal with him. Nobody fucks with Clint or his crew. I bet he sends him packin'," I said.

Hunky Bill watched the blocks at the back end, to make sure that everything went smooth. Slim tight-lined the butt-rigging out of the landing and was going to clear the lines all the way to the blocks but they wouldn't clear so I blew for him to skinner back. "Looks like we've got a si-wash in the haul-back, fella's, so let's hook up a turn and see if we can clear the lines," I said.

We headed into the turn. "Jimmy, grab that big hemlock. Tim, hook-up that cedar and fir together." I said.

The guys finished setting their chokers, but I needed more slack to set mine. "Step up out of the way. I'm going to go ahead easy on the riggin'." We were all standing on the high side, a few feet from the turn, when I gave the signal to go ahead easy.

That was the last thing I remember until I became aware of voices coming closer.

"Where the hell are they, Hunky?" screamed Clint.

"They got hit with the haul-back, Clint."

"All three of them?"

"Yes, there must have been a si-wash in the haul-back because it came at them like a tightly strung bow. It hit all of them and flung them over the rock bluff forty feet down to the logs below!"

"Sonofabitch, let's get down to them. It'll be a miracle if no one is dead!" Clint said.

Clint wasted no time. "Here they are, under these logs. LaSal's face down and there's blood everywhere. Looks like a head injury. Tim's sitting up, but Jimmy is down and not moving,"

"Hunky, get the bug off of LaSal and blow seven long. This is a helluva accident! We'll need the ambulance from camp. I'll see how I can help these guys. You head into the landing and get on the radio and inform camp to get a doctor coming from town. I think we may have a fatality on our hands!"

"Jed. Jed, are you alright?" In and out of consciousness, I could faintly hear a voice. I tried to open my eyes but they seemed glued shut. I shivered and felt cold. Then a warm feeling came over me. I felt as though I was in another world and everything was peaceful. There was something walking towards me. Its face was green, red, and white, and it had long hair flowing down past its waist. It was Bakwus', and in his outreached hand was an eagle feather that he waved over me.

Ghostly, this supernatural being looked down at me. "Son, you'll be fine," I thought this eerie thing said to me. But its voice seemed distant and soft. I felt as though I was in a different land, time and dimension, but it felt good. Was I dead?

"Let's get these guys on the stretchers and the hell off this side-hill. LaSal's in the worst shape, don't know if he'll make it. Poor bastard! Can you walk out Tim?"

"Yes I can, Clint. The haul-back didn't hit me as hard. LaSal took the full brunt of it because he was standing in the front of us," Tom said.

I regained my consciousness in camp – but barely. The doctor stepped into the ambulance to check us out. I heard my dad's voice. "Jed, are you OK?"

"I'm OK, dad," I weakly said.

"Are these guys going to be OK?" dad asked the doctor.

"The other two will be fine. Your son, I don't know, he's lost a lot of blood. He's in bad shape, Frank. It's a head injury and we need to get him to the hospital!" the doctor said with urgency.

I layed on the stretcher in the ambulance and noticed my dad as he looked through the side window, staring at me. When I turned my head to look at him, he had a tear in his eye. It scared me so I closed my eyes. When I opened them again, he was gone. But something else looked at me through the same window. I blinked my eyes to clear them and see who it was. It was the Bakwus′!

CHAPTER 11

Road Block

When I woke up in the hospital Genevieve was there and sitting next to me. She held my hand gently between hers. "Jed, glad to have you back in the land of the living," she said reassuringly. "How are you feeling?"

"A bit groggy and I'm hungry, but otherwise not too bad. How long have I been in here?" I asked.

"It's been ten days. They've kept you sedated so your body could heal. You sure gave us a scare," she informed me.

There were tubes attached to my left arm and a bag of clear fluid hung off a stand beside my bed. I felt my head because my face seemed to be quite swollen. "Gee, I guess I must look funny, eh? How many stitches?" I asked my girlfriend.

"Yes, you sure do look different. They put in over a hundred stitches in your head, so don't look at yourself in the mirror, it'll scare the pants off of you. The doctors have said that you're not out of the woods yet and it'll take some time for the swelling and bruising to fade away. Now that you're awake, they will run more tests to make damn sure everything is fine. So you may be in here for a while," said Gen.

Those words were not comforting so I kept my thoughts to myself.

The days in the hospital turned into weeks but I was definitely on the mend. All the tests and x-rays came back clean indicating that there was no lasting damage. It was going to take time to heal! In the meantime, I did my best to give the nurses a bad time. And I had lots of visitors from work mates, friends and relatives, and of course Genevieve. I was discharged from the hospital with a clean bill of health and a little wiser about working in the woods.

Damn it felt good to be out and about again. And right then I was waiting for my friend. "How you doin', Jed?" asked my buddy Drew. "The newspaper article said the accident was one of the worst they have had in the valley. You're a lucky man, my friend!"

"Shit, it would take more than that to put me down. Besides someone has to look out for your sorry ass," I poked fun at my friend.

"Guess you've got someone upstairs looking after ya," said Drew.

"More like something down here," I said as I looked out the window of Walt's Drive-In. I looked at Drew and continued. "One of the things that stuck out in my mind about the accident was my vision of the Bakwus'. I'm starting to believe that there just may be something to what the Indians have said to me."

With an inquisitive look on his face, Drew asked, "What's this about?"

"Ah never mind. Are you going to the protest in Victoria tomorrow?" I asked.

"Yes, you can come with me, if ya want? It'll be a hum-dinger. There's supposed to be quite a number of people showing up to support the Indians and just as many to support the logging company. Should make for an interesting mix of arguments on both sides of the fence – eh? I heard your old buddy Hanson and his buddies will be there."

"He's no fucking friend of mine! If that prick shows up there's bound to be trouble. It seems to follow him wherever he goes," I quickly pointed out to Drew.

The drive over the Malahat took forty minutes or so and by the time we arrived at the parliament buildings there was hardly a place to park. Drew was right, there was going to be a few thousand people here to either protest the logging of Sleeping Beauty Mountain or people taking a stand against the protesters. In any event it promised to be interesting.

After parking some distance away we briskly walked to the parliament buildings, not wanting to miss any of the speakers. A huge crowd was gathered on the lawn where the organizers had set up microphones and speakers. We were a bit early and had to wait for the first speaker to take the podium but this allowed us time to mingle. Drew pointed out some of the politicians and prominent First Nations in the crowd.

The Indian people were dressed in traditional attire and there was a procession of drummers which entertained the crowd with traditional spiritual songs and dances. The politicians shook hands and schmoozed the crowd with fake smiles and pretended that they cared about the issue.

"Hey LaSal!" hollered a familiar voice. "How the hell's she goin'?" Without looking I knew exactly who it was. Hunky Bill. That meant one thing. Freddie Hanson would be here as well and that spelled trouble.

"I'm doing okay," I acknowledged.

"You're one lucky sonafabitch," said Hunky Bill. "Thought you guys had met your maker. Well I'm glad to see that you are going to be fine."

This act of kindness was unusual coming from him. "Thanks," I said. "It was as close as I ever want to come to shaking hands with St. Peter. It's a tough way to learn, but that's never going to happen again."

"Well young fellow, I've had my share of bumps and bruises from working in the woods and I've learned a great deal from them. I'm just glad you're okay. When are you coming back to work?"

"Not sure. I've got to see the Doc once more. But the way I feel, it will be soon."

"Great. We're still logging over on Sleeping Beauty. That's why I'm here. Those fuckin' Indians think they can stop us from making a living. But we're going to show them a thing or two," he said meaningfully.

Not knowing what to say I gave him a slight smile and turned to listen to the first person at the podium. It was an Indian fellow from the local Band and by the tone of his voice he was going to rally the protesters.

With his hand held high in the air his strong words reverberated. "We'll never let the logging company log Sleeping Beauty! They think they destroy our traditional burial grounds? No way! Our people will fight this to the very end. That mountain has...."

"Go to hell!" hollered someone from the crowd.

"We need to feed our families!" bellowed another.

"Ya, you have no right to stop us from making a living!" shouted Hunky Bill.

It was about then that the people against the logging started to jeer back at the loggers. There were yelling matches in different parts of the crowd and things seemed to be getting out of hand.

I noticed Freddie Hanson and a couple of his drinking buddies coming our way.

"Hey Hunky! Do ya think we should kick some ass!" he said loud enough for all to hear.

Freddie slid in next to Hunky Bill and I saw him pass a small brown bag to him. It was a bottle of hooch. When those idiots drank there was trouble. I could tell he was itching to get a fight going.

He noticed me. "Hey LaSal. What side of the fence are you on, ya little fucker!" Hanson meanly hollered. "Are you with those goddamn lazy Indians? They want to stop us from making a living."

I was scared but needed to stand my ground. "Look Freddie, I don't know much about..."

Hanson abruptly cut me off. "Fuck you! You're a logger now. So ya better get your act together and stand up for what is right. The company is right and not these good for nothing bunch of slackers!"

"Back off Freddie," said Hunky Bill. "Leave the kid alone. He's been through enough lately. Besides, when he comes back to work he'll be logging right beside us, on Sleeping Beauty."

Freddie was a little tipsy and as he took a step back he tripped and bumped into a Hippie. "Hey man, watch what you're doin'," the fellow said.

Without hesitation Freddie let his fist fly. It struck the fellow so fast and hard that he hit the ground immediately. His buddies saw what had taken place so three of them jumped Freddie and the fight was on. Freddie's work-mates stepped in to give him a hand. A couple of the Indian fellows joined in to support the Hippies. I was surprised at how well the Hippies, with their long hair and ragged clothes, handled themselves. I guess looks can be deceiving. Fact is one of them looked as though he had spent some time in the ring because he gave Hunky Bill a good go. Much to the embarrassment of Hunky!

Drew looked over at me. "Let's get the hell out of here. Here come the cops. They're sure to arrest us along with those assholes."

We quickly made our way over to a retaining wall and climbed up onto it so we could watch the goings-on. The crowd heckled each other from both sides of the issue as the cops came through to break up the donnybrook. It didn't look like much of a fight, mostly pushing and shoving and a few punches. It didn't take the cops long to break it up and send those people on their way. By the look of it, Freddie and his mates came out ahead. As they left the grounds Drew and I could hear them laughing and joking with each other. They accomplished what they came for: to disrupt the logging protest.

The protest went on as if nothing had happened. All the guest speakers had a turn up on the podium and made their case against the company for not logging Sleeping Beauty. They did make some good points but it was definitely one sided because most of the pro-logging supporters had left. When all was over we made our way back to the vehicle. We followed a small crowd of Indian fellows and overheard them talking.

"We had better organize a road block out in the woods," spoke up one of the fells.

"Why?"asked the fellow that walked next to him.

"Well, I don't think they will stop logging the mountain. Did you hear what the politician said? All smoke and mirrors. If we don't take the bull by the horns ourselves, nothing is going to change. Those fuckin' loggers have no right to be logging on our land. They are all a bunch of red-neck white ass mother-fuckers. We'll show them!"

I was a bit taken back to hear the Indian fellas talking like that. I expected that kind of talk from the likes of Freddie Hanson and his crowd, but not from the Indians. It was then I realized that discrimination knows no boundaries.

After spending the next two weeks at home relaxing, the Doctor gave me the okay to go back to work and I found myself on the town crummy heading to camp Monday morning, ready for work. My mind was awash with all kinds of thoughts and I was unable to concentrate on any one thing. Oh well, I thought, once I get back out on the side hill and shake out the cob-webs I'd be fine.

When we arrived at camp we noticed a crowd had gathered in front of the office. I wondered what the hell was going on?

"Alright fellows, this is the situation," said Phil Harmon, the camp manager. "Looks like we've got a bunch of protesters blocking the road at Branch 20. They're going to take direct action against the logging on Sleeping Beauty and ..."

"Damnit! I've got a family to feed and those bastards are not going to stop me from going to work!" shouted someone from the crowd.

"Ya!" hollered another. "Let's head out there and kick some ass! Those fucking Indians are not going to stop us from working just because they claim to have an ancestral burial ground on Sleeping Beauty."

"Hang on fellas. We've got to do this right. I've already got the RCMP coming in from the Foot. The protesters don't have a legal right to do what they are doing and the cops will remove them when they get here. In the meantime we have to wait," said Phil

"Fuck that! Let's go to work. We'll get rid of those lazy rubies," spoke up Carl Jorgensen the old Swede. "If we let them get away with this now, they'll be back again and it'll never stop," he said.

The majority of the men voiced their approval and wanted to go remove the blockade.

"Listen fellows, we…"

As Phil was about to address the men a crummy whizzed by the crowd of angry loggers and headed for the woods. It was Freddie Hanson and he wasn't wasting any time.

"Goddamnit!" shouted the manager. "We don't need any trouble. Look. You fellows head out there and keep things in order. Don't let that crazy bastard get carried away."

With that order coming from the camp manager, the crowd dispersed. Not all the men were working up Branch 20, so those crews headed in a different direction. The rest of us that were working on Sleeping Beauty Mountain loaded into the crummies and started the short dive to Branch 20 and uncertainty. Damn that Freddie Hanson!

We arrived at the start of Branch 20 and by the look of the tire tracks on the gravel road Freddie didn't waste any time in getting to the blockade. We rounded a sharp corner and found Freddie's crummy in the middle of the road with the door open – and no sight of him.

"Wonder where that crazy fucker is?" said Slim.

"Look's like that sonofawhore is headed into the woods. See his foot tracks going up the bank," said Clint. "I bet he's going to go around the protesters blocking the road."

"Ya, but it's a long way to go cuz he's got to go over that big ridge, and it's full of rock bluffs," said Slim with a bit of a grin.

"That's right, but he's crazy enough to do it. And wholey fuck will those fucking protesters be surprised," said Clint with a chuckle.

We drove up the road and it wasn't long before we approached the road block. All of us were quiet with anticipation. In a couple of minutes the crummies had come to a stop and we all bailed out and started to mingle forty feet or so in front of the protesters.

"Listen up guys!" bellowed Clint with his meanest logger's voice he could muster up as he tried to intimidate the people on the road block. "The cops are on their way. They'll move you cocksuckers out of the way!" he informed them as he turned to glare at the sixty or so people blocking the logging road. That's when the name calling started.

"Hey, white-ass!" hollered a native fellow "You guys are not going to destroy our land."

Clint stepped towards the protesters and gave them the middle finger. "Fuck you! Why don't you go get a job, ya lazy bastard?" Clint said sarcastically.

With those words most of the protesters started to yell and taunt the loggers. Racial slurs were coming from both sides and the tone was getting angrier. There was still no sign of Freddie Hanson. I wondered where he'd disappeared to?

The loggers and protesters were nose to nose and screamed at each other. It looked as if there was going to be a rumble.

The Woods Forman, with the cops in tow, wasted no time as he got out of his crummy. "Alright, everyone calm down!" he yelled. "Clint, take your crew and get back in your crummy before all hell breaks loose!" ordered Custy and the crew followed his orders.

Two RCMP officers made their way to the crowd. "Listen up! We'll arrest anyone who doesn't obey us." said one of the officers. "I want you all to calm down and take a step back from each other. Then I'll explain what is going to happen here."

Those words seemed to defuse the situation somewhat, but there was still some name calling and racial insults that came from both sides.

"Everyone be quiet," spoke the RCMP officer. "What you protesters are doing is against the law. The company has a legal right to log this mountain. I understand you don't agree with the logging. However, that being the case, you do have a legal avenue to get an order from the court to stop the logging. Without that, this protest is against the law. Are you going to leave peacefully?"

An old Indian fellow stepped up in front. "You'll have to pack me off this mountain, because I'm not going to go on my own. And it's a safe bet that that goes for all of us here blocking the road," he intently told the cop.

"Alright then. Here are the straight goods. If you all are not going to go on your own free will, I can't remove you. The company doesn't have an injunction from the court to stop you from blocking their road, so until they obtain one I can't order you to move nor can I arrest you," he informed the protesters.

With that statement the crowd erupted with a loud cheer and the Indians beat their drums. For now the protesters had won!

"Custy, until the company gets an injunction, all I can do is keep the peace," the cop said.

"No problem. I'll send the crew home and the big-wigs from head office will have to deal with the court order."

As we headed for camp we came across Freddie Hanson sitting on the side of the road. He looked as though he had seen a ghost. His hands trembled and he sweated profusely.

"Freddie, what the hell's the matter?" inquired Slim, with a concerned look. Freddie looked up slowly and shook his head. He couldn't say a word and his face looked like he had aged twenty years.

I looked out the window and our eyes met and we stared at each other briefly. Freddie knew damn well that I knew what it was that scared him. Something unexplainable, probably something supernatural.

CHAPTER 12

Strange Happenings

The word came down from head office that we would be off for a week and a half. This would allow the company time to seek an injunction to remove the protesters from Branch 20 and Sleeping Beauty Mountain. It would also give me time to go fishing.

I was on my way to Skutz Falls on the Cowichan River a few miles south of Lake Cowichan. My Dad had been there a couple of weekends ago and said he couldn't keep the trout off his hook. After I parked my vehicle I followed the path down to the Cowichan River. The noise of the falls was intoxicating and lured me closer to my intended quarry held within its churned up crystal clear and cold water. I noticed someone further downstream, looked as though they were sitting on a small outcrop into the river. Not many people know of that spot, so they must have known the river well because the pool they were fishing always produced nice fish. I think I'll wander on down there and see if they have caught anything, I thought.

"Hello," I greeted the older looking person. "How's the fishin'?" I asked. Much to my surprise Elsie turned around to greet me.

"Well hello young Jed," said Elsie. "I haven't seen you since the dancing at the Longhouse. How are you? I heard that you were in a very serious logging accident?" said my Elder friend.

"I am well, Elsie. And yes, I was in a bad accident and spent some time in the hospital but everything is fine now."

"Well, I'm very pleased to see and hear that you are ok. Sit down and let's talk a while, Jed," she calmly said.

Elsie looked right at home on the bank of the river. By the way she handled her fishing pole I could tell she had done this for many years. And she had caught a couple of nice trout as well.

"Looks like you had some luck, Elise," I warmly said.

"Yes, but they're not biting as well as they should for this time of year, Jed. But I do have a good feed for supper. So tell me, how are things with you?"

"Oh, same old, same old. I'm back at work. You know how that is. The side hills wear a guy out and I've been spending more time with Genevieve."

"Speaking of work, were you at the road block, Jed?"

"Yes, I was there," I said awkwardly.

"Wish I could have been there, but I'm getting too old for that type of thing. Maybe if some of us older Elders were there it may have been friendlier. It's too bad it has come to this kind of protest. It's not what most of the Elders at the village wanted and I blame the government. They should have had better judgement to let the logging company log in there without consulting us first. All we want is to protect the old and sacred burial grounds. They can log the rest," she said.

"I agree, Elsie, but I have to work with those people so for the most part I've kept quiet. The company says the best wood is near the burial grounds and to make it feasible all the wood has to go. I think most people want a proper compromise. There's lots of wood to log so why not protect a historical site. What I'm concerned about is how this issue has the people in the Cowichan Valley split. And the racial discrimination is very disturbing. Why are people like that, Elsie?"

Before she had a chance to answer my question, a fish took her line. "Hang on a sec, I've got to land this fish."

Elsie played the fish like an expert to bring it closer to the shore. Her face lit up like a youngster while the fish danced back and forth and launched from the water in all its silver glory. And then ka-sploosh, it hit the river on its side which sent spray everywhere. For a brief moment the years appeared to melt away from this wonderful woman. It didn't take long before she had her quarry beached and ready to take home.

"Jed, discrimination is a curse besieged by people. Why? I don't know. In a perfect world we would all be tolerant of each other, but our world is not perfect. People are not perfect. So all we can do is try and learn about each other and respect our differences."

Those were wise words that I would heed. "Well I've got to go, Elsie. It has been very nice to see you again."

"Here, take this fish, you never even wetted your line. I guess you got caught up listening to this old woman. Well at least you'll have fish for supper," she said with a laugh.

"Thanks. It'll taste mighty fine."

"Say, did you put that Northern Flicker feather I gave you in a special place?" she asked.

I inquisitively looked at her. "Yes I did," I said, "Why?"

"Remember what I told you about that feather? It'll help protect you."

"Oh?"

"The dancers held a secret ceremony at the Longhouse. They have asked the creator for help in protecting Sleeping Beauty. It was a powerful ritual that involved both the Bakwus' and Tsonokwa masks. It is said and believed that strange things will take place out there, Jed. So be careful."

The logger in me didn't want to believe her, but the tone and conviction in her voice was believable – was something going to happen? And when?

"Say, when you have time, would you like to come and have supper? And bring Genevieve. I'd like to meet her."

"I'll give you a call soon. It'd be nice to have dinner with you and I'm sure Gen would enjoy it as well," I said to my Elder friend.

I took my fish and said goodbye then headed up the trail to my vehicle. I paused and looked back at Elise. She was in the same spot with her line in the water, a sun-dog rained down on her that silhouetted her body, which gave her a comforting ancestral look. After our conversation there was a peaceful calm shadowing me, something I didn't really understand but it felt good. I wondered what she meant that strange things will happen.

It took the company about a week to obtain an injunction from the court. The judge was very specific within the order regarding the blocking of the road – there was no legal justification to block the road stopping the workers from going to work. However he did say that the protesters could apply to the court for an order to cease logging while the issue was being sorted out. To date no application had been made so we were going back to work.

The call came that work would start the following Monday. So back to the grind, again. When we arrived at camp a meeting had been called.

Once all the crummies were in camp the men gathered outside of the office. "Well fellas, over the weekend the RCMP came and informed the protesters that the company had an order from the court to put an end to their blockade. The protesters left peacefully. So for now everything should be back to normal – normal as it can be for you bunch of rag-tag hay-wire loggers!" said Phil Harman with a tongue-in-cheek laugh.

Everyone was in a good mood, itching to get back to work. "Hey Phil! How many of those tree-huggers did you stump-break last weekend?" hollered someone from the crowd.

Everyone roared a hearty laugh. "The last thing I would do is bugger-a-hugger," expressed the camp manager and he headed back into the office.

The men dispersed. Each headed for their crummies and back to work out in the woods. Everyone's frame of mind was good because the loggers had come out on top, for now.

"Does anyone know where the hell Freddie Hanson is?" asked Slim before we took off.

"I heard he's taking some time off. Rumour is that whatever he had seen that day out at the road block scared the livin' shit out of him. Hunky Bill says he's never seen Freddie like this before," Clint informed everyone.

"Bet he's on a piss-up," chuckled Tim. "Hope the fucker never comes back."

I was glad to see Tim back after the accident and setting chokers again. "No-shit! I hope the prick never comes back. He's nothing but a troublemaker," I said.

As we approached the area where the road block was Slim brought the crummy to a stop and we all got out.

"Goddammer. Look what the hell those sonsawhores left here?" said Clint with a surprised look on his face.

"What the hell? Never seen this kind of thing before," said our new chokerman, Ray Newman. "Nice caving though. What is it?"

"Fuck if I know. But they went to a lot of work to create it," said Tim.

"That's right, but they had fuck-all to do anyway. None of them ass-holes work, so they had all week to fuck-around," Emile angrily mentioned. He was not a happy camper having lost work and with a large family to feed he couldn't afford to miss time. "Let's cut the ugly thing down," he said.

"For chrissake no. We'd better not do that. It'll just cause more trouble and rub salt in their wounds," said Slim.

"Whaddya mean no? I don't want to drive by this damn thing everyday," mused Tim mordantly.

"Look fellas. I've seen this totem before when I was at the Longhouse in Duncan – it's a Bakwus' figure. And I'd leave it alone," I sternly informed them all..

"Why? You superstitious, Jed?" enquired Ray.

"There could be sneak-arounds out in these here hills, Jed!" said Slim teasingly.

"Not quite. But I think this carving is something that should be left alone. Besides, do you see any Indian folks working here?" I pointed out – not wanting to reveal to the crew anything I knew about Indian folklore.

"Let's get the fuck out of here. We've got some logging to do!" ordered Clint.

We all got back into the crummy and then we heard a power saw. It was Pete Logan, our landing bucker. He had grabbed a saw out of the back and was going to cut the carving down. Pete was an ex-faller and close to retirement. He was a quiet man that spoke few words. Fallers were a breed unto their own and they were often called the princes of the woods because of their elite status in the job category.

In a flash he had an undercut in the totem and was putting in the back cut. The seven foot Bakwus' hit the ground with a mighty thud! I'd say it was all over within thirty seconds or so. We all stood there dumbfounded in disbelief.

Clint was pissed off and had a mean scowl on his face. He never said a word, never had to, he just motioned with his hand for everyone to get going and we did.

We started to log our first road. "Tim, Ray, follow me, we're going to tag a couple stragglers to the right of the rigging. Gonna be a nice day fellas. It's nice to see the sun is shining. Can ya smell the fresh cut fir? It's the smell of money," I informed my chokermen.

I blew for the butt-rigging and spotted it and slacked it down. We took out a couple of the chokers out of the bullhooks on the butt-riggin' and set them on the hard to reach logs. Then we headed away and clear of the logs and sent the turn into the landing. For the next hour all went well and it didn't take long before we had quite a pile of logs built up in the landing – the Woods Foreman would be happy.

Ray wiped the sweat from his brow. "Hey, Jed. Look what's coming over the hill behind us? Looks like it may rain," he said.

"What the hell are ya talking about?" I said and turned to look. "What the hell? You're right. Shit. The sun was just out and the weather report said it was going to be clear skies all week."

"Ya, well they're wrong. And by the look of the nasty clouds headed our way we're in for a helluva piss-cutter of a rain storm," said Tim, grimly.

The wind started to pick up and the skies turned an ugly black. And there looked as if a fog was coming down from the top of the mountain. Strange!

Clint came down from the back end. "Let's head for the crummy. If there's lightning with this squall we'll be safer away from the lines. One time I saw lightning strike the main-line. It killed two guys on the crew because they were holding onto the chokers."

"Right-on, let's get out of here. I don't like the look of things anyway. D'ya see the strange fog up the hill, Clint?" asked Ray.

"Never seen that kind of fog before and I've been in the woods all my life," Clint informed us.

The wind increased which whipped the surrounding timber into a wild frenzy. And the rain started to pelt down with such a force that it seemed to bounce off the ground.

"Looks like we made it to the crummy just in time, fellows," said Slim as he slammed the door of the crummy behind him.

He no sooner got those words out when all hell broke loose. The deafening fierce wind slammed us and in an instant we were engulfed with the mysterious fog that came from the top of the mountain. This bizarre misty fog was a greenish-blue that had bolts of reddish-orange lightning infused within its life-like being. The lightning intensified and cracked all around us. The noise was defining and the rain pelted the ground with such force that deep furrows were sliced into the earth as it ran down the logging road. And there was a foul odour that oozed into the crummy which eliminated any sense of realism and added to our anxieties.

"Let's get the hell out of here!" hollered Clint. "I've seen enough of this bull-shit! Don't know what the fucks going on and frankly I don't give a fiddle-fuck. Let's go, Slim." ordered our hooktender.

We all sat in silence with our own imaginative demons that raced through our minds. Slim started the crummy and sped off down the road. He wasted no time and didn't let off till we were off the mountain and on the mainline headed for camp. Were we a crummy full of scared wimps or was there something else in control of our minds?

In twenty minutes or so we arrived in camp, only to be met by the camp push. "Why the hell are you in camp?" asked Phil, with a puzzled look on his face. "Are the protesters back out there?"

"No. There's one bitch of a storm out at Sleeping Beauty, Phil. It's full of lightning so we can't take a chance with safety," expressed Clint.

"Bull-shit! Look at the sky. It's clear as a bell, so there's no way it can be storming at Branch 20 – can it?" the camp manager said angrily, not wanting to miss a day of logging.

"It was the strangest storm, hard to explain, Phil, but you have to take our word for it," an embarrassed Slim backed what Clint had said.

The suspicious manager looked my way. "LaSal, whadda you have to say, Jed?"

"Oh it's stromin' all right. None of us wanted to stay."

"No-way. I don't believe that it's that bad. Head over to the cook-shack and have a coffee. I'll send Custy out there to see what's going on," Phil said. And walked away with a disgusted look on his face.

We all looked at each other sheepishly. None of us were going to mention to the camp manager about what the storm looked like – he'd think we're all crazy. And we felt crazy, too.

Custy pulled up in his pickup ready to head out to Branch 20, so Clint walked over and filled him in about what had taken place. By the look on the old geezer's face he thought we were all fucking nuts!

"LaSal, come'on with me. Let's go have a look at what the hell's going on," said the unconvinced woods boss.

The drive out was quiet. We didn't say a word to each other. We turned the corner up Branch 20. "Well the weather looks fine now, LaSal. I see a squall had gone through though. Between you and me, Clint filled me in on what took place out here. Don't believe him for a minute. Clint is a respected logger and a stand-up guy, but how can I believe a person when they say something supernatural must have taken place. I called bull-shit!"

"I don't know about that. We all saw the same stuff and I have to tell ya, it was strange."

"Well to each their own, Jed. It'll take more than a bunch of loggers to convince me that the storm was brought on by something ghostly – for fuck sake!"

As we approached the carving it was standing straight up like it had never been cut down. "I thought Clint said that Pete had cut the sonnofawhore down?" said Custy, with a puzzled look on his face.

"He did," I said, with a look of disbelief.

"Goddamn liar! It's standing up like a stiff prick," said Custy.

Without a word the woods foreman slayed on the breaks and got out of his pickup and grabbed a power saw from the back. "Fuck-it. I'll put an end to this crap once and for all," he said. "Those fuckin' Indians aren't going to flaunt this kind of thing in our face. They're not going to stop us from logging!"

"I wouldn't do that!" I hollered, and quickly made my way to the back of the pickup, to try and stop him. "There's a better way to remove the carving, Custy. Really, I can't believe my eyes. Pete cut the damn thing down. So someone or something must have stood it back up," I said stepping in front of Custy.

"To hell with it. I'm going to take care of this thing once and for all. Get out of my way ya little pip-squeak!" ordered the woods foreman.

Custy's eyes looked wild and it was apparent that there was no way to stop him. In a flash the carving hit the ground, again. And with a satisfied look on his face Custy got back in the pickup. "Be-goddamned, it had been cut down, Jed. What's going on around here? Is someone or something messing with us?" he asked.

As Custy turned the truck around to head back to camp, we couldn't believe our eyes. There was another storm brewing over the mountain, with a creepy greenish-blue fog in its wake.

"Let's get the hell out of here, LaSal, I'm beginning to think this mountain may be cursed," said a concerned and somewhat frightened Custy. "Maybe we shouldn't be logging Sleeping Beauty after-all," he mused out loud.

I looked over at Custy, his hands gripped the steering wheel hard and sweat ran down his face. He had a look on his face like he'd seen a ghost.

"Maybe the mountain's being protected. The Indians said things would happen if the company logged Sleeping Beauty." I paused a moment. "I wonder what's next?" I said.

CHAPTER 13

Open Defiance

"Waitress! Another round of beer for our table!" hollered Pete. "Hell with it, if we can't work we maz-well drink," he enthusiastically encouraged his friends.

"Damn right, Pete. The carving is still laying where Custy fell it and the company has to meet with the Indians to work out a deal to get them to remove the bloody thing," said Face-Powder Frenchy, an old falling partner of Pete's.

Face-Powder Frenchy continued. "I was talking to the Bullbucker on my way down here and he said the Indians didn't want to remove it. But the company told them if they didn't take it away it would be burnt."

"No shit – I can't understand how they get away with interrupting our work. Guess the company doesn't want to rock the boat, politically," said John Ferguson, another faller at the table.

"LaSal. Maybe you should go help the company? I hear you've gotten a little cozy with the Indians these days," John said to me.

"What makes you think I'm cozy with the Indians?" I said.

"Well Custy told us guys you tried to stop him from cutting the carving down," said John

"That's right. I did try and stop him, but that doesn't mean I'm cozy with them – now does it," I said, ready to defend myself. I wasn't going to let anyone push me around anymore.

"Ya little piss-ant," spoke up a quiet faller sitting with the guys. "How'd you like me to kick your ass?" he said, as he pushed his chair back and stood up.

I never expected that kind of reaction so I, too, stood up. "If you want a scrap, I'm game!" I said, fuelled by the beer in my belly.

Before he could answer me the door to the beer parlour opened with a loud bang and in walked about six or so Indian fellows. They hesitated and looked around, then walked straight towards the table of fallers.

A large tough looking fella was in the lead. "You Pete Logan?" he asked with a stern look on his face.

"Hell no," said John. "Why?"

"I am!" growled Pete back at him. "What the hell do ya want?" he said and took a swig beer.

Without a word the Indian fella sucker punched Pete. The force knocked him over backwards and on to the floor. In an instant the other fallers were out of their chairs and squared off with these marauding fellows bent on revenge. The fight was on!

Everything happened fast. The fallers were out numbered and needed a hand . . . so I jumped in! These fallers worked at the same camp as I did. If I didn't lend a hand I wouldn't have lived it down. Drew, who sat with me, moved away. He wanted no part of this.

I'm not much of a scrapper but I did my best to help out and threw punches and wrestled with the attackers. The tables were knocked over and beer was spilled, which soaked the floor. The crowd in the bar loved it. They hooted, hollered and cheered like it was a hockey game. Hell, I think the bartender even turned up the music.

It wasn't long and the cops showed up and broke up the fight and separated us into our respective groups. Without much fanfare they sent the Indian fellows on their way and kicked us out of the bar as punishment.

Out in the parking lot the quiet faller offered me his outreached hand. "Young fella, put her there. My name's Ben Simms. Thanks for your help – you're alright! If you ever want to break in fallin', let me know. You'll fit in with us princes of the woods," he went on to say.

"Thanks," I said, and shook his hand. I felt proud that he thought I would fit in with the falling crew. Princes of the woods? From what I was beginning to understand, fallers were held high on the prestige scale. Is it because they have a very dangerous job? Or is that that they work by themselves? Is it because they are marshalled by themselves separate from the rest of the logging crew? I didn't know. But what was clear was that when people spoke about fallers it was usually with a tone and sense that they were a different breed of men.

The fallers went off in a different direction and Drew and I headed next door to the Lake Café for some Chinese food. Before we went inside the Indian fellows pulled up in their car.

One of the passengers rolled down his window. "This isn't over!" he screamed. "Let your buddies know that we'll see them again and it's not going to be nice next time." And they sped off towards Duncan. I ignored them and quickly stepped through the door, not wanting any more trouble.

***

The time off went fast and it wasn't long and we were back at camp and ready for work. "Fellas. We had the Indians come and they reluctantly removed the carving from Branch 20," Phil informed the crew. "Hopefully this issue is over and we won't have any more work stoppages. So head out and have a nice day. And be safe," he warmly but firmly encouraged us.

We rounded the corner on Branch 20, headed for the tower in anticipation of another day spent out on the sidehill. I looked out the window of the crummy and much to my surprise I saw what looked like a white tarp. It appeared to be strung in between two trees at the back end of our setting. "Have a look at this," I pointed out to my workmates in the crummy.

"What is it?" asked Ray curiously.

"Not sure. But we're about to find out," said Carl, our landing bucker.

Slim pulled the crummy up close to the tower and got out. "Well I'll be goddamn!" he exclaimed. "Looks like we've got some tree-sitters at the back end. Some people will go to any lengths – won't they?" he continued.

"For chrissake! Looks like those protesters have gone to a helluva lot of work to stop the company," said Clint, with an unbelievable look on his face.

We all gathered around the tower because we couldn't start logging with those guys at the back end. "Radio camp and let them know that we have more protesters out here and we can't work," Clint ordered reluctantly. "When Phil hears this he's going to be some pissed-off."

"If it's not one thing it's another. Those bastards!" said Emil. "We've all got a living to make and those sonsabitches are making it very difficult. Why don't we take care of these guys, once and for all?" he meanly provoked the crew.

"No sense in getting carried away, fellows. I'm sure Phil and the boys will be out as quickly as they can. We don't need this to escalate," said Slim.

"Let's go to the back end and have a look at what's going on?" I suggested, being curious.

"Good idea, Jed. Take your rigging crew and have a look around. When Phil gets here you'll be able to fill him in on what the hell is going on out there," said Clint. "The rest of you stay in the landing," he advised the others.

"Tom, Ray, let's go. We'll head up through the fell-and-bucked on the walk logs Clint had been using – follow me," I gestured.

We nimbly made our way through the felled timber and by the time we made it to the back end all of us had a good sweat on. "Let's head through the standing timber. It'll be an easier and quicker approach to where the protesters are," I said.

"What do you think they are up to, Jed?"

"Not sure, but let's go find out," I replied. "By the look of it they came in over top of the mountain cuz I don't see any sign of them going up through the slash or fell-and-bucked – guess they didn't want anyone in camp to find out. Smart move hey?"

"Should we sneak up on them?" asked Ray.

"No, that's not necessary. They know we're on our way. I think I can see someone up in the tree. Do you?" I asked.

"Ya, in fact it looks like they have both trees rigged," informed Tom.

"Well, a couple of more minutes and we'll be there," I said with a little uncertainty.

We arrived at the bottom of the two trees that had the banner strung between them and there was no one at the base of these trees. "Hello!" I yelled. "How's it goin'?"

Tom and Ray found a stump and sat down to watch the goings on. "Goddamnit, look at all the rigging they have up there," said Ray with a surprised look. "They've got both trees rigged up with some type of platforms – guess they plan on staying a while," Ray continued.

I shook my head in disbelief. "No shit," I said. "That took a lot of work to get all that material here and up those trees."

"Hey! Anyone home up there?" I amusingly hollered up the tree again. We kept our eyes peeled for any movement. The trees the protesters had rigged were around thirty feet apart and eighty feet up. They strung a large white banner between them which read, in big, bold red letters: Stop the Logging - Indian Land.

Platforms were built just under the banner on each tree and by the look of it there were people on these platforms. But as of yet they hadn't shown themselves.

My first thought was that these guys were dug in for the long hall. "I wonder how long they plan on staying?" I asked my work mates.

"Bloody-hell," said Ray. "Looks like we're going to have more time off."

I stepped onto a stump to get a better view when I noticed two fellows looking down at us from one tree and one guy over on the other. "Hello down there!" one of the Indian chaps hollered.

"We're not come'in down. We've got lots of food and water so you might as well fuck off home," he said mockingly.

"We're here to just have a look so we can let the camp-push know what the hell the score is," I politely informed him.

"Well there's no sense in hanging around because we're not leaving," he said defiantly.

"Tom, Ray, let's head back down to the landing. We've seen enough," I ordered.

I lifted my hard hat off my head to wipe my brow when I noticed another fellow up there. He was in the tree that

I thought only had one guy – so I took a better look. "Well I'll be goddamn. I don't believe my fucking eyes. Do you guys see who I see?" I expressed.

Tom started to laugh out loud. "I wouldn't have believed it if I'd not seen it first hand," he roared with a belly laugh.

"You're right. This is going to be big news on the coast. Let's get to the landing so we can tell everyone!" said Ray very excitedly.

I couldn't believe who we'd seen so we hurried as fast as we could down to the landing. My thoughts were running wild. Damn this is unbelievable news. As we approached the landing we saw the camp manager. He sure didn't take long to arrive from camp.

The men gather anxiously around us at the front of the tower. "Ok, LaSal. Fill us in what's going on up there?" asked a concerned Phil Harmon.

"They've got two trees rigged with platforms on them that they can stay on and they told us that they're not coming down, but here's the best…"

"How many are there?" asked Phil abruptly.

"As I was about to say, here's the best part. You won't believe who is up there protesting?" I continued.

"Who!" hollered Slim.

"Ya, who?" asked Phil.

"Freddie Hanson!" I informed them all.

Everyone in the crowd roared. "What the fuck is that all about? Are you sure?" asked Phil.

"Ask Tom and Ray."

"That guy is off his rocker. He was always a little crazy," said Clint. "Guess he's gone off the deep-end."

All the fellows were dumb-founded and chattered among themselves like a bunch of hens. Custy stepped out into the middle of the crowd. "Ya know fellas. I've been trying to reach Freddie for some time. I wanted him to come back to work but no one knew where he was. An old flame of his that I ran into in Duncan said that whatever he saw that day out on Branch 20 scared the livin' shit out of him and he's not been the same since."

"What's new? He's always been loonier than a shit house rat," said the loader operator.

"Was she a red-headed broad with a fat ass?" asked Emil.

"That's the one. If the cops get involved with this issue they may want to interview her," said Custy.

"She's just an old ditch-pig that can't be trusted," said Emil. "The cops know who she is."

"Whaddya mean? She looked like a decent gal," said Custy.

Emil had a goofy look on his face. "She never married and hung out at the bars all her life. None of us know her name, all we ever called her was Red. She has a reputation for taking different men home whenever she wants her fancy tickled. Hell, if she had as many pricks sticking out of her as she had stuck in her she'd look like a porcupine," he said and slapped his leg and began to laugh.

Everyone joined in with the laugh but it was strange to know that a guy as hay-wire as Freddie could change his stripes. Something must have gotten to him and I had an idea what that something may have been.

"No sense hanging around here, fellas. Let's head for camp. You can head home until we figure this mess out. We'll be in touch," said Phil as we all went on our way leaving the tree-sitters and Sleeping Beauty to themselves – for now.

After a few days at home I thought I would take Elsie up on her offer for dinner so I gave her a call. Elsie readily invited me and said to bring Genevieve as well. It had been a while since I had seen Genevieve so I thought I would head to Duncan for a visit too.

I gave Genevieve a call. "Hi, Jed," she warmly greeted me on the phone. "Yes it's been a while since we went out. What's that you say? I'd love to have dinner with Elsie tonight. I'll be ready by four. Thanks – see you then," said Genevieve passionately.

I arrived early at Gen's house and she greeted me at the door with a hug, "Nice to see you, Jed. How are things?"

"Everything is going great except that we are shut down again. It could be for a while as the protesters are tree-sitting."

"It made the newspapers so I had a bit of an idea of what was going on. Think the company will put you to work in another area?"

"There's talk of it but they said they would ride it out for a bit. If they do scatter our crew, I've asked if I can go work with the fallers."

"I didn't know you were interested in falling, Jed."

"I've been watching them fall a setting across the valley and I think I would like to give'er a try."

"Well it's a dangerous job, so if you do please be careful," Gen said with a concern.

Gen snuggled up next to me as we drove to the Indian reserve to have dinner with Elsie. She rested her hand on my knee and her dark hair fell side-ways and touched my shoulder. Her perfume was light and very pleasant – which seduced me. It was nice to feel her warmth and share pleasant conversation on our short drive. It was so nice that I took my time driving, wanting this moment to last.

"Come on in, Jed!" Elsie greeted us at the door. "And you must be Genevieve?"

"I am. And it's very nice to meet you, finally."

"Follow me and make yourselves at home," she said. "Dinner's just about ready. Have you ever had moose meat?"

"No I haven't," I said. "Have you Gen?" I looked at her.

"Yes. I lived in Ontario as a young girl and my dad went moose hunting once in a while. Can't say I remember what it tastes like though," she informed us.

"I thought I'd cook a moose roast with all the trimmings, including bannock," said Elsie, with a sparkle in her eye.

"What's bannock?" asked Gen.

"I've heard of it but have never had it," I added.

"It's traditional Métis bread, much like a small biscuit but not cooked in the oven. We often call it fry-bread. I've got an open fire out in the back yard to cook it.

One day I'll show you how. It's easy," Elsie eagerly enlightened us.

"Where'd you get the moose, Elsie?" I asked.

"I got it up on my trapline in northern BC. Every year my husband and I go up and trap, hunt, and fish. We always bring home a moose. Maybe someday you can come with us," she said.

"Could I?"

"Of course. You are welcome anytime. But I warn you . . . it'll get into your blood and you'll want to go every year."

The dinner was excellent. It was the first time I had moose and I vowed to make sure it wouldn't be the last. Elsie was entertaining. She fondly reminisced of her younger days in Manitoba. Elsie told us numerous stories about hunting and trapping and fishing. I was spellbound by these fascinating tales. Gen took to them as well and asked lots of questions. I was pleased that Gen took an interest in the things that interested me. We all got along great.

The evening went by fast and it was time to take Gen home. "Thank you very much, Elise, for cooking such a nice meal," I said.

"Yes, thank you. I, too, enjoyed the moose meat dinner and I really enjoyed the conversation afterwards," said Gen approvingly.

"Anytime – we'll do it again," and gave us a hug.

We were saying our goodbyes at the door when Elsie tugged at my sleeve. "Jed, when you go back to work, I want you to be careful," she said with a concerned look.

"Why's that?" I asked.

"I overheard one of the dancers say that some of the young people have formed a traditional warriors group. He said that they're going to defend the sacred ground at any cost."

"Any cost?" I asked.

Elsie looked me in my eyes with a disturbing and concerning look on her face. "Talk is . . .," she hesitated. "Guns could be involved."

CHAPTER 14

The Silver Bridge

"Hey look over there?" said Drew with a puzzled look. "What's written on the side of that bus?" he inquired. We were going through the Indian Reserve on our way to Cowichan Bay to pick oysters at low tide.

"I'm not sure but I think it said Indian Warriors or something like that," I told Drew.

"Did you ladies see what it said?" I asked Genevieve and Sherry Hill, Drew's date for the afternoon.

"No. I didn't get a very good look at it. All I saw was some big black lettering," Sherry let us know.

Gen and I looked at each other. We both saw it and knew exactly what it was. "Don't say a word to anyone," implored Gen as she directed her comment to Drew and Sherry. "When Jed and I went for supper with Elsie John, she informed us that a number of young people on the Rez had formed a group to protest the logging on

Sleeping Beauty. She called it a warrior group and, by the sound of it, these warriors are very militant and that trouble was brewing – she spoke of guns."

Both Sherry and Drew were shocked at what Gen had told them.

"Remember the Mohawk blockade back east? They did the same thing. Someone was shot and the army was called in because the cops were outnumbered," said Drew.

"I remember that. It made headline news for weeks," I said.

"Let's all hope that nothing like that happens here in our peaceful valley," said Genevieve hopefully.

The tide was low, perfect for gathering oysters. We all were hungry for a good feed and it didn't take long to gather our supper. "Let's shuck them right here. One of the Indian fellows at work told me to always do that. He said to leave the shells right where we picked them and they create a surface for juvenile oysters to attach to and produce more oysters – cool hey?"

Our bucket was full of nicely fresh shucked oysters and we were on our way home when we saw that big yellow old school bus rambling down the road towards us. And it was full of people.

"Wonder where they are going?" asked Drew.

"I don't think they are going fishing!" I said satirically.

I squeezed Gen's hand. She winked at me and I nodded back. We both saw the same thing but would wait till we had some privacy to talk about it.

I drove Gen home from Sherry's place, satisfied that we had a great oyster feast.

"What did you see on the bus, Jed?" asked my girlfriend.

"As we went by a fellow held up what looked like a goddamn gun! I wonder if they are going out to the tree-sitters. If they are, we're in for some trouble. Should I call the cops?" I asked.

"I don't know if that's the best thing to do. They might say they are just going hunting," said Gen.

Even though my gut feeling told me to call the cops, I resisted. I dropped Gen off at her house with a promise I'd stop by later. We were still off work and waiting for the company to sort out the growing mess about logging Sleeping Beauty and I had a hunch that things were going to get worse.

On my way home I saw the Riverside Hotel and Bar's parking lot was full so I thought I would stop in and have a beer or two. It was the place where you could get caught up on all the gossip.

I was hardly in the door and not even at a table yet when a familiar voice holed at me. "Sit down ya little-fucker and don't be cheap. Buy us a round!" slurred Ben Simms. By the look of it he had half a load on already.

"Nice to see ya, Jed. So tell me, when the fuck are you going to break-in falling?"

"I don't know. I asked Custy if it was possible but he hasn't gotten back to me yet," I said.

"Once you go fallin', you'll never work on the rigging again. It's the best job in the woods, Jed, and I think you'd fit in. They say you're a hard worker and have a good head on your shoulders," said Ben.

I waved for the waitress to bring us a round of beers. "Say, could you please put the hockey game on? It's going to be a hum-dinger."

"Sure thing," she said.

The hockey game was half way through the second period and everyone in the smoked filled bar cheered heartily for their respective team. In between plays the chatter was deafening and the tinkle of glasses as the patrons emptied them was almost musical. It was a good excuse to stay, drink and finish watching the game.

The game was unexpectedly interrupted by a special news bulletin. "We interrupt the hockey game to bring you this breaking news," said the news anchor. "The

Island highway in Duncan has just been blocked. Reports are that the local Indians have moved a number of vehicles on to the Silver Bridge, blocking traffic in both directions. The RCMP have cordoned off an extensive area for the protection of the public. People are advised not to go near this vicinity. I have just been handed an update. It has just been reported by the RCMP that the people blocking the highway are armed. CHEK TV NEWS has a crew on the way to the Silver Bridge area and will bring you a live update soon – so please stay tuned."

The bar went momentarily silent. People seemed to be confused and somewhat shocked. This couldn't be happening in our quaint valley was the look on most folks face.

"Well, I'll be goddamned," said Ben. "Looks like those bloody Indians have gone and done it this time. We were just talking about that yesterday, that all across Canada there seems to be more radical protests. If they have guns, no tellin' what the hell will go on. Things are sure goin' to hell-in-a-handbasket."

"Ya, this definitely kicks it up a notch. Sure hope level heads prevail," I optimistically said. I purposely mentioned nothing about what we saw earlier in the day.

The hockey game came back on and the bar returned to normal once again, but the mood had noticeably changed. The people weren't cheering as loud and there was a more serious demeanour which cloaked the smoky old beer joint. A few got up and left silently and knew full well the gravity of the situation and probably wanted to get home to their families. A protest like this had never happened in the Cowichan Valley. Most believe that it only happened in other places.

I got up from the table and made my way over to the pay-phone. I wanted to give Genevieve a call to find out if she had heard yet. The phone only rang once before it was answered. It was Genevieve. "Gen, you watching the news?" I asked.

"Yes we are. It's on all the stations, Jed. Now we know why they had written Indian Warriors on the side of their bus. Doesn't look good, Jed. Where are you?"

"At the Riverside. We were watching the game, but I see it's not on now and the... Hang on a sec, Gen."

"What's that you say?" I asked one of the two cops that just walked in the door and approached and spoke up to me.

"You Jed LaSal?" one of them inquired.

"Sure am."

"Would you step outside with us? We need to talk to you."

"Gen, I've got to go. Some cops just came in and I guess they need to talk to me or somethin'. I'll call you back when I know what the hell is going on," I said and hung up the phone.

"What's up, fellas?" I politely asked apprehensively.

"Let's step outside where it's quieter," said the taller of the two.

I followed them out the door and over to the squad car. "Are you available to go to Duncan right now?" one of them asked.

"How come?"

"Do you know about the Indians blocking the Island highway at the Silver Bridge?"

"Sure do – the hockey game was interrupted with news about the blockade," I said.

"The situation is serious and by the reports coming in from dispatch, it's getting worse. The Elder's from the Band are putting together a few people to try and talk to the protesters to find out what their demands are. One of the Elder's asked if you could accompany her. Elsie John. Do you know her?"

"Yes I do. I've been to one of their functions at the longhouse and she was there and my girlfriend and I just had dinner with her, not that long ago," I said.

"Would you be interested in helping out? But I have to tell you it may be dangerous," the cop said.

"I suppose so," I said, hesitantly.

"Leave your vehicle parked here and come with us, Jed," they said. And we all headed to the cop car.

It was my first ride in a cop car and it was interesting to hear all the chatter on the police radio. "Calling squad 377. Did you manage to find Jed LaSal?" asked the dispatcher.

"10/4, dispatch. We are transporting him right now and will arrive in Duncan in twenty minutes."

"Take him to the mobile command centre set up north of the bridge," ordered dispatch.

I sat in silence and listened to how the cops had surrounded the protesters, blocking any way for them to leave. I had started to have second thoughts about my decision to get involved, but I trusted Elsie and if she needed my support, I'd do it.

The command centre was set up in the middle of the road and there were cops everywhere. Some looked like they were from a special squad as they were dressed in full gear with helmets, rifles and dark clothing. I had a quick look around and there were cops on top of roofs, behind trees and poised behind squad cars. All were at the ready, guns aimed towards the bridge and the young warriors. Some of the cops were keeping the curious onlookers back as that crowd was growing and the traffic was being re-routed.

As the crowd grew so did the jeering. It was apparent that the non-aboriginal people didn't like the natives blocking the road which caused a huge inconvenience for people coming and going into and out of Duncan.

One of the bystanders was quite vocal. "Shoot the bastards! They have no right to block our road. You goddamn Indians don't deserve any special treatment. You're nothing but a bunch of terrorists!" he continued with a steady rant.

With arms raised and fists clenched others in the crowd shouted obscene and racial remarks. The mood was dark and hate seemed to cloak the dampened air.

The cops looked nervous and on edge. "Follow me, LaSal," spoke an older grey haired cop.

We snaked our way through a maze of cops, all of which were focussed on the bridge some distance away. He led me to a large and official looking bus, which must be some sort of command centre because the roof was loaded with radio antennas and communication dishes.

The cop opened the door for me. "Step inside, Jed," he asked.

The inside of this mobile command was abuzz with what seemed like organized confusion as this veteran cop guided me past a number of other cops that were busy. All of which were either on a phone, mobile radios or strategizing with the commander.

In the back there was a small room where three Elders sat, silently. "Hi, Jed," softly spoke a recognizable voice.

I turned to find Elsie. Her eyes looked sad and I saw that she had been crying. I walked over and gave her a long and reassuring hug.

"How can I help, Elsie?" I asked and broke the uneasy silence.

With a very concerned look on her face she spoke gently."The three of us are going to go into the roadblock and I need you there to support me, Jed. We know everyone of those young people, most ever since they were born. But things have changed. They don't listen to us Elder's much anymore. We have to try, Jed," she said with a cracked voice.

"It's time to go," said a strict looking cop. He led us out the back door. Not a word was spoken as we filed out of the command centre.

Outside the air was still and there was an army of cops everywhere. One of them approached us. "Listen up," he said. "We've been in contact with the protesters and they have said that the Elder's may enter the roadblock.

I'm cautioning you though. It is a very volatile situation we have here. If it keeps escalating there are bound to be people that will get hurt. Once you enter that area you all may or could be held as hostages. So this is your last chance to back out," he vehemently warned us!

One of the Elder's, without a word, made a move towards the Silver Bridge and immediately the rest followed. Elsie took my arm and we all slowly walked towards these young militant warriors that had guns at the ready!

CHAPTER 15

An Outsider

My legs shook uncontrollably and I sweated profusely and my heart pounded so hard that it felt like it was in my throat. "I feel like I'm going to be sick, Elsie!" I said.

Elsie squeezed my arm reassuringly and we kept walking. It was only a short distance to bridge, but the gap between the militant Indians and the hordes of cops felt like an eternity. Steadily we made our way towards the Silver Bridge and impending danger!

"Hold it right where you are!" screamed a raucous voice form behind the overturned car in the middle of the road. "LaSal, turn around and walk backwards to us... and put your hands up in the air where we can see them!" An Indian fella ordered.

I did as he asked but this only added to my anxiety. The Elders never broke their slow stride as we approached the barricade. All of us were quiet in our own thoughts.

"Step this way," said one of the Indian fellows.

In an instant there was a hand on my shoulder and I was on the ground. I looked up at an Indian warrior. "LaSal, you wouldn't be foolish enough to have a weapon would ya?" he asked.

"Peter! Let him up and quit this nonsense," said Old Joe Simon, one of the Elders. "He is here with Elsie, so leave him alone!"

Peter let me up, but not before giving me one of the meanest looks I've ever had. There was no question he meant business.

"Okay, I'll let him up but he'd better not be spying for the cops," Peter informed Old Joe.

"That's nonsense," said Old Joe. "He's here on his own free will...to see if he can help us."

Even though I was scared I managed to hide it, or so I thought. This was not a time to look or act weak. If I had learned anything about the Indian people it was that they didn't like a coward-like person as it was a sign of weakness – so I had to suck it up and be brave.

"Listen, Peter," spoke Elsie in her usual soft manner. "I have a lot of respect for Jed and he's a nice young man, that's why I asked him to come with me. He will be able to relay to the authorities what your wishes are."

"I don't trust him. But I respect you so I will do as you ask, for now."

"That's right! Or we could hold him hostage," cut in another young warrior.

"I don't believe you trust anyone right now, Peter," said Elsie.

"Leave him alone!" shouted Old Joe. "Even though I may agree with you, this type of action is not the way to go. If you hurt this young man the cops will start shooting and everyone will lose. Do you understand?"

Peter never said a word but the look on his face said it all. He and the rest of the protesters were not about to listen to reason right now. I sure hope I made the right decision by walking into this volatile situation.

They were dug in good. Their stronghold was in the middle of the bridge which was blocked on both ends by overturned vehicles. With a quick look around I saw that they had plenty of food and the Cowichan River which robustly flowed under the bridge would supply all the water they needed and possibly an escaped route for these twenty-five or so protesters. However by the look of it they could hold out for weeks.

I wasn't surprised that the Elders were welcomed with respect. All were offered a place to sit and some dried salmon, which is custom amid Indian people. The Elders, in the midst of themselves, talked quietly in their native tongue. This seemed to bring calmness to the situation. But not for long!

Two fellows approached me. They were dressed in camouflage clothing from head to toe and had bandanas covering their faces so that only their eyes showed. They firmly took my arms and escorted me to a small fire that was burning in the middle of the bridge and sat me down.

"Put your arms behind your back, LaSal," one of them ordered!

"Screw it! Let's hold him hostage," the other one said.

I held my composure as all eyes were on me. These guys meant business!

"Damnit! Leave him be!" blurted out Old Joe Simon, once again, "Jed will do you no harm. He came here to help."

"If you guys continue on like this, us Elders are going to pack-it-in and head out of here," said Ernie Johnston, one of the other well respected Elders. Ernie is one of the top carvers for the Band and works with the youth teaching them the skills needed to create traditional carvings in Coast Salish style.

Elsie got up and walked over and stood between me and the protesters. "This will not solve our problems," she spoke with a more stern voice, "Jed will be able to help you. He can be trusted."

The protesters spoke in a low tone among themselves. "Alright, we'll leave him be for now. Jed, are you willing to help us?" asked Peter.

"I'll do what I can," I said, "What would you like me to do?"

"Nothing right now till we talk things over with the Elders," said Peter.

I sat by the fire and quietly listened to the ringleaders and the Elders. Peter was definitely the head honcho and the spokesperson for the group. I didn't know much about him but saw him around town ever so often.

The conversation was blunt and to the point. "We want all the logging to stop on Sleeping Beauty Mountain. And for those white guys to leave the area alone. I am tired of them raping our land," said Peter, in a very direct manner.

"They have been logging on our traditional lands for years, Peter," said Elsie.

"Well it's about time they stopped," Peter told Elsie.

"Maybe so, but do you think the way you're going about it is the right way?"

"Elsie, how long have we all been trying to get the government and the logging companies to listen to us?"

"You're right, a long time, but this type of protest could get someone hurt…there may be a better way," offered Elsie.

Peter, quietly paced back and forth and his body language said it all, he meant business. I had the feeling that there was no turning back now. These young warriors were here to stay until the logging company stopped logging Sleeping Beauty.

"Listen to reason, Peter. There are a lot of us that have been fighting for our rights long before you were born. Even before our time the Band has struggled with the loss of hunting grounds and fishing places. I remember when they took away our right to fish with fish traps and weirs on the river. How do you think that made us feel?" said Old Joe. "But we never considered a violent protest like this."

"Ya, my Grandmother told me about stuff like that, but that was then and this is now. I don't trust the white people – and never will!"

One of the Elders that hadn't spoken a word finally broke her silence. "If I may say a few words. What you are saying and doing is wrong. Your words are the same as some of the white people, full of discrimination. And your actions are putting a lot of people in danger, Peter. Our people have always welcomed newcomers into our homelands. We have always shared our land, our food and our knowledge of the area. What you young people are doing is out of frustration and I do understand. But this is not the way to go about it." said this kind hearted Elder.

Her soft spoken words had everyone's attention and pointed out that discrimination knows no borders and people of all races can fall victim to it.

"What do you want us to do?" asked Elsie.

"Ya, let's get this show on the road, Peter," said Old Joe.

Ernie, known for his dry wit spoke up, "Besides, there's a hockey game on the tube tomorrow night – wouldn't want to miss it."

Everyone had a good chuckle but the mood didn't last long. "Our demands are simple, stop logging our sacred ground," Peter informed the Elders and stood there with his arms crossed and a stern glare on his face.

No sooner had he finished his demand when two other young warriors started to beat on their drums, and chanted to the rhythms – all of which added to the mysterious shroud of emotional drama that filled the air.

The warmth of the fire seemed to take me to a different place and time and as I watched the thin ribbon of smoke linger its way skyward it was strangely mesmerizing. A weird and wonderful relaxed feeling cloaked me witch released primal thoughts of my ancestors. Was it because of the aboriginal blood running through my veins – I wondered? I had never felt this way before but it felt natural.

I was startled out of this trance-like metaphysical state by the distinctive yet distant sound of a rifle! "Those bastards took a shot at us!" hollered a native girl from behind the overturned bus.

Everyone hit the ground and hid as best as possible. At the same time a helicopter flew low and hovered over the bridge and shone down a bright spotlight which illuminated the whole encampment.

"What the hell is going on!" screamed Peter.

"Don't know but keep down!" Old Joe hollered back.

I laid still and wondered what was coming next. Where we under attack? The only noise I heard was the crackle of the fire and the low rumble of the Cowichan River that ran under the bridge. Everyone was either sprawled out on the ground or where hidden behind the overturned vehicles. I could hear the cold sound of bullets being loaded into guns. The young warriors loaded their firearms – ready for what may come next.

CHAPTER 16

Straight to Hell

One night turned into three, then four. I felt as though I was held captive. After that rifle shot the other day the protesters were at the ready, poised for anything. It was vividly apparent that they were putting it all on the line by taking shifts 24/7 to keep a watchful eye on the outside enemy. It was chilling to be surrounded by loaded guns! And my fears were heightened knowing that these young warriors, alert and agitated, were ready to shoot at the drop of a hat.

As the days went by the tension was thick which made everyone edgy. Uncontrollably my thoughts turned to leaving this place, but sensible logic won out for now, so I stayed put. The Elders persisted with their encouragement to the young warriors to end this protest. But to no avail the young Indians held their ground and all were ready to die for what they believed in. Goddamnit, I was scared!

Early on the morning of the sixth day the Elders called another meeting by the fire. Old Joe spoke passionately. "There are a couple of things some of us Elders want to get off our chest, so if I may start first, I would like to say to you that, I, in some way support you for being brave enough to do what you are doing and you all know that I wish you the very best. But I think you should send LaSal with some demands. That way at the very least you will have started the process to negotiate some type of settlement. I want you to know that I will be here to the very end to help out in any way I can. Thank you."

Old Joe took his place by the fire.

One of the warriors approached the fire, dressed in dark clothing and his face painted like he was at war. As he approached he held his hand high above his head, his fist was clenched tight and he shook it angrily. "I'm prepared to die! We are tired of being bullied around by the fuckin' government!" He looked my way. "And I will take him with me!"

No one said a word, not wanting to agitate him further and I felt as though I was going to pass out. I had to concentrate hard to keep my composure.

Next to speak was the silent one, Judith May. "Young people. We come from a very proud Nation, with deep roots that are unmoving. Our ancestor's spirits are with us on this journey. They are with us all through this valley, we call home. Right or wrong, their spirits will help guide you. They will protect you on this troubled journey. So think long and hard and the answers will come," she said and raised her hands upward to the sky.

Next up was Ernie Johnston and he looked mad. "I am real disappointed in you young people. Fact is I am down right pissed off! I know each and everyone of you - most since birth. I don't agree with what you are doing. This type of action is a step backwards, as far as I am concerned. Some of us have put in a lot of time at the negotiating table with the government. We have made some gains, small ones, but all the same, some gains.

But now I don't know, I think those gains will be put aside. This is just plain craziness." Ernie glared at the young people for a moment. "What if the cops start shooting at us? Peter, what if you are killed? Or you Rosie! I am not in favour of what you are doing and I think you should shut it the hell down!" He turned and walked away and kept his back to the protesters. I am told that this is a gesture indicating displeasure.

Elsie stepped forward – there was a long silence. "I know each and every one of you, well. We have fished together, danced together, feasted together, and we have cried together. I don't want us to die together," she said as she looked over at the young punk that made that disturbing remark. He knew she was not happy about his remark, but he glared back defiantly.

"Elsie," cut in Peter, "Last night some of us talked it over and we have decided to send out LaSal with our demand. Jed, will you do this for us?"

I stood at the back of the crowd, but I moved closer. "Yes, I will help in any way I can."

"It's straight forward. Let them know that we want all logging to stop on Sleeping Beauty Mountain. Tell them that we are prepared to close down our resistance camp immediately if they meet our demands. If not," he paused, "we are prepared to die here!"

The drumming started. It was loud and vibrated through out our bodies. Some of the young dancers moved to the rhythms around the fire and started to chant to the tempo. The Elders looked sad, but calm. Their words had fell on those young, deaf ears so it was now up to me. I was going to walk out of this camp and convey to the rest of the world what the protesters wanted.

As I prepared to leave the camp Elsie and Old Joe approached me. "Be brave Jed," said Elsie. And she gave me a hug.

"You may be young, Jed, but Elsie has told me that you have a good head on your shoulders. So take their demands to the police and let them know also that we are doing what we can to help." Old Joe shook my hand and nodded his approval.

I made my way to the overturned bus and was about to step out to the other side when Judith May stepped my way. She handed me an eagle feather. "Take this, young Jed. It is a sign to those people out there that what you say is said with truth. It will also give you strength to be brave."

I took the feather, clutched it in my hand and with one glance back headed for the cops. Even though I felt as though I was being set free, my thoughts were with the Elders and the rest of the people in the protest camp. They had a reasonable demand. There were lots of other areas out in the woods for the logging companies to log instead of the old Indian burial grounds.

"Stop where you are, LaSal!" hollered a cop from behind cover. "Put your hands in the air where we can see them, then keep coming."

As I got closer I could hear them talking. "What's that he's got in his hand?" asked a cop that was leaning across his cruiser, his gun at the ready.

"Don't know. But I don't think it's a gun," said another.

"Looks like a feather or somthin'!" hollered the guy from behind the cop car. "LaSal! Stop, turn around and put your hands behind your back!"

It was confusing to me. Suddenly I was light headed and my legs felt weak, but without question I did as they asked.

I could hear the cops coming for me and I was scared shitless. "I'm going to co-operate – for Christ sake! Put your fuckin' guns down."

"Shut-up! And stand still!" hollered a cop.

In an instant I was on the ground and handcuffs were being put on. No sooner were the cuffs on when I big cop jerked me to my feet and escorted me behind their line of defence.

I was back at the command centre sitting on a stool surrounded by cops. One had a movie camera on me. And another straddled a chair in front of me and glared, which added to my nervousness. But I held my composure and still clutched my eagle feather.

He slid his glasses down to the tip of his nose. "I'm Sergeant Major Crosby. So, young man. What do those goddamn Indians want?" he asked sarcastically.

Instantly my anxiety turned to anger. What the hell did this guy mean? My long angered gaze faded and I regained my composure somewhat. "It's quite simple," I said, "They want the logging to stop out on Sleeping Beauty Mountain."

Without hesitation the Sergeant angrily blurted out, "They can go straight to hell!"

"They stop logging, and the road block comes down," I reiterated calmly.

The cop sat up straight but was restless fidgeting with his glasses and tugging at the collar of his shirt. There was no doubt this request got under his skin.

"I thought the Elders could stop this thing?" he asked me.

"They said they would do what they could. They didn't say they could stop it. And they are trying."

"I don't believe you, LaSal. I think they are all in cahoots. If this doesn't stop soon the order will be given to put an end to it."

"How armed are they?" he asked.

"I'm not going to answer that," I said.

"If you don't, you'll go to jail for aiding and abetting – ya little fucker." He was not happy.

"Look, I'm not here to rat on those guys, I'm here to relay a message. If you think you can pressure me into supplying you with information, you're wrong!"

He turned to the others and said: "Take that damn eagle feather away from him and put him in the cell! We'll let him sit it out for a while. That will change his mind."

"Goddamn Indian lover," someone said. I looked around but all was quiet.

"Sarg, the Inspector is on his way, he'll want to have a chat with him," said one of the cops.

I looked out the side window. There were a lot of people gathered. I saw TV crews and cameras, cops dressed in black swat gear, and regular RCMP scattered all over the place. As I sat there my mind wondered and I thought about Genevieve, my family, and friends. Sure would be nice to have a beer and a bullshit at the Riverside.

My thoughts were also with everyone of the Elders and protesters.

The door slammed and in walked a fellow dressed in a suit. "Hello, Jed, I'm Inspector O'Neil. I have to ask you a couple of questions. Are you OK with that?"

"Sure thing." He seemed to be more pleasant than the others.

"Are you hungry?"

"Not really, but I could use a cup of coffee."

"Get him a coffee," he ordered. "Do you take anything in it?"

"A little bit of milk, please."

Inspector O'Neil turned a chair around to face me. He sat back and relaxed. He crossed one leg over the other. "OK, Jed, tell me – what are they after?"

The coffee tasted good, hadn't had one in a few days so I sipped it slowly and savoured one of my favourite beverages. "Mr. O'Neil, it's simple, if the logging stops on Sleeping Beauty they are willing to close down the protest."

The inspector took his time to answer. "It's not that simple. We can't give in to their demands. It's against the law to do what they are doing. Do you understand that?"

"I do. But there must be a way to compromise. Look, I'm just a logger. All I want is things to get back to normal so we all can go back to work. I'm not here to negotiate with you guys, I'm just the messenger."

"That's correct. But you are holding information that will help us," he said.

"Maybe so, Mr. O'Neil, but I was asked by the Elders and the protesters to bring a message to you guys. That's all. How do I go against those people? They trust me."

"And rightly so. However it would be in your best interest to help us," he said.

"Throw the little prick behind bars – that will jog his memory about whose side he's on," cut in the Sarg.

The Inspector smiled but ignored his comment. The door opened and in walked Genevieve. She calmly walked over and gave me a hug and kiss.

"They asked me to come and keep you company. Thought it may help," my girlfriend said.

She stood there and held my hand which calmed me down. It was nice to have the support.

"How are my Mom and Dad holding up?" I asked her.

"Fine, they know you are OK and doing your best. How are Elsie and the rest of the Elders doing, Jed," Gen asked.

"Everyone's doing well. Of course they want this to end. But they are fine," I said reassuringly.

"LaSal, are you going to co-operate with us? We need to have our questions answered," asked Sergeant Crosby.

"I am," I politely said. "What would you like me to take back as a reply to their demand?"

"You're not going anywhere, LaSal!" he sternly informed me. "If you think you are going to help those bloody Indians, you're crazy!"

I was shocked. This guy needs to be put in his place. The room was quiet. "May I speak my mind?" I asked the Inspector.

"You certainly may," he said.

Turning slightly to face Sergeant Crosby, I let loose. "You piss me off! It's one thing to do your job. It's another to have the kind of attitude you do and you know what I'm talkin' about. Goddamn discrimination.

This kind of stuff has to stop! I admit there are some on the other side that think the same way, and that's not right either. It's absolutely wrong that people are not tolerant of each other. It makes me sick to hear you openly degrade my friends and I don't have to put up with it, they are decent people!"

I found myself in the back of a cop car headed for jail. Guess they didn't like what I had said, but I had to get it off my chest. We made our way through the police line that they put up. People were everywhere. I recognized a number of folks as we drove by, and by the look on their faces they were worried.

This was going to be my first time in jail. The junior cop led me into a begrimed cell. By the look of this cold and dingy place, it had seen its better day. Oh well, I know that Genevieve will be doing what she can to get me out.

Exhausted I pulled a musty blanket over myself and fell asleep the minute my head hit the grimy pillow. Weirdly I dreamed as though I was floating through time. I was out in the woods effortlessly hovering above Sleeping Beauty Mountain, looking down, and the trees were brilliant green and glistened. I smelled the pungent earth below, which reminded me of the days spent on a side-hill, logging. There was a light gentle summer wind and the sun shone worm and bright. I could hear birds chirping and watched them as they played in the updrafts of the mesmerizing breeze.

Then suddenly this calm state of mind turned to chaos with everything appearing to be blurred and ugly. The birds were silent and the sky was dark and menacing – there was an eerie calm! Sleeping Beauty started to shake and sway, violently. I broke out into a cold sweat and started to fall toward the mountain. As I fell uncontrollably I saw an image of Bakwus' through the dark misty clouds. Strangely, I felt safe.

I awoke soaked in sweat but had a smile on my face. From that moment on I knew that something beyond the white-mans comprehension or control was going to protect Sleeping Beauty Mountain.

CHAPTER 17

Town Hall Meeting

"LaSal!" hollered a cop. "Let's go. You've been released. Head out to the front desk and sign yourself out."

The officer escorted me out to the front counter where another cop had some papers for me to sign. "Well, LaSal, was this your first time in jail?" he asked.

"Sure was," I said. I didn't want any idle chit-chat with any of these cops.

"The Inspector may want to meet with you again, so don't leave town. If you do, you'll find yourself back in here and you will be staying with us for a while. Do you understand?" he ordered hard-heartedly.

"Yes," I said without looking at him. I didn't want to cause any ruckus so I kept my comments to myself.

He handed over my belongings, which included my eagle feather, and I made my way out to the front door where Genevieve had waited. She had driven my car to the police station to pick me up. We embraced and she gave me a passionate kiss.

"Let's get the hell out of this place, Gen. I'm starved."

"The Greenhaven Café is open and they serve the best breakfast in town. Hopefully we can get a seat," she said.

"Doesn't your mom cook there?"

"Yes, she should be there now. Mom will cook us a great breakfast," she said.

I felt free. It was nice to jump in behind the wheel of my car with Gen snuggled up close. As we drove towards the main part of town there were more cops than I had expected to see and by the look of it the army had been called in too. They had blocked off the main highway and all the streets that lead towards the Silver Bridge. Lookie-loo's were everywhere, but the cops made sure they were kept way back out of potential danger and to insure they never got in the way. The traffic was still being detoured around. I could only imagine how pissed off everyone must be. What an inconvenience. We pulled into a gas station to fill up the vehicle.

I was busy at the pump but heard a voice. "Hey LaSal, how's she goin'," greeted the familiar voice.

"Not bad considering I spent last night in jail. How are you, Slim?" I grinned at him. Slim never asked why I was in the hoosegow. And I never explained to him why either.

"We're not back to work yet. The company moved a few fallers and machinery into Branch 36 but most of us don't have enough whiskers to bump anyone so I'm at home doin' odd jobs for the Old-Lady. I hope this bullshit ends soon," he informed me.

"I think everyone hopes that it ends soon, Slim."

"I'm not sure," Slim frowned and shook his head. "Rumour is that the cops are going to let them sweat it out for a while."

"Where did you hear that?" I asked.

"My Sister-in-law is the receptionist down at the cop-shop. She gets all the scuttle-butt."

"No shit," I mumbled.

"There are a lot of pissed off people around here. Some have talked about taking things into their own hands," said Slim.

"That would be a big mistake. They are armed, ya know."

"Maybe so," admitted Slim. "But you know how some of the radicals are. I hear that there is going to be a town hall meeting tomorrow night."

"Where at?" I requested.

"In the Union Hall. Ya goin'? I think it will be packed. Might be a barn burner, Jed."

"Ya, I can just about imagine, every nut case in the valley will show up and stir the pot," I said.

"Maybe see ya there," said Slim, and grinned at me. "My Old-Lady says she's goin' so I'll be there too," he said and chuckled.

"Nice to see you, Slim, and I'll probably see you at the meeting," I said. "Say, have you heard anything about what's going on with Freddy Hanson?"

"As a matter of fact I have. That idiot is the only one still protesting up on the platform. Custy and a couple of other fellows tried to talk him down but he told them to fuck off and pointed a rifle at them – silly bastard," he said sarcastically.

"He's always been a loose cannon, Slim," I said in agreement.

"My Sister-in-law told me that the cops are thinking of taking his old flame out to the tree stand. You know the one, that big tited red-headed old mattress he's been banging and see if she can talk some sense into him."

With a nod I finished my fill up and we headed to the Café.

"It looks like it's packed to the nuts, Gen" I said as we drove by slowly.

"Probably because the food is good and free coffee fill ups," said Gen.

"Let's go anyway. We'll find a table sooner or later," I said.

The air was thick with cigarette smoke and the chatter was nonstop. The odd table paused from their meal and took a look at us as we walked by. "Do you know any of those people?" I asked Gen.

"No. But they must have seen your picture in the newspaper," she replied.

"What the hell do you mean my picture in the paper?"

"I wasn't going to say anything," Gen informed me. "Because I thought it may upset you. But while you were at the barricade the paper printed an article. Somehow they got a photo of you and included it."

"I bet it was the photo they took at the logger's sports last June at the Foot."

"Come to think of it you were dressed for work," Gen said.

"Great! Now everyone in the valley will know I was behind the barricade," I grumbled disgustingly.

"Don't worry, Jed. I'm sure it will all work out. Most folks are sympathetic to what the Indians are going through. It's only a handful of people that are hard-nosed," my girlfriend said reassuringly.

Interrupting us, Gen's Mom, Bea, stepped up to the table we now sat at. "How are you kids doing?" she said with a warm smile. "Have you ordered yet?"

"Yes we have Mom."

"How are you, Jed?" Bea greeted me warmly.

"I'm fine. But I'd be better if this protest and all the things around it would just end," I said.

"Yes, it sure has turned our community upside down. Everywhere you go it's the talk of the town – some for it, some against it. I see and hear it in here. Some of the conversations are quite heated. Heck, there was even one fist fight. Are you going to the meeting tonight, Jed?"

"Sure am. Have you heard what time it starts?" I asked.

"It's been advertised on the radio and they said the meeting will start at 7:00 sharp. Stop in at the house,

Jed. Reg wants to see you before the meeting," Bea informed me.

"No problem. We were going to stop by anyway."

We finished our meal, paid and left the café. Gen took my arm and we walked snuggled up to the vehicle. It felt good to once again be close to my girlfriend.

As I unlocked my vehicle a red-neck truck rumbled down the street and slowed going past us. "LaSal!" someone hollered out the window. "We're going to get you! Ya Indian lover!"

I glared at them to let them know that I wasn't scared. Immediately I raised my hand and gave them the middle finger. They kept going. I was glad because I'd had enough excitement over the last number of days.

"Let's get out of here, Jed. I don't want any trouble," Gen said.

Without a word we got in the vehicle and drove off. We arrived at Genevieve's house. It was a cozy little place in the old part of town. Reg kept the yard groomed nice and everything was in its place. I parked the vehicle and was just getting out when that same truck roared up and slammed on its breaks. "OK, LaSal, let's go!" yelled a fellow as he stepped out of the truck.

I never hesitated and stepped towards him ready to defend myself. "I'm not scared of you fuckers! Let's have-at-er!"

The punk took a swing. I stepped back slightly and then came at him with a left hook. I hit him with a good shot right in the side of the head, which knocked him back and down. He got up slowly and looked shaken with a dribble of blood running out of his nose. He never made a move towards me again.

"We'll get you, LaSal! You're going to die the same as those fucking Indians!" screamed the long haired driver.

"Fuck you!" I said and gave him the middle finger.

They sped off and peeled rubber half way down the block. Reg stood at the edge of his driveway, broom handle in hand. "Thought you would need some backup, Jed. I may be old and slow but I'm still pretty to watch."

"Got any cold beer, Reg?" I poked fun at my future father-in-law.

"Now that's a dumb question. You know that my beer fridge in the garage is always full," he said with a twinkle in his eye.

On the way back to the garage Reg gave me a friendly nudge. "How you doin' young man?"

"Pretty good, everything considered."

"Don't let it get to you. You are doing the right thing," he said reassuringly.

"Ya, that's what some say but it gets a bit trying when jerks like those guys come a callin'."

We popped the tops on a cold one and I tipped mine back and downed half the bottle. Wow! Did it ever taste great.

"I'll grab a couple more and let's go in the house. The TV is plastered with coverage about the protest. They are reporting that the army may be sent to help. If that happens, people will change the way they think. I was down at the Legion the other day and the crowd in there was split on the issue. But if the army is sent in most will be sympathetic to the Indians, seeing the government as bullies. Are you going back into the barricade?" Reg asked.

"Don't know. The cops are not too pleased with me right now so they might not let me go back in. I did promise Elsie and the bunch I would do what I could to help out. But I don't know if it will work out," I said.

Gen already had the TV on. The cameras had good vantage points from on top of Village Green Hotel. The panoramic view covered the entire area. Everything from the Command Centre to the overturned bus on the bridge was in plain sight. But the cameras were far enough away that you couldn't see the people very well.

A reporter came on. "The Army has been called in to set up and monitor a larger perimeter round the Silver Bridge. We have reports that there are a group of local people that are threatening to take things into their own hands."

Gen turned down the TV and said, "This has gotten way out of hand. I saw a bunch of red-necks over at the A&W yesterday, and it looked like they were having a meeting or something. I thought I saw Freddie Hanson's buddy with them."

"I hope not. Anybody that hangs out with Freddie is trouble. Bet they are stirring the pot. Has there been any word about how Freddie and the tree sitters are doing?" I asked.

"Apparently Freddie is the only one left out there, according to the news. A number of people have tried to talk him down but had no luck. It was reported in the paper that he is armed and dangerous," said Reg.

"He's a loose cannon," said Bea as she walked into the room.

"You're home early, Mom." Gen got up and gave her a tight hug.

"Yes, the gal that cooks on the afternoon shift came in early so I thought what the hell, I'd come home early. Have any of you heard anything about Red going out to where Freddie is?" she asked.

"No, but we ran into Slim at the gas station and he mentioned that the cops were thinking of taking her out there," I said.

"She came in for a coffee today and told folks that she was going out to the woods with the cops. No one believed her but I'm beginning to think she was telling the truth," mentioned Bea.

"Did she say when she was going out to see Freddie?" I asked.

"She said maybe tomorrow," said Bea with a sigh as she sat down and fixed her hair and put her feet up on the footstool.

"I hope she can talk some sense into him," said Gen.

"I have my doubts," said Reg. "The cops must be getting desperate if they are thinking of taking her out there. Do you know her, Jed?" he asked.

"I've met her. She's polite with me, considering that she's Freddie's flame."

"I wish her luck if she goes. She's probably the only person in the valley that has any influence over that man," Bea pointed out.

"What time is it, Mom?" asked Gen.

"It's getting late. You guys had better get going to the Union Hall, if you want a seat. The place will be packed to the rafters. I'm tired so I'll stay home and get some rest," she said. Bea was one of the hardest working people I knew. She held no less than two cooking jobs at a time. I often saw her come home from doing the breakfast shift at the Green Haven to grab a couple of hour's rest and then head out to the Doghouse Restaurant and do the afternoon shift.

Gen didn't live very far from the Union Hall so the drive there didn't take us long. We quickly parked and headed inside. It looked as though there were over three hundred people jammed into the hall. At the head table sat the mayor and a representative from the RCMP. There was a microphone set up, separating the rows of chairs.

"Greetings, folks. I would like to call this meeting to order. Sitting next to me is Sergeant Maxwell. He is here to fill you in about what has taken place and to answer any questions you may have. So with that I would like to hand the mic over to Mr. Maxwell."

"Good afternoon. Because the media has covered this matter extensively I will be brief with my presentation. I feel it is more important to open up the floor and let you ask questions. For the most part, we have set up and protected a perimeter defence line around the Silver Bridge. This was done to protect the general public. To date we have only had one demand from the protesters…they want all logging to stop on Sleeping

Beauty Mountain. The RCMP have brought in an experienced negotiator to spear-head the talks when and if the protesters are willing to talk. The government has also sent a number of army personnel to assist us with this issue. The situation, as I understand it, out in the woods is stable for now. A local gal, Ms. Betty Campbell, known as Red to most in the valley, has offered to help us with negotiating with Mr. Freddie Hanson, her boyfriend and who is the only tree-sitter on the platform. Mr. Hanson is armed and is considered dangerous. Thank you and I will take your questions."

"How long do you think this situation will last? It's a big inconvenience for a lot of us living on the other side of the Silver Bridge," asked a polite young lady.

"Unfortunately, that is a question that cannot be answered. It could end today or it may be still going three months from now," The Sergeant said with trepidation.

There were cat-calls and boo's coming from the crowd, especially from the guys that stood next to the doorway. We were tucked in close to the front but I had a good view of those fellows and it looked like it was those same guys, and more, that stopped at Genevieve's house.

The line-up for the mike was long. "Have negotiations started?" asked another.

Before the question could be answered an agitated looking guy pushed his way to the front of the line and pushed the speaker out of the way. "I'm not going to be so polite," he aggressively let everyone know. "This is bullshit! When are you guys going to get some balls and storm the blockade? I don't give a rats-ass how many of those bastards are killed. They want to play with fire. I say we fight it with fire. And if you don't soon do something...well, by god, I know people that will," he said.

He stepped back from the mike and waited for an answer. The crowd voiced their opinion from their chairs. Some were for it, some were against. And those guys in the back were the loudest and tried their best to get the crowd going and cause trouble.

"Calm down!" the Sergeant said sternly. "To take matters into your own hands will only make things worse. We are doing everything in our power to rectify this issue. So I'll put it to you directly. If you take the law into your own hands...we'll arrest you and you'll be charged. Now Sir, would you please step back from the mic and let someone else ask a question."

"Fuck you!" he said, giving him the finger.

The cop leaned over to the mayor. Covering his microphone he whispered something to the mayor. The mayor nodded to the security guards and they stormed the fellow that stood unmoving at the mic. The scuffle was short and the security guards escorted the fellow out of the hall. The other guys at the back followed.

I leaned over to Gen and whispered, "I bet we've not heard the last of those guys."

"I bet you're right," said Gen. "Those guys are nothing but trouble. Let's get out of here. I've heard and seen enough."

We got up to leave when the Sergeant hollered. "Mr. LaSal, may I see you for a moment?"

My heart started to pound and I nodded in agreement. As I approached him, I saw one of Freddie Hanson's side-kicks. He glared at me meanly and took off out the door. There was no doubt that he would pass on to those red-necks that I was going to speak with the cop. All that was running through my mind was what they had said to me earlier . . . that I could die!

CHAPTER 18

Vigilante Justice

Sergeant Maxwell didn't want to talk at the town hall meeting so he slipped me a note which simply said: Please come to the RCMP station in the morning. I had a pretty good idea what it was he wanted to talk to me about, based on what Bea told me. I was apprehensive but, oddly, I could not turn him down.

When I arrived at the police station at around nine o'clock in the morning there was a cruiser out front warming up and the Sergeant was standing next to it. As I approached it, the Sergeant spoke to me. "Climb in, Jed. Let's talk in the vehicle," he politely suggested.

I did as he asked.

"Jed, we would like your help. Freddie Hanson's girlfriend will be here any minute now and we are going out to the tree stand. Would you be interested in going? From what his girlfriend has said, you may be of some help. If you don't want to go, I understand," he explained.

All I said was, "I'll go."

"Thanks, Jed, I know this isn't easy."

I no sooner relaxed back in a plush seat in the cop car when Freddie Hanson's girlfriend walked up to the cruiser and opened the door. "Shove over, kid," said the pleasant older woman as she slid in next to me in the cop car. "My name's Red. What's yours?"

"Jed," I said.

"I have heard of you, Jed. My Freddie has spoken of you, often."

"I hope he said nothing but good things," I kiddingly mentioned.

"Don't worry, dear. He spoke kindly about you. Matter of fact, it's one of the reasons I asked Sergeant Maxwell if you could come with us out to the woods to talk with my Freddie," she mused, chomping away on her bubblegum.

"That's nice but I have to tell you, whenever I'm around Freddie, he's not very friendly," I let her know.

"It's all an act, sweetie. Deep down, Freddie is a softy. He likes to put on the tough guy act. But that's not to say that he won't stand up for what he believes in," she smiled and touched me lightly on the arm.

"He does it well," I said with my eyebrows raised.

"Trust me, Jed. He likes you. Over the last while Freddie has changed. He knows that the booze fogs his mind so he doesn't think straight. So he's really trying to make amends."

"He has a strange way of doing it," I said.

"Do you think he'll listen to reason?" asked Sergeant Maxwell.

"Don't know. I guess we'll find out soon, won't we," said Red.

"That's one of the reasons I thought it was best to take a couple of people he may trust. We know he is armed and we certainly don't want to see him get hurt from making a bad decision," Maxwell informed us.

"Have you heard anything about some other people going out to the woods, Sergeant Maxwell?" asked Red.

"No I haven't. But at the meeting the other night it was apparent that there was a group of people that may take things into their own hands."

"Last night at the bar, I overheard a few guys talking about just that - taking things into their own hands," she let him know.

"Do you know those people, Red?" inquired Sergeant Maxwell.

"No . . . I don't," she hesitated with her answer.

By her response, there was no doubt that she knew them. We drove in silence. Red gazed out the side window. She knew more but held back with any information.

It didn't seem to take long and we were at camp 3 and stopped in front of the office.

"How's it goin', LaSal?" asked Custy as he greeted our arrival in camp.

"Not bad considering all the bullshit that's going on," I responded.

"Ya, I've heard that you've been involved," said Custy, with a puzzled look. "Take these folks over to the cookhouse, Jed. I'm told that we're going to have a meeting prior to heading out to Branch 20."

It felt good to once again walk through the cookhouse door. The coffee was on so we all poured a cup and sat down at one of the long tables.

"So, Red, I have the feeling that you do know those fellows that made those accusations in the bar," the Sergeant prodded the old babe.

Red sat in silence at first but then she spoke. "Look, I'll be honest. I do know those guys but not that well. They hang out at the pub quite a bit. The one with long hair, I believe his name is Nick, is the loudest. Causes trouble all the time and seems to be the ringleader," she opened up but was noticeably fidgety.

"Is his name Nick Ivanov?" inquired the cop.

"Yes it is," Red quickly let us all know. "And yes he belongs to the Russian gang," she offered, but hesitantly.

The cop nodded his approval but said nothing and recorded what he heard in his notepad. Custy and a few other company men came into the cookhouse. They all sat down and all had concerned looks.

After brief introductions the meeting started. "I received a call from the night watchman late last night," said Steve Wallis, the company's CEO. "He informed me that a truck had sped through camp and looked like it was loaded with guys and was headed in the direction of Sleeping Beauty."

"Did he see how many?" asked Sergeant Maxwell.

"No. They were going too fast and it was dark," the CEO said.

"Maybe they were just a bunch of fellows taking the back road to Port Alberni," mentioned Custy.

"I doubt that," said Wallis. "The watchman followed them past the turnoff to Alberni. He said their tire tracks went towards Branch 20."

"Is there any logging going on right now?" asked Maxwell.

"No, we shut'er down till this matter sorts itself out. The mechanics in the shop are the only ones working," said Wallis.

"I sent one of them out to Branch 20 to have a look around. He should be on the radio any time now," spoke up the company's master mechanic.

"Good. That'll help," said the Sergeant.

The conversation turned to some of the logistics, safety, and Freddie Hanson. The cop suggested that we were going to be the only ones going out to the woods. He didn't want to scare Hanson by having a parade of crummies showing up. It was agreed that only the Sergeant, Red, and myself would go but we would have radio communication for backup.

In walked the receptionist from the office. "Tim has called in from Branch 20. He said that there is no sign of that truck or the people in it," she informed us.

"We'll still have to be cautious. If that was Nick Ivanov . . . we could be in for some trouble," Sergeant Maxwell said with a concerned look. "Ivanov is known to the police."

"It may be best to take my crummy," suggested Custy. "A cop car showing up out there may signal trouble. Another thing, do you people have rain gear? If not you may want to stop in at the dry room and pick some up. For the most part, the weather has been great but for some odd reason there are strange ominous looking clouds hanging over Sleeping Beauty," he said and gave his head a scratch.

I smiled to myself. I knew what was going on. The Elders said that the mountain would be protected so I wondered if their prediction would come true.

Custy handed me the keys to his bush crummy. It was nice to be heading out to the woods once again, albeit for the wrong reason. "Sergeant Maxwell, do you want me to drive right up close to the tree stand?" I asked.

"I think it would be a good idea to get as close as possible. But if you see anything out of the ordinary, stop immediately!" he ordered firmly.

Red sat quietly and stared out the window. Her thoughts must be of Freddie and what might happen to him. We turned up Branch 20. The road was a little rough and as we climbed the abrupt grade the wind picked up. We all saw those clouds Custy talked about. He was right - it was clear and sunny on the way there but by the look of those menacing clouds all hell could break loose.

We drove by the statue. "What's that, sweetie?" Red asked me curiously.

"It's a Bakwus´. It's there to protect Sleeping Beauty," I let her know. Red didn't say a word.

"Did you see those tire tracks heading off onto that side road?" asked Sergeant Maxwell.

"Sure did," I agreed.

"Where does that road go, Jed?" the Sergeant asked.

"It winds its way around Sleeping Beauty," I explained. "I heard the company put in some new right-of-way in order to access a nice stand of fir," I said.

"Does that road dead-end?" he asked inquisitively.

"Yes it does. The only way out is back the way they went in."

Sergeant Maxwell grabbed the mic and turned up the radio. "Calling camp," he called over the airwaves.

"Go ahead, sergeant," said the receptionist's voice on the other end.

"Will you call the Lake Cowichan Dispatch and ask them to send backup," the Sergeant instructed her. "And let them know it is urgent!"

"Roger, "Came back the response."

I drove as close to the protesters' tree stand as the road would allow, parked the crummy and we all stepped out and looked up the hill. The tree stand was much the same as I remembered it. There was a slight breeze which made the limbs dance lightly in unison and with the dark clouds that loomed over us it made for a vivid scene right out of the movies. Prompted by the breeze, the standing timber swayed in unison, much like an artist would graciously apply even stokes of a paintbrush.

"Get the hell out of here!" hollered a familiar voice from way up in the stand. Some things never change – Freddie Hanson hadn't lost his flare.

"Don't say a word," ordered the sergeant. "Red, you stay here while Jed and I head up there and find out if Freddie will talk with you. If we're lucky, he'll come down out of the tree stand to talk knowing that you are here."

"Right-o," Red anxiously said while she fidgeted in her seat. I could tell by her body language that she was very nervous. And for good reason. She knew Freddie Hanson better than all of us put together.

It wasn't far up through the fell and bucked timber to where the tree platform was. "Let's go up that draw on the right. It will give us a bit of protection," I suggested to the sergeant. "Be careful, you don't have any caulk boots on," I also told him.

He didn't say a word but he did unbuckle the snap to his handgun and looked me in the eye and said, "You ready for this?"

"Absolutely!" I never hesitated to say. Even though it was unnerving, I wasn't going to let him know that I was concerned.

We started out up the hill with me in the lead. It felt good to be back walking on fell and bucked logs. I only wished that it was under different circumstances. I could hear the sergeant breathing hard as we exert ourselves. "You OK? Do you want to stop and catch your breath?" I asked.

"No. Let's keep going. I don't know how you guys do this all day at work," he said and paused to wipe the sweat off his brow. "I'll let you know when I need to stop, Jed."

The draw was beginning to peter out so I stopped climbing. "We have to cut over this ridge and drop down into the other gully. That gully will take us to the bottom of the tree stand," I informed the Sergeant.

"It's going to expose us, Jed, so hustle," he said.

As we both topped out on the ridge at a dead run we were startled by a loud bang...bang...bang. I instinctively dove for the dirt and rolled down into the gully! And the sergeant was right on my heels.

"Jesus Christ!" I hollered. "What the hell was that?"

"Gun shots! Stay down!" he unequivocally ordered. "It's not coming from Hanson. Must be from those fuckers that come in during the night. Those bastards!" he snarled and drew out his hand gun.

"LaSal, do you think you can make it down to the pickup, safely?"

"I think so. If I follow this gully down I can stay out of sight," I said.

"OK. Head back to the pickup. Radio camp and have them call in a helicopter with backup, and hurry!" he said apprehensively.

I crawled on my belly until the gully deepened. I bounded from log to log, not missing a step. I had to make it to the crummy and the radio. Again, the gully petered out, but at least I was close to the crummy. I sprinted along a buckskin log. When again I heard, bang . . . bang, pause, and bang, I hit the dirt! Breathing hard, my legs shook and I was soaked in sweat but I mustered strength and took off once more for the crummy.

I flung open the door. "Red, hand me the mic!" I yelled. She didn't answer and was laid out on the seat, blood trickled from underneath her. "Fuck me! She's been hit!" I bellowed out loud.

I grabbed her arm and checked her pulse. Thank Christ she had one but it was faint. She must have got hit from a stray bullet, from the volley aimed at me. As I reached further past her for the mic I was poked hard in my back by a sharp object. "LaSal! You touch that mic and you're dead!" It was Nick Ivanov with his rifle jammed in my back!

CHAPTER 19

Mystical Bedfellow

I woke up slowly, fading groggily in and out of consciousness. Damn my head hurt and throbbed nonstop. My hands and feet were bound tight and the goose egg on the back of my head explained why I felt so bad. Those bastards! Why did they do this to me? How was Red doing? I hoped she was alive. I wondered if Sergeant Maxwell and Red made it out of the woods. And how did I get here in this old run down room? I was betting I was back in Duncan, somewhere. My mind ran wild with questions.

As the minutes ticked by I regained some of my composure and I heard muffled talk in the next room, but it was audible. "Hey Nick, what's our next move?" asked a raspy voice.

"Boris, pour me another drink will ya?" asked Nick. "Alex...you, Shorty, and Lenny head down town and find out what's going on. Try and find out what the cops are up to. And don't screw up. Those fuckers are always after us so we've got to stay a step ahead of them if we're going to pull this off . . . there is a lot riding on it."

"No problem, Nick. We'll snoop around," came the reply.

"Boris and I are going to rough up that prick, LaSal," said Nick. "We think he's in bed with the cops and we need to get some information out of him. Then he'll be crab-bait. The movement of the drugs won't take place until they start logging again. Until they do there won't be enough logs to fill the barge and a lot is riding on this. We are going to stash it on the log-barge that is headed down the coast to L.A. If I only had a bit more time when we were out in the woods I would have had Freddie Hanson in my sights and it would have been the end of that prick once and for all. With him gone out of that tree stand the company would have started to log," he explained to his gang. "Now head down town and find out what's going on," Nick ordered.

I couldn't believe what I heard. By the sound of it they were running drugs and without the company logging it was putting a wrench in their plans to use a log barge. Was my time on this earth running out? This gang needed to be stopped. Somehow.

The door flung open and in walked Nick and Boris. They paused and stared intently. The sweat poured out of me and down my face. I thought to myself, "I've got to get through this." Boris tipped up his drink and guzzled it. He finished and hurled the glass against the wall. "Come-on ya little fucker, stand up," he said and untied my feet only.

A large man, Boris manhandled me like a ragdoll. If I was going to get out of this situation I had to dig deep within me for an inner strength like never before.

"Fuck-off!" I screamed. Immediately, he nailed me with his big fist. I hit the floor and, just as fast, stood up again. "Untie me and I'll teach you some manners your mother never taught you . . . ya sonofawhore!" I hollered at this mammoth of a man.

"Undo him, Boris," ordered Nick. "Let's find out what this cop-lover's got," he said.

I turned around and Boris undid my hands.

"Alright you fuckin prick, let's have at'er!" I shouted.

I fought like a madman. Fists and feet flew, some connected and some missed. If they were going to kill me, I was not going to make it easy for them. For a moment I had the upper hand but Boris lunged and tackled me to the floor. "That's it, Boris," I heard Nick coach him on. "Soften him up for me."

"I'm not scared," I taunted and struggled, but he was just too big and too powerful.

He pinned me to the floor and with both hands gripped my throat. I flailed away with both hands but it was useless. "I'm going to choke the life right out of you! Die, ya little shit, die!" he yelled.

His eyes bugged out and drool ran down his chin as he choked the life out of me. I started to fade and his voice seemed slow and garbled. I was going to black out!

Out of the corner of my eye I vividly saw the mystical Bakwus' suspended in the air that was a weird green, blue and black. His face was amazingly clear and colourful and there was a bright light that surrounded this larger than life creature. Oddly, the room appeared peaceful.

I was overcome with an inner calmness and felt energized and empowered to deal with these two villains. Indian-like, I cried out like a warrior, "Arrrrrrrrr!" and threw my attacker over my head with an unexplainable ease. I glanced over at Nick. He stood frozen, his eyes fixed on Bakwus'. Immediately I focused on Boris and spoke to him with authority. "Stop!" I yelled and held out my open hand. "If you quit now I won't hurt you."

He paid no attention to me and struggled to get up off the floor. Without hesitation I scurried over to him and elbow dropped him between the shoulder blades. He fell and didn't mov. Nick looked over at me, no words were spoken. He turned around and put his hands behind his back. He gave up. I quickly tied these scoundrels up with the same rope they had used to tie me up with. Boris laid flat on the floor out cold and Nick sat in the corner with his hands tied behind his back. He was white as a ghost and his eyes were fixed on my mystical helper. As I stepped through the doorway and glanced back over my shoulder, Bakwus' was still suspended in the air, on guard. I was free.

I made my way out of the gloomy borstal, free at last I had to go for help. I sprinted down the street and immediately recognized where I was. Those idiots had kept me right downtown, not far from the cop-shop.

"Hey LaSal!" hollered a voice from a vehicle that came my way and stopped. "Jump in. Shit, everyone in the valley has been on the lookout for you," said the driver.

"Ivanov and his gang had me tied up in an old house a block from here. Take me over to the cop-shop, and hurry!" I said.

We pulled up in front of the police station and I quickly went inside. The cop at the front counter needed no introduction. "LaSal! Glad you are OK," the officer greeted me.

"They held me captive just a couple of blocks from here," I said.

"Do you remember which house?" he asked.

"It's the old vacant house at the end of Front Street. And they are tied up."

"What do you mean they are tied up?" he asked.

"I tied them up after a bit of a scuffle," I said humbly.

"How many are there in the house?" he asked.

"There are only the two I tied up. Ivanov ordered the others to go downtown and find out what's going on," I said. 'So I don't know when they will be back."

Without a word he turned and disappeared into the back of the office. I stepped back from the counter and took a look out the window. Damn it felt good to be out of the hands of those gang members.

"LaSal," came a familiar voice. "Are you OK?" asked Sergeant Maxwell as he extended out his hand.

We shook hands, firmly. "Yes I am, thanks," I said.

"Follow me," he said and opened the door that led to the back of the police station.

I could hear the chatter on the two-way police radio. And by the sound of it the cops had closed in on the house. The take-down went off without a hitch with Nick and Boris tied up and the only ones in the house. The cops stormed the place and took care of business – Nick and Boris were now in custody.

"Jed, tell me, how did you manage to escape?" asked Sergeant Maxwell.

"I had help," I said matter-of-factly.

"What do you mean you had help?" he asked.

At first I was hesitant to discuss what had taken place, but I thought what the heck and opened up to the Sergeant. I explained to him what had taken place from the moment I woke up. When I came to the part about the Bakwus´ he stopped, turned and faced me.

"Hold on a minute, Jed. Are you telling me that it was a supernatural aboriginal being that helped you?" he said and scratched his thinning hair.

"I am," I said boldly.

"Those guys must have given you some first-rate drugs, eh?" he said tongue-in-cheek.

I ignored his remark and decided that there was no use in trying to explain anything to him. For that matter, most people wouldn't understand but then, why would they.

"Dare I ask how Red is?" I asked.

"She's doing fine but is still in the hospital. I guess that when they were shooting at us a stray bullet must have got her," the Sergeant explained.

"Well that's good news. How long do they expect she will be in the hospital?"

"She's a lucky gal, Jed. The bullet grazed a vital organ. The Doctor said that if it was a direct hit she'd be dead."

We heard some commotion at the back of the police station. "Wait here, Jed. I'm going to go give those guys a hand. Sounds like they are here with Ivanov," he said and took off.

I stepped out of the room so I could see what was going on and they were bringing in Nick and Boris. Both were in cuffs and the cops wasted no time in putting them in separate jail cells. It was nice to see those criminals locked up.

The back door was flung open again and in came more cops escorting the other fellows and, even though they were restrained, the cops were wrestling to get them into jail cells. Shorty spotted me and stopped struggling with the cop and looked my way. He paused and stared briefly at me.

"LaSal, you had better leave town because we're going to get you ya fuckin' Indian lover!" he yelled as the cop stuffed him into a cell.

Sergeant Maxwell motioned with his head for me to leave the room. On the way out I hesitated by Shorty's cell. "You guys will not be able to hurt me," I said.

"Ya think so!" he blurted back, giving me the middle finger.

"Ask Nick," I wryly said and left.

CHAPTER 20

Tales of the Past

It started to sink in how close I had come to being rubbed out by that violent gang of drug dealing thugs. If the last few days had taught me anything, it was how quickly circumstances could change so I made a vow to myself to live life to the fullest. From that moment on I would pack all I could into the years ahead of me.

I needed some time to myself. With all that had been going on lately I headed to the Green Haven Cafe' to have a quiet breakfast by myself. "Hello Jed," spoke a warm and recognizable voice. "May I sit and have a cup of coffee with you while you finish your breakfast?" asked Elsie.

It was nice to see and hear my Elder friend. "You're very welcome to join me, Elsie. What brings you to the Green Haven?" I asked.

"I was looking for you and thought you may be here. Do you have time to come over to the Longhouse?" she

221

asked. "The keeper of the old masks is going to explain the power that comes from those ancient mystical creatures. Other people from around town will be there as well, Jed."

This was just what I needed - a reprieve from the stressful goings on that has dominated my life lately. "Yes, I would love to hear those stories. What time would you like me there?"

"Anytime after lunch would be fine."

"Did all the Elders leave the roadblock?" I asked.

Elsie continued. "No. A couple of them stayed behind. We did what we could but those young people were not going to listen to us. I guess they will have to learn on their own. I just hope that no one gets hurt."

"Have the two sides got together yet, Elsie?" I asked.

"No. They are as far apart as ever. We got word that the cops and the army are ready to storm the blockade, to put an end to it, so that was one of the reasons we decided to leave," she said with a very concerned looked on her face. Elsie raised her coffee cup up to take a sip. She looked out the widow and seemed to stare off into the distance, lost in her own thoughts.

I broke this silence. "Well let's hope that it works itself out. The last thing anyone wants is for people to get hurt," I said. But my gut was telling me that things may get worse before they got better.

I finished my breakfast and visit with Elise. Before we parted I gave her a hug and told her that I'd see her this afternoon. As I strolled down the street towards my vehicle I felt a certain sense of connection with Elsie, the Elders and the First Nation Peoples. I guessed it must have been the native blood running through my veins.

As I strolled down the street back to where I parked my vehicle my thoughts were interrupted by a loud vehicle speeding down the road. It appeared to be picking up speed and was erratically all over the road from one side to the other. I stopped and turned to watch what was going on. The vehicle swerved towards my side of the road and was aimed right at me. Instinctively I stepped back and out of the way. Just before it hit the sidewalk the vehicle again swerved back towards the middle of the road and slowed down a bit. A person inside this projectile stuck his head out the window and yelled my name. "LaSal!" Was that a gun I saw being held up in the window? If so, I guessed Nick Ivanov and his gang were hell bent for leather to get me. I didn't recognize anyone in the car, so I'd have to watch my back from here on out. This freighting incident shook me up mentally. When would this bullshit end?

I had a couple of hours to waste so I thought I'd head down to the police line and have a look at what was going on. I arrived and stood behind the line and looked down the street towards the Silver Bridge. There were cops and army personnel everywhere. By the look of it they had beefed up their numbers so the rumours must have been true – they were getting ready to attack the protesters and put an end to the blockade.

"Hello George. How's it goin´?" I greeted the Bullbucker, George Peterson, from camp. "What brings you here?" I asked.

"Oh . . . I'm just curious what the hell is going on, Jed. I hear that you've had your share of excitement," said George.

"Yes it's been quite a ride and it's not over yet. I don't like the stress and all the bullshit and can't wait till things get back to normal in the valley," I said.

"We all can't wait, Jed. I was born and raised in the valley and have never seen anything like this. People have taken sides and have drawn lines in the sand about who is right or who is wrong. This protest has brought out feelings and misguided thoughts from a lot of people. What it boils down to is discrimination – sad but true. Never thought that I'd see and hear it in our little town and valley. It just goes to show you that even in a small place like here we are not immune to the ravages of terrible human behaviour and bad choices. Maybe someday people will come to their senses and learn to live together as equals," he said.

"I agree. What do you think it will take to change things, George?"

"I really don't know. Maybe something catastrophic has to happen to bring everyone back to their senses. By the look of what's going on here, the cops and army are going to attack the protesters," he said with a sad look on his face.

"If they do . . . people will get hurt or, worse yet, killed," I said.

"Let's hope it doesn't come to that, Jed. Well I've got to go. See you when camp gets back to work," said George and he turned and walked towards his car. He walked with a slight forward lean. It must have been from all those years of packing those heavy power-saws around the side-hill. I wondered why he said he would see me in camp. The fallers are kept separate and we lesser-mortals on the rigging, for the most part, don't mingle at camp with those guys. Maybe I'd get a chance to break in falling.

I sauntered down the road and back to my vehicle. It was time for me to head to the Longhouse and listen to the Elders and the oral legends.

The drive to the gathering place didn't take long because I took the old and scenic road that winds its way along the bottom of Mt Tzouhalem. The parking lot was full. The Longhouse was as I remembered it. As I walked through the arched and decorative entrance, a warm rush ran through my body. It felt good and as though I belonged. Even though my Indian ancestry came from a place far from here, I felt a common bond. This place had a special spiritual glow.

"Welcome, Jed," spoke an Elder. She gestured for me to follow her. "Please . . . sit. The others will be out in a moment. My name is Phyllis. I live over on the old part of the reserve, down by the mouth of the river," she said.

"Nice to meet you, Phyllis," I said.

Phyllis pointed to the Elders that entered the big house, two of them held masks in their hands. I recognized those masks immediately as Bakwus' and Tsonokwa. There were also other non-aboriginal people that accompanied the Elders. We all made our way to the fire-pit in the middle of this magnificent building. The fire was lit and its embers, a brilliant orange, glowed and radiated a comforting heat which added to the suspense within this dimly lit and time-honoured abode.

"I would like to welcome you all to our Longhouse," said an Elder that was cloaked in a traditional button blanket robe and wore a woven cedar headband. "My name is Stella and I am one of the keepers of these ancient masks. We have invited you here today because the Old One, our oldest Elder made the request. On occasion we bring to life these ancient masks and share the oral history that has been handed down for thousands of years."

The Old One sat back from the fire-pit and in the dimly lit Longhouse the silhouette of this ghostlike elderly person added to the anticipation. Her weathered and primordial face had a sense of wisdom that only comes from time. The Old One looked not only wise but had a sense of peacefulness that surrounded her.

The drums, with their low and guttural tone, put all of us under a relaxed spell and ready for Stella to carry on. "Bakwus', the wild man of the woods is unpredictable. He can take on many forms and the ancients say to be wary if you are a bad person because he will haunt you. It has been said that you will go crazy and never be the same if he comes for you. He may even take you away . . . never to be seen again! The ancients have said that Bakwus' is a protector of good people and will shadow you your entire life, appearing when you least expect it. Tsonokwa, the wild women of the woods is a body snatcher and will come to the village and take people that are not of good mind and quality. She will hide them in the deep and gloomy woods until those who are bad turn good. It is said that Tsonokwa will snatch bad kids and take them away, only returning them when they are good. She, too, will also protect you from bad things if you are a good person. The Old One remembers a long time ago when something very unusual happened in the village."

There was an eerie silence and pause as the Old One stepped up close to the fire. Adorned in a very old and tattered but decorative button blanket, she wore a scarf neatly tied on her head. It was apparent she was very old by her slow and uneasy movement, but there was an air of perspicacity that filled this large room as she stood and looked around, silently. Everyone waited with patient eagerness for her to speak.

"One time . . . long ago, my great-grandmother told me the village was under attack from vicious warriors from a far away land. They had many big war canoes that held lots of painted, fierce looking men with weapons. Each canoe had a large war drum that signalled their bold approach to our peaceful village. The noise from those drums vibrated through the villagers' bodies and, with each stroke of their paddles, the war cries from the invaders sent chills through the settlement.

Death was on the doorstep! Fearing for their lives our people ran wildly for the safety of deep woods – only to be followed by those killers with their weapons. They were going to kill all the men and take the women and children as slaves . . . our village would be destroyed. My great grandmother spoke of the chaos. She said the young kids cried hysterically and women screamed for help as they heard the echoes of death from the men that defended the shores of our community. The men's defence was to no avail. They were being overtaken. Outnumbered and out fought . . . our ancestors' lives would be changed forever. The women and kids gathered on a high ridge that overlooked the village. They saw the devastation. But they also saw a strange, eerie greenish-blue fog that came in from the sea and brought with it tremendous winds and reddish-orange bolts of lightning – and the thunder was deafening! Within the ominous fog the ancients saw two vivid faces. They were of Bakwus' and Tsonokwa. Bakwus', with his bold green and black face was framed with long dark hair. The greenish-blue fog flowed from his mouth as he swooped in and over the warring villains and defenders. Tsonokwa, in all her majesty, was jet black with orange striping that ran down her face. Her eyes were brilliant orange and the source of the lightning bolts that struck the ground with thunderous cracks. This sight would be ingrained in the oral history of our nation for eternity," she spoke softly, but vividly.

The Old One paused. Everyone gazed at the fire intently and was mesmerized by the oral history and how the Old One brought to life this believable legend.

With an eagle feather in hand, she continued. "The creepy fog which held Bakwus' and Tsonokwa plunged down and engulfed the marauding villains from afar. The ground shook violently and the wind transformed the tall fir trees that surrounded the village into lethal weapons that cascaded down onto the trespassers, which sent the attackers into a retreated frenzy. They dropped their weapons and ran for their canoes, to flee our village in fear for their own lives. Some disappeared within this nightmarish scene, their cries faded into the distant – never to be seen again!"

The drum tone changed and in came masked dancers. Each held a very old weapon. They circled around us to show off these impressive implements of prehistoric war on the coast, left behind many years ago. No sooner had the dancers encircled us when the door at the end of the Longhouse opened swiftly and in ran a young Indian fellow. "There has been gunfire at the blockade. Peter is dead!"

CHAPTER 21

Trigger Happy Punks

Everyone left the Longhouse in such a hurry that no one had time to reflect on the oral history presented by the Elders. My mind was full. I was worried, much like the others at the Longhouse, about what was happening in our community of Duncan. With the news of Peter's death I had visions of war in our valley. I could not help but think that there was going to be more people hurt or worse yet, killed.

As I approached the intersection of the Island highway that leads to the Silver Bridge I heard the sound of sirens. I stopped and waited as cop cars and emergency vehicles sped through the junction with all lights flashing - all but one, that is. I waited as a lone ambulance went through the intersection, slowly. It didn't have any lights or siren on. A chill ran through my body. Instinctively, I knew that this vehicle was transporting Peter's body.

I rolled down the window in my vehicle and immediately heard the distinct and frightening sound of gunfire!

Were my nightmarish visions of injured or possibly other dead people real? My hands shook as I gripped the steering wheel to maneuver my vehicle through the crossroads. I felt slightly dizzy and sick to my stomach, so I pulled into the gas station on the opposite corner. The thought of this bizarre situation was overwhelming.

I hardly made it out of my vehicle and was on my knees vomiting when I heard a voice. "You okay?" asked someone. I looked up and found a couple of cops standing over me. "You're going to have to vacate this area," said one of them. "We're securing a larger area surrounding the bridge, so when you're done, get in your vehicle and get out of here!" he ordered, abruptly.

I wiped my mouth with the sleeve of my shirt. "No problem. I'll take off right away," I told the cop. No sooner had those words come out of my mouth when another cop car pulled up.

The cops slammed on the breaks and were out of their cop car, quickly. "Are you Jed LaSal?" Asked one of them.

"Yes I am," I said. It was pointless to ask them how in the hell they knew I was here at the gas station.

"LaSal, leave your vehicle here and come with me. We've been looking for you. Sergeant Maxwell wants to see you," said another cop.

"What's up?" I asked.

"The Sergeant wants to have a chat, so he'll answer that question."

The ride was brief as we pulled up to the command centre. "Follow me," the cop said bluntly.

I could hear the odd pop of gunfire and there were cops and army personnel everywhere, so it was reassuring to seek the shelter and safety of the command centre. I walked directly up to the Sergeant. "What's up Sergeant?" I pointedly asked, then stood there with my arms crossed. I was not happy.

"Thanks for coming, Jed. As you can see we have a very serious crisis on our hands and I may need your help. I am going to call a cease fire because I think there are wounded in the blockage and we need to get them out and to the hospital," he said.

"What happened? Who started the shooting?" I asked.

"They shot first and my men and the army personnel were given the order that if any shots came from the blockade to shoot," he made it clear.

"What the hell can I do?" I asked and shook my head in discontent.

"We want you to go in with the paramedics. Those people in the blockade know and trust you, so we feel that it would be safer for all concerned if you would accompany them."

I stood for a moment, silent. "All right. I'll do it," I said. "But how will they know I'm coming with help?"

"The Elders have suggested that you carry a talking stick. But I have to warn you that there are no guarantees. This will be a very dangerous situation."

He showed me the decorated First Nations symbol. It was nicely carved with aboriginal figures and had a bundle of eagle feathers neatly secured on the top. "The Elders have said that those that carry this talking stick are safe. They also said that the young warriors will recognize the talking stick and not shoot," said Sergeant Maxwell.

Even though I understood what the Sergeant had said, I was still very nervous. I took the talking stick in my hand. "Where are the paramedics? Let's get this done," I said.

"They are waiting out back. Good luck, Jed," he said and shook my hand.

I turned and headed out the back door where two others waited. "Hello, Jed," they both greeted me. "I'm Burt Jones and this is my partner Faith McMillan."

"Hello," I greeted them with urgency, but confidently. "Are you ready to go?" I asked.

"Yes, let's get this over with," said Faith. She was nervous and for good reason.

We stepped out and headed towards the Silver Bridge. I led the way with the talking stick in hand. The Elders were right. I felt safe, but more than that, with every step I felt confident. We made our way to the blockade.

The encampment was the same as I remembered it. The fire in the centre smoldered, sending a thin plume of smoke skyward and it was unusually quiet. A young girl lay covered up beside the fire. Old Joe Simon, one of the Elders that stayed behind, approached us. "Hello Jed. Thanks for coming. Sue is wounded. She took a bullet in the leg and has lost a lot of blood and is weak," he said. "We let the cops and the ambulance come in and get Peter. There was nothing that could be done for him, Jed."

Old Joe's hands shook as he informed me about Peter. Everyone was on edge but the encampment had an air of defiance, too.

The paramedics were already at her side. "This girl needs to get to the hospital right away!" exclaimed Faith.

While Burt and Faith worked to stabilize the young protester the others at the camp looked traumatized and never said a word. The gravity of this situation had hit home. In the truest sense, they understood they all could die.

"Why did the cops start shooting?" asked Old Joe.

"What do you mean the cops shot first?" I was puzzled by his comment.

Old Joe gave me a strange look. "With no warning, a shot came from over there," he pointed to the right of the camp at a clump of trees up the river. "One shot and it hit Peter. He never knew what hit him," he paused. "Then all hell broke loose," said Old Joe somberly.

"Something's not right, Joe. I don't think that the cops had anybody up the river. To the best of my knowledge they are all spread out towards town," I said.

"Well Peter was hit from the left side as he sat by the fire. He never even had his gun in his hand. The second shot hit Sue and all hell broke loose. These young people manned their guns and started shooting back at the cops. That's when gunfire came from out front. And lots of it. Jed, I've never been so scared in my life. These young people were in a fight for their lives, defending themselves."

I was shocked to hear Old Joe's explanation about how the battle started but there was no time to quiz him further because that young girl had to get to the hospital. "Joe, I'm going to explain to Sergeant Maxwell what you've said and, if everyone agrees, will he be allowed to come into camp and talk to one and all?" I asked.

One of the young warriors overheard me with the request. "LaSal you tell the cops that if they want to talk we'll listen to what they have to say," he paused.

"But it better be good. Peter's dead and someone's going to pay for it."

"I'm going to go out and talk to Maxwell," said Old Joe. "The time has come for talks to start to put an end to this awful mess. I don't want any more people hurt," he said with a forceful tone. Not one of the protesters said a word and, by the solemn look on their faces, I got the feeling that they too wanted this over. But they were proud people and in all likelihood they would stick it out.

We headed back to the police line.

The young girl was transferred to an ambulance and Old Joe was talking with Sergeant Maxwell. They looked my way and gestured to me to join them. "Jed, from what Joe has told me, the altercation started with a shot that came from up the river," said a concerned Sergeant Maxwell.

"Yes. All the protesters back up what he is saying."

The Sergeant stared at the ground and pondered this new and disconcerting information. We stood there awkwardly and waited for his response. After a long silence he looked up and gazed out towards the river. "Ivanov," he mumbled.

"What's that you say?" I asked.

"Nick Ivanov. If I were a betting man, I would bet he is behind the first shot that came from up the river," said Sergeant Maxwell.

"What the hell! I thought he was in jail?" I quizzed him.

"He was. But somehow he made bail. On the way out the door he made some threats, but the guy is always threatening someone so we never paid any attention to him," he said and turned and gave orders to another cop to go find and arrest Ivanov and any and all of his gang members.

With Peter dead and the others behind the blockade wanting revenge, the situation was desperate.

CHAPTER 22

The Old One

I was in shock so I headed home for some much needed rest and a home-cooked meal. Every one of my friends had been encouraging me to leave home, to fly the coop, to get my own place and that would happen one day. But for now, it was really nice to help mom and dad out by paying for room and board.

My own bed felt good. I slept reasonably well considering all that had been going on lately. I hadn't been eating all that well, so I was looking forward to my mom's home cooking.

"Young LaSal, your breakfast is on the table!" hollered my mom. "You've slept for 10 hours. Hope you are rested, son." My mom summoned me for breakfast.

After I washed up, I headed to the kitchen. I didn't have to be asked twice when a home-cooked meal was set on the table in front of me. "Thanks, mom." And I dug in.

"Your father has gone to town for some parts for the car. Will you be home for dinner?"

"Don't know. I hear a rumour that we may be going back to work. If that is the case, I will be here."

"We got a call from Custy, the woodsforman. He says the company has an area to log away from the entire ruckus. It's on the other side of the valley. Apparently you'll be able to see the tree stand where Freddie Hanson is still hanging out," said Mom.

"That'll be interesting," I said. "Maybe I should take the binoculars."

"The rumours about going back to work must be true if Custy called. I'll try and find out today," I said.

"You keep your head up, son. We support you with what you have been doing but there are people out there that have voiced their opinion against you. So please watch out," said my concerned mother.

"Thanks, mom." I finished my breakfast in silence. I could tell by the concern in my mother's voice that she was worried and rightly so. My Dad had been very quiet about this whole matter. But he never was one to voice his opinion much anyway.

"I will be meeting Gen for lunch at the Green Haven. If Dad calls from town, let him know he's welcome to come."

"Will do," she said and came over and gave me a big hug. She squeezed me firmly. I knew that mom had been worried and didn't want me or anyone else in our family involved in the troubles that plagued our communities in the Cowichan Valley, especially when discrimination was involved. But out of respect for my independence, she didn't say much.

I stopped at the Chinese-owned corner store on my way to Duncan to pick up a couple of things. "Hello, Mr. Chow. How's things with you?" I greeted him. I knew Lee Chow well. Our family had patronized his store ever since I was a little boy.

"Good as usual, young Jed. I have been reading in the paper all about what you are doing to help with ending the road block. Very honorable, young Jed, but you will have made some enemies in the valley as well. Stick to what you believe in because this may be over sooner than you think," Mr. Chow said.

Puzzled, I asked him, "What do you mean this could be over, Mr. Chow?"

"I saw the Old One the other day down at the beach in Cowichan Bay. Do you know her?"

"I've listened to her speak at the Longhouse," I said.

"She is a very wise and calm person, young Jed. She told me that a vision had come to her in a dream. That vision was of destruction and mayhem." He paused and looked out the window. "The Old One said that soon it will be over."

I knew better than to ask him to explain more about what the Old One had told him. He was a man of few words and probably wouldn't tell me anyway. I paid for what I came for which included the weekly newspaper. The headline read "Provincial government calls for a cooling off period." Below the headline there was a large photo of the Silver Bridge and the protesters peeking out from behind the overturned bus. It was a dramatic and explicit-looking image that, in my opinion, gave the readers the wrong impression.

I could see within the photo young Indian warriors in full camouflage with their guns pointed towards the cops and military personnel. This photo took up almost half the front page. There was no doubt it painted a bleak picture of the situation and painted the Indian people with the wrong brush.

I sat in my vehicle and started to read the article.

"The provincial government today announced a cooling-off period to help defuse the escalated situation in Duncan. The protesters will remain in their position on the Silver Bridge and the RCMP and army will remain steady as well. There will be no talks, said the Minister of Aboriginal Affair. "Due to the tragic circumstances, today the government has called for a cooling-off period. This will give everyone time to step back, take a breath, and evaluate what has taken place and hopefully start what the government considers an end to the protest."

When asked what the tragic circumstances were the Minister commented bluntly: "The arrest of Ivanov. Allegedly, he and his gang are the cause of the gunfire that tragically has taken place."

Those were strong words that pissed me off so I tossed the paper into the passenger seat and took off for Duncan to meet Gen for lunch. I drove in silence and reflected on what I had just read. The cooling off period the government had called for was all smoke and mirrors. What was wrong with those bastards in government? Nothing had changed. They only seemed to say what they thought the majority of people wanted to hear. What happened to fairness and just plain common sense? All the First Nations wanted wad to preserve an ancient burial ground. Given what the Minister said in the newspaper, I wondered how long they would wait before the government gave the order to take down the blockade? After contemplating the short newspaper statement by the Minister, I turned on the local radio. Mr Chow said that the Minister was going to be giving a statement further to the news article on the front page.

I was half way to Duncan, around Hill 60, when the Minister came on the airways.

The radio announcer introduce the Minister and asked him to explain the governments position on the roadblock. The Minister went on to further stated.

"Look, this roadblock has not only created poor relations between the government and the First Nations, but it has created a split between most folks not only on southern Vancouver Island but around B.C. in general. The government will not accept this type of terrorist tactics. We will not be held hostage by a group of protesters. We understand the concerns put forward by the protesters, however, simply put, it is against the law to do what they are doing. If they take down their roadblock we would be willing to talk. The forest company has a legal right within their forest tenure to log the timber on Sleeping Beauty Mountain and the government has an obligation to honour its legal commitment to that company. What everyone must understand is that the timber will be logged in that area. What the protesters have to understand is that there is a treaty process in place and the government will honour that process, too."

I turned the radio off and drove the rest of the way to Duncan contemplating what the Minister had said. It didn't sound like the government was going to be flexible with this matter any time soon. This was not good news! I turned at Burkies Corrner and headed for down town.

I parked along Main Street and got out of my vehicle and turned to lock the door. I had my head down and was fumbling with with my keys when I heard a familiar voice.

"How's it goin, LaSal?" asked a fellow. I knew right away it was the woods foreman from camp.

"Hello Custy," I greeted the woods foreman from camp. "Not bad considering all that has taken place," I said.

"I've heard that you have been involved with the goings on. No matter what people say, good or bad, you have made yourself a name in the valley. I think that once most people sift through the bullshit they can see that it's the government that needs to step up to the plate. They hold the cards, Jed. They could approach the company with an offer to log someplace else until this whole thing is straightened out. I've been around this game a long time and when the government wants the company to make changes they are more than willing to trade off timber from one area to another," said Custy.

"Most people I've talked with felt this whole thing could have been avoided if the government had approached the company with that offer. But no, they choose to flex their muscles and show the protesters and everyone who the big boss is, and look at what has happened. Peter is dead and discrimination is rampant, on both sides," I voiced my opinion.

"You're right," Custy said. "Not to defend the company, but they did approach the government with a proposal, which was turned down. From what I am told, since that young man was shot, they changed their mind and gave us an area to log across the valley from Sleeping Beauty. That doesn't mean that the company will abandon their plans to log Sleeping beauty. It just means that we can get back to work until this whole thing straightens out. And that's why we're puttin' together a skeleton crew and we are goin' back loggin'. Do you want to chase on the pipe?"

"Sounds good to me. Who's hookin?" I asked.

"Larson's gonna hook and Stant will pull riggin and we'll find some chokermen," Custy said. "Ya up to chasin'?"

"I will be on the crummy in the morning," I said, feeling elated that I was going back to work. But I wondered what was going to happen in our valley? How long would the government wait until they gave the order for the cops and army to storm the blockade? My elated feeling turned to one of concern for everyone this situation had affected, especially the protesters.

"Great, we'll see you at camp in the morning. Have a good day, Jed," Custy said and headed towards his vehicle.

Wow, it would be nice to get back to work. My thoughts drifted back to the protesters. How long would this cooling off period last? Would someone get impatient and start shooting again? Would the government order the blockade dismantled by the cops and army? I had a lot of questions in my mind. Most of those questions were out of concern for the safety of everyone I got to know at the Silver Bridge blockade.

Genevieve came walking down the sidewalk. She looked great.

"Hi Jed," Gen warmly greeted me. She gave me a tight hug. "Let's go eat. I'm starving," she said.

"I just ran into Custy. Looks like we'll be goin' to work in the morning," I told her.

"Yes, dad said that the company was going back to work. Are you ready?"

"I sure am. He asked me if I would chase on the tower. They've put together a small crew to take out some wood on the other side of the valley from Sleeping Beauty. I know the area. It will give us a clear view of the tree stand."

"Will you be able to see Freddie Hanson?" Gen asked.

"We won't be able to see him clearly, but we will be able to watch him move around up in the tree stand," I said. "Ya have to give him credit, he has stuck it out."

We sat down at the table in the Green Haven Cafe.

"He's a nutcase, Jed."

"I know, but the guy has got guts. I don't know too many people that would do what he is doing. It will be interesting to watch what is going on from our vantage point across the valley."

"Did you hear that the Elders are going to have a gathering on the beach down at the Bay?" Gen asked.

"No I didn't. What's up?"

"Apparently the Old One has asked all the Elders to come to the beach this coming weekend for a traditional salmon feast. Ethel, who works with mom, said that the Old One has had a vision and wants to tell the Elders."

"Did she say what this vision was about?" I asked.

"No. But Ethel said the rumour is that the Old One said the protest will end soon," Gen informed me. I'm sure Gen believed there was going to be a battle with people getting hurt or killed. She may be right. It didn't look good with both sides unwilling to give in and the government, at this point, was not willing to sit down and talk.

The Old One was wise. Some people said she had powers, powers to see and hear things into the future. Most non-aboriginal people thought this kind of thinking was outrageous. But on the other side of the coin, aboriginal people since their inception believed strongly these insightful powers exist. Who was I, or anyone else, for that matter, to argue with thousands of years of belief and tradition?

"Ya want to head to the beach and see what's going on?" I asked Gen.

"Sure, I'm not working this Saturday. It would be a nice way to spend the afternoon. Which beach?"

"Most of the gatherings take place at the mouth of the Cowichan River. The estuary is a special place for the tribes. It has a long finger of sand that is exposed when the tide is out and is at the bottom of Mt. Tzouhalem. This mountain, I am told, is one of the most sacred places for the Cowichan peoples. It stands overlooking the sea and the start of the Cowichan Valley. Much like a sentinel it is on guard protecting this precious warm land. Let's go and have a look and listen to what the Old One has to say. Are you into it?" I asked.

"Sounds like a nice place. I'm looking forward to it," Gen said. "You looking forward to going back to work, Jed?

"Yes I am. It will be nice to shake out the cobwebs and get back to the woods and work, but I wonder what Sleeping Beauty Mountain will have in store for us? Seems that damn mountain is always full of surprises."

"Sleeping Beauty Mountain and logging it is not the biggest problem, Jed. In my opinion, the biggest problem is Nick Ivanov. The word on the street is he's a drug dealer and needs to move drugs and is pissed off because no logs are hitting the water and being loaded out on a log barge to head south to Los Angeles. People are saying that millions of dollars are at stake and he will do anything to make sure his plans are not foiled," Gen said.

"I have heard the same rumours. And by the sound of it, he could be responsible for Peter's death. The cops are looking for him and his gang as we speak. Since the shooting and uproar at the Silver Bridge they have been nowhere to be seen."

"If they find him, he won't go easy," Gen said.

"Yes. And because he is a loose cannon," I paused. "I will have to be extra careful. He would think nothing of shooting me too. Let's not forget he had a gun in my back not that long ago."

CHAPTER 23

Branch 6

I was half asleep when the crummy arrived at the gate to Camp 3. Most loggers that commuted to work had a long and bumpy ride to camp. Standard practice for some men was to sleep. It took me a while to learn how to nod off while the crummy gently swayed back and forth to miss the ever-present potholes on a washboard gravel road. I felt the crummy slow down and make a sharp turn. We must have been turning into the marshaling yard at camp. The crummy came to a smooth stop and the familiar squeak of the mechanical door was a signal to get my ass up and out of the seat. It was time to go logging. Our limited crew was quiet as we filed out of the bus, lunch buckets and pack sacks in hand. With all the time off recently, everyone was slow to get going. The woods boss stood like a sentinel in the middle of the marshaling yard ready to direct his crew. He sauntered back and forth, head down and gently kicking the odd rock. He was deep in thought.

With a shit-eatiń grin and his tin hat worn angled back on his head, Custy walked towards us. He approached Ollie Larson. "Ollie, the tower is rigged and ready to go but you'll have to put in an eye-splice in the haulback. And make sure you check the guyline stumps. Wouldn't want one of those fuckers to pull. The yarder's up Branch 6. Do you remember the setting we started and had to pull out of because of the snow?" Custy asked.

"It's the setting at the end of the short road off of Branch 6, the one with the big landing," said Ollie. His voice was gravelly and his eyes looked like two piss-wholes in the snow. No doubt he drank and partied it up during the time off. For most old single loggers it was a way of life; they don't know any better. A good percentage of them, when they got too old to log, ended up drinking the rest of their life away in some old stinky seedy bar on Davey Street in Vancouver.

"That's right. You'll have to string straw-line but the blocks are where the hooker left them on the last road he was on. Make goddamn sure you check the guy-line stumps! Remember last year when that old piss tank hooker from up the coast we hired pulled tower 37 over? It was because he was too funckin lazy to check the guyline stumps. There will be some hard fuckin' pulls, Olli. The wood is big. There will be some long stuff but the fallers did a good job bucking up the setting," Custy said.

With a nod and a grin Olli buggered off to the smaller woods crummy. He didn't want to endure any more lectures from the grizzled woods boss. It was a signal for the rest of the crew to load up and head to the woods and spend the day logging. Everyone was anxious but in a good mood.

Slim, the donkey puncher, was already sitting in the driver's seat and waited for the crew to get into the crummy. He swung the door open. "How's it goin' Jed," he said as I climbed in. Tall and lanky, Slim barely fit in behind the steering wheel because his knees seemed to always get in the way. He was a chain smoker that always had a cig hanging out of his mouth.

"Great," I said. "Looking forward to getting back to work."

Custy was talking to a new fella they hired and pointed towards our crummy. The new fella, caulk boots in hand, walked over to our woods bus. "Find a seat young fella," Slim told him. "What's your name?"

"Tom," he said. "Tom Spencer."

"Nice to meet you," replied Slim. "You settin' beads?

"I am." And the new chokerman found a seat in the back of the crummy.

I was tying up my caulk boots and sipping a cup of tea I had poured from my thermos when I noticed a familiar figure in the marshaling yard. He was talking to the woods boss then made his way towards us.

The fella climbed into the crummy. "Sam!" "How the fucks she goin'?" I asked my old workmate. It was nice to see Sam back at work.

Sam grinned. "Thought I'd come and check out the mountain and see if that old prick Freddie Hanson is still up in the tree stand."

"No shit. Gotta hand it to him. He's stuck it out. Who the hell has been bringing him food and water, Sam?"

"Let's just say he has been looked after," Sam said with a wry look on his face. I could read between the lines and knew better than to quiz him anymore.

Custy approached the crummy and climbed and stood in the doorway. He hesitated and flicked his cigarette off into the dirt. "Jed, Stant never showed up. I guess he's quit and moved on so you'll have to pull rigging. You okay with that?"

"No problem. I'll head over to the office and grab the bugs."

"The landing bucker will chase until we can round up another fella," said Custy. He turned and headed for his truck. Custy shook his head and he looked discusted that Stant was a non show for work. I think he probably found a camp job up the coast. Can't blame him, because there seemed to be no end in sight with things getting back to normal around here.

I picked up the bugs at the office and headed back to the crummy. "Mornin' Jed," said landing bucker, Pete Stromberg. Pete had been landing bucking as long as anyone around these parts could remember. I have worked with Pete many times. Calm and always smiling, he was a dependable and capable logger.

Pete was a small man in stature with a weathered face from years of working on side-hills on the coast. Up until Pete hired on at Camp 3 as a landing-bucker, he worked as a faller. From Sooke to the Charlottes, Pete had worked in many camps. He was well known on the coast for his ability to lay the timber down. What he lacked in size he more than made up for with finesse and years of experience.

"Morning Pete. Good to see ya."

"Nice to be back to work, the bills are piling up," said Pete.

"Yes. I know what you mean. My bank account is getting skinny," I said. "Come to think about it, my bank account is always skinny."

Pete had a chuckle about what I had said. "Let's head to work, young man," he said and we headed for the bush crummy.

The crummy bounced along at a steady pace as we headed out to the woods. We hit the odd pothole which sent all of us lightly into a relaxed wobble. Heads bobbed and bodies swayed. If you weren't trying to nod off, you were trying to sip tea or coffee. You learned very fast over the years how to stay relaxed while riding on those pothole ridden and washboard gravel roads. Most loggers could sleep like a baby while going to and from the job site.

The steep climb up Branch 6 was long, narrow and full of switchbacks. The sun peeked over the mountains to the east which cast long shadows. It looked like it was going to be a nice day. We leveled off somewhat at the top of the mountain and made a left turn down the short spur road where the tower was. We no sooner had stopped next to the pipe and both Sim, the yarding engineer, and Red, the loader operator, were out of the crummy and warmed up each of their respective logging machines. From our vantage point at the end of this spur we overlooked the entire Nitinat Valley, which ran east and west. Sleeping Beauty Mountain stood majestically across from us. Being the tallest mountain in the valley, some of the old time loggers describe it as sticking out like a sore prick. And right smack dab in the middle of it we could see the tree stand and large sign that still hung off of it. It was too far to see Freddie Hanson but we all knew he was there. He stood there on guard in the tree stand and would stay there until this standoff was over.

We all had our bush boots and hard hats on and were ready to go logging. I strapped on the bug, ready to blow the long standing whistles that gave Slim direction as to what we wanted him to do for us side hill gougers as we went about the business of logging.

"Jed, you take the snotty end of the strawline and head up the hill towards that big o'l buckskin," Larson gave the order. "Tom and Sam will pull slack for you."

There was a corner left to log on the high side of the road. If everything went right it would only take the rest of the week to finish it off. Tom and Sam were spread apart and pulled the strawline off the drum on the tower. Sam was close to me and Larson was with the new guy, showing him the ropes. I could hear the old hooktender as he barked out orders to Tom about how to pull and string strawline. It reminded me of my first few days in the woods. The one thing that had stuck with me was the first thing the hooktender had said to me: keep your eyes and ears open and your mouth shut and you'll make out alright young fella. It was good advice. Most hooktenders will take new guys under their wing if they heed their advice. If the new guy didn't pay attention, he'd be in for one hell of a ride. Or, the hooktender may say to a greenhorn, "Up the hill or down the channel." That's logging terminology for get your ass in gear or you'll be fired.

I picked my way up the hill through the fell and bucked timber towards the buckskin log Larson pointed out to me. I had to stop often because I was not in logging shape. Too much time off and you will pay the price for a few days or so.

I finally arrived at the back end and saw the block still hung where it was left when they pulled out of this setting. I paused for a moment before I yelled down to Sam, "Line." This meant I had reached my destination and to stop pulling slack.

Larson wasn't far behind me. He packed a coil of strawline and his axe. "Fuck! Am I ever out of shape," he said.

"No shit," I said. "Me too!"

"I gotta quit drinkin," Larson said.

"How many times have you said that over the years, Olie?" I asked.

"Too many fuckin' times, by-golly," he said. We both were soaked in sweat and our legs were a bit wobbly.

Larson checked the block to make sure it was hung right. "Looks good, Jed." He took the end of the strawline and strung it through the block, pulled a bit of slack and handed me the end. I knew exactly what to do and headed for the other block at the back end while Larson fed me slack.

I strung the strawline through the block and headed back down the hill to meet Sam and Tom. I met Sam halfway down the hill. He took the end from me to hook the two ends together. The ends were spliced with a strawline-eye and hook for a quick hookup. "Put a wrap in it Sam. Larson will come unglued if it comes apart and we have to re-string the lines."

Sam was quiet. He fumbled a little putting a warp in the spliced eye of the strawline. "Little rusty, Sam," I teased.

"Yes it's been a while." Sam continued with a mischievous look on his face. "I've been busy, my friend. Maybe one day I will tell you about it."

I was curious but we had some work to do first. "Let's move out of the bight so we can run the haulback around."

We headed across the fell and bucked logs to the slash. I rested my hand on the bug and took one last look around to make damn sure everyone was clear. I looked down at the landing and could see Larson down there putting in a new eye in the haulback. So I held off giving the signal to go ahead on the strawline.

All three of us "pulled up a stump" to have a bit of a rest.

Immediately, the conversation turned to Freddie Hanson and Sleeping Beauty Mountain.

"Sam, fill me in about what you have been up to?" I asked.

Sam gave me a blank stare look and slowly turned and gave Tom a stern look. "You keep your mouth shut about what you hear me say," Sam bluntly told him.

Tom's body language changed. He took Sam's stern warning to heart as he began to fidget. "I will," he nervously committed to Sam.

Sam turned his attention to me. "Jed, I have been very busy. Most people don't know there is an old hidden trail into Sleeping Beauty from the coast; it was used years ago by our ancestors to access the ancestral burial grounds and to hunt and fish this area."

"No shit," I said. "I am not surprised."

Sam continued. "Myself and a few of the other dancers have been helping Freddie. We brought him food and kept him company some nights. We have also been doing some special ceremonies in the area. Ceremonies that call on our ancestors to protect the mountain."

"Ya know, Sam, when I was in the office this morning, picking up the bugs, the personnel man told me that company side-rods out and about on the claim said that they thought they heard what sounded like drumming and chanting coming from the mountain. They brushed it off as nonsense."

Sam smiled and continued. "An old Elder hiked into the mountain a little while ago. He spent a few days on the mountain. When he came back to the village in Duncan, all he would say is "It won't be long.""

We sat in silence contemplating the information Sam revealed to us. If I had learned anything recently it was to never underestimate what the Elders said. They seemed to be connected to a higher presence and see and understand things with an uncanny sense.

The silence was broken with the whistle on the machine. Slim gave us the signal to go ahead on the strawline. They were ready in the landing to start logging.

I blew three short and one short. "beep, beep, beep… beep." It signaled the engineer to go ahead on the strawline to run the haulback around and back to the machine to be hooked to the butt-rigging.

Slowly, the stawline started to move. Once the lines came tight, there was the puff of thick black smoke and a roar from the diesel engine on the yarder as Slim went ahead on'er.

The new chokerman was quiet and watched what was going on intently. Sam sat on a stump and waited for the riggin' to be tight-lined and skinned back to begin sending logs into the landing. His eyes had a distant look. He was unusually but noticeably calm. I worked with Sam a lot over the years and he generally was fidgety first thing in the mornings.

I looked down towards the landing and saw Pete busy as always. Slim had run the strawline in which pulled in the haulback, with its new eye, into the landing. Pete hustled over to unhook the strawline. With a neat flip he swung the slack haulback towards the butt-rigging. With shackle in hand, he proceeded to hook the eye of the haulback to the butt-rigging and scrambled out of the way. Slim tight-lined the riggin', and with a roar of the engine the riggin' was sent up the hill towards us. We could hear the choker bells and butt-rigging jingling as they came up the hillside.

My hand rested on the bug and I measured the chokers as they whizzed their way up the hill. With one short beep I stopped the dangling chokers. Instantly, Slim stopped the rigging.

We walked briskly into the turn. "Tom, you grab the back choker and head towards that short chunk of fir," I said and pointed. Sam needed no orders, he knew his job and took hold of the middle choker and backed out of the way, and waited for me to blow the signal to slack the rigging down so we could hook up the first turn.

I held the bug in one hand and the front choker in the other. I blew slack the mainline. Slim slowly eased the butt-rigging down. We all tugged on and grunted to set our chokers. Sam was done first so he went over to lend a hand to Tom. When they finished they headed out of the turn and waited for me. The fir peeler was large so I struggled to button up the snotty end of this kinked up inch and an eighth steel necktie. It was like wrestling with a large python snake!

I hustled out of the turn. "Fuck I'm out of shape," I mentioned to the guys as I stepped up and onto a stump next to them. With three short bursts of the whistle I blew to go ahead on'er. The butt-rigging moved slowly at first until the chokers tightened up, then Slim widened on it. The turn of logs bumped, slid, and channeled a groove in the dirt down towards the landing. Pete was Johnny on the spot to unhook the chokers so the rigging could be sent back up the hill to us for another turn. The loader operator swung his machine around and grabbed the logs, one at a time, and stacked them neatly; ready to load once a logging truck backed into the landing.

Slim tight-lined the rigging up and started to skin'er back, but stopped. Ollie had already checked the square guyline and moved on the back quarter. I saw him give Slim the hand signal that all guy stumps were good.

Beep, and the rigging stopped abruptly and we scrambled in to set another turn. This was how the morning went. Turn after turn of logs was sent into the landing. Custy was right - the fallers did a good job of bucking the trees they fell into logs. The logging went fast. We were soaked in sweat from the hard work. Surprisingly, Tom kept up with Sam and I as we set the pace.

After we ate lunch and started back up the slash to finish the day, Ollie too hiked up through the slash towards us, but stopped often to rest. Once he got to where we were he sat on a stump and waited for us to finish setting a turn.

Tom seemed to have gotten his side-hill legs. He beat us out of the turn. "This young fella is a keeper, Jed," Ollie said.

"Ya, he's getttin the hang of'er."

"Can you make do without him for a while? I need some help at the back end to set up the next road change."

"Go ahead and take him. We'll finish this road and head towards the landing. Do you need a hand stringing line?" I asked.

"No. It's going to be an easy change. Then we'll swap lines for the next one before I jump the lines over that big gully," Ollie said. "Then we'll put the scab-block on." He continued.

Tom buggered off with Ollie and Sam and I kept logging. We had to clean up the chunks and small logs that fell out of the chokers before we could change roads.

"The old prick is sure organized, ain't he," offered Sam.

"Yes he is. You don't work in the woods as long as him and not understand what needs to be done. It's instinctive. Even at his age he moves cat-like through the slash and fell and bucked. He is always on the lookout to make sure the logging is going smooth. Old loggers like him never miss a click," I told Sam.

Ollie and Tom were busy at the back end getting ready for the road change. Sam and I worked our way down the road we had just finished logging and cleaned up as we went. Once we were just outside the landing and there were no more logs or chunks to pick up, I blew for the strawline. Sam and I moved to the side out of the way of the lines and waited for Ollie and Tom to move the one back-end haul-back block and string strawline for the road change. Sam sat on a stump but I didn't. I stood with one foot up resting on a piece of wood next to Sam's temporary resting spot. It was my job to not let my guard down and keep a watchful eye and ear out in the event something went wrong.

We noticed that Custy had pulled into the landing in his pickup. He walked over towards the tower. Slim stood on the running board and greeted him. They talked for a couple minutes and Custy got back in to the pickup and buggered off. Slim summoned Pete and they too talked for a short bit. Something was up?

Pete turned and headed our way. He only climbed a short distance out of the landing, stopped, cupped his hands around his mouth and hollered up to us. "Custy's shuttin'er down for the rest of the day, Jed. Seems the dump is broken down and they can't unload the logging trucks. So once Ollie's finished changing roads, we're heading home."

I raised my hand in acknowledgement. It didn't take long for Ollie and Tom to finish their work and we heard Ollie blow go-ahead on the strawline. No sooner had Slim started to run the haulback around when he blew a shave and a haircut. That was the signal that we were done logging for that day. With that, Ollie and Tom headed towards the landing.

Sam and I had already made our way to the crummy and waited for the rest of the crew. As I untied my caulk boots Sam said, "Something I didn't want to tell you while Tom was around and keep this to yourself, Jed. Freddie Hanson is armed and told me that he will not be taken alive. And with Nick Ivanov on the run, our valley will not be the same any time too soon, Jed."

I sat in silence and contemplated what my Indian friend had said. I could tell by the tone of his voice and his body language that he respected Freddie Hanson but would still like to hear that Nick Ivanov was shot dead.

CHAPTER 24

Birds Eye View

Morning arrived quickly - too quick - and I found myself back on the crummy headed for camp. Being tired and worn out from the first day back at work, I had eaten dinner and went to bed. Day two at work would be as hard or harder. The mussels are sore and fatigued. So, like an engine on a cold day, it would take a bit once we started logging to warm up and work the kinks out.

The routine was always the same at camp. Once the town crummy pulled up to a stop at camp, a flurry of activity took place. Men scurried around. Some paused to talk with others or to Custy or another side-rod.

I noticed a new guy standing next to Custy. I stood next to the crummy with bugs in hand. Custy and the new fella came our way. "Jed, like you to meet the chaser," he said. "This is Vasko."

When Vasko reached out to shake hands I noticed a slight smirk on his face. Immediately I recognized this guy and turned my back to him and stepped up into the crummy.

This caught Custy by surprise and he approached and stood in the crummy doorway. "What the fuck's your problem, LaSal?" Custy asked bluntly.

As I tied my caulk boots, I looked up. "That fucker's Ivonov's cousin! He's part of the gang that's caused a lot of grief around the valley," I sternly told Custy. He knew by my tone that I meant business.

This was the first time Custy had seen me concerned and ticked off. "Well Jed, he's the only one we could find with any experience. So try and work with him, will ya?"

I nodded approval to Custy but I knew it wouldn't take much for the fists to fly. The ride out to the yarder was quiet. I was sure that everyone in the crummy sensed my dislike for the new chaser. Once we arrived, Slim got out and started the yarder and stayed in his cab. He too felt the discontent I had for this troublemaker.

The crew stepped out of the crummy to start the day and we all, almost at the same time, noticed some activity across the valley on the road below the tree-stand. Looked like a couple of pickups had pulled up into an old landing on the road. We watched as the people in those trucks got out, and from what we all could see, looked up towards the tree-stand and Freddie Hanson.

"Let's get at'er boys," ordered Ollie.

We all hesitated and lingered because we were curious about what was going on across the valley. From what we saw, it looked as though there may be a plan in place. The people in the trucks were interested in the area and how they may approach the tree-stand.

"Get your fuckin' ass's up the hill!" Ollie again ordered sternly.

We wasted no time and stepped off the road and into the slash and started to log. I could sense that both Sam and Tom were on edge because they never spoke a word. After several turns, the sweat rolled down our faces and out from under our hardhats. Our hair was soaked as if we had jumped in a shower.

I broke the silence. "Say, fellas. I know what went on this morning has everyone on edge but we have a job to do here so let's try and forget about who that fucker in the landing is and do our job. Otherwise, someone may get hurt."

"The only piece of shit that could get hurt will be Vasko!" Sam harshly said.

I was surprised by Sam's outburst. "I agree, Sam, but you heard Custy. He was the only experienced chaser he could hire."

"Maybe so, but this changes things for me. I like working with you and the rest of the crew. But I won't be able to work with that prick!"

I knew better than to push my luck and try and convince Sam to let it go, for now.

After our talk, the logging seemed to get back to normal, somewhat. We sent in some turns of big logs and it wasn't long before there was a load of logs ready to be sent to the dump. Red was busy positioning logs in the landing to put a load on. Larson was up at the back end. He had moved and hung a block and strap and sat on a stump to overlook the logging. He was a good Hooker and kept an eye out for his crew. Nothing got by the old prick.

I hollered up to Ollie. "We'll be done in a half a dozen turns or so!"

Ollie stood up on the stump. "Blow for a straw line extension!" he bellowed down to us.

We sent in another turn of logs. As it hit the landing, I blew three short and one long, which signalled the chaser to send out an extension. Vasko was nimble and never missed a step. It was apparent he knew his way around the landing. Vasko hooked up the staw line extension to the butt-rigging and Slim tight-lined it out, landing and skinned'er back to Ollie at the backend. We took time to rest as he pulled the extension up and coiled it at his feet.

There was no sight of the two trucks across the valley. As fast as they came, they were gone.

"Sure would be nice to know what they are planning," I said.

Tom, who was normally quiet, spoke up. "I heard the other day, at the coffee shop, the army was going to put an end to the tree-stand. The word on the street is that the government wants to put an end to it."

"Maybe so, but this issue has made the national news and has gained strength with grassroots people," Sam said confidently.

"Yes. I saw it on late-night national news, Sam," Tom said.

"One of the Elders told me that First Nations people from across Canada are going to come and support us," Sam informed us.

"I wonder what will happen to Freddie Hanson if the army storms the tree-stand?" asked Tom.

Sam smiled. I knew Sam knew Old Freddie and, with some help, had an ace in the hole. A backup plan in the event something like this happened.

Without a word, Sam stood up and fucked off down the hill towards the landing. I knew better than to try and stop him. "Watch this, Tom," I said. "If I were a betting man, I'd bet Sam stops in the landing and gives Vasko a-talkin' to."

"No shit. Sam doesn't like that guy. Don't be surprised if the fists fly," Tom said and gestured with his clenched hand.

"Sam's usually a quiet and kind person. This issue has a lot of people in the Cowichan Valley pissed off and on edge. It's also changed people, Tom. No matter what side of this issue people are on, siding with the Indian Band or not, there are some people whose thoughts cannot forget about the discrimination that has been revealed and brought to the forefront," I said to Tom.

"That's true, Jed. Discrimination has torn this valley apart. When will people wake up and understand we all have differences and we need to respect those differences. No matter what side you are on, no matter what nationality you are, people need to embrace and respect other people and cultures."

I didn't realize my young workmate thought about discrimination or this issue the way he did.

It didn't take Sam long and he was in the landing. From our vantage point, we had a bird's eye view. No one yelled or waved their hands, but the minute Sam approached Vasko, the fists began to fly! I was surprised at how well Sam could handle himself. He moved with the speed and cunning of a seasoned boxer, which didn't take long for him to dispose of Vasko.

With Vasko on the ground, we heard Sam yell, "Stay down!" as he shook his clenched fist at him. Vasko rolled over and sat up, but didn't even try to stand up. He knew he had met his match. Sam hesitated and stood over top of his quarry. Then, without a word, he turned and headed down the logging road. Sam was once again going to vanish into the timber.

Ollie blew for Slim to go ahead on the rigging. I stood up and waited to spot it. But Slim was out of the cab and stood on the deck of the yarder so he never moved the butt-rigging. He waited for a pickup that came up the road and stopped in the landing. It was one of the other side-rods, Ed. Slim and Ed talked for a short bit and then Ed got into his truck and fucked off.

Slim got back into the cab, but instead of skinnin'er back he tight-lined the rigging and blew a shave and a haircut. Tom and I looked at each other and knew that we were finished logging for the day. I motioned with my head to for us to move to the landing. So we started to make our way through the freshly logged slash to head back to the landing. Larson was already partway down, as he made his way through the fell and bucked timber.

Once everyone was on the landing, the crew gathered around Slim. "The company is shutin'er down. From what Ed told me the army is on the way out to the tree-stand. He has asked us to wait here until he radios us that all is clear on the mainline for us to head in."

Larson spoke first. "I guess the fuckin army is going to put an end to the tree-stand?"

"Not sure, Ollie. All I was told is we have to get the fuck outta here," said Slim.

We all sat in silence and watched across the valley. The parade of camouflage green army trucks was impressive. There had to be close to thirty vehicles lined out and headed up the branch road towards the tree-stand and Freddie Hanson. In the lead were two RCMP cruisers.

"Looks like there will be a showdown," said Tom.

"Don't know, but it sure doesn't look good. From what I have heard, Freddie's not going to give up without a fight," I said.

"If Freddie shoots first all hell will break loose. The army won't fuck around," said Slim.

"Never thought this situation would escalate to this point. This all could have been avoided if the company had changed their logging plans," said Red, the loader operator.

"Maybe not," said Ollie. "The Indians have been on the warpath for some time now. They are trying to protect their historic lands," he continued.

"You are right about that, Ollie. The government has refused to sit down and discuss this issue with them. So what are they to do?" I asked.

Ollie smiled, took his hat off and ran his hand through his hair. "Everyone loses," he said.

"Couldn't agree with you more," said Slim.

"Will it ever get back to normal?" asked Tom.

"Not sure what it will take, but this sure has divided the people in the Cowichan Valley. It will probably take years for people's memories to fade but it will never be forgotten," I said.

"Jed, where do you think Sam is headed? Surely he's not going to walk all the way back home to Duncan?" asked Tom.

"No, he won't head for Duncan. The one thing you have to understand is Indians like Sam are at home out here. They know how to survive in the woods. My gut is telling me that he will head for the tree-stand."

"No shit," Ollie said. "If you remember last time he fucked off he disappeared for weeks. No one saw him in town or any other place around the valley."

"I think he was helping Freddie Hanson. There's a rumour that the Indians have a trail into Sleeping Beauty Mountain from the coast," said Slim.

"It's the only way Freddie could have food supplied to him," said Tom.

"It's a long way to come in from the coast but the old Indian burial grounds have been there since before any roads were built in this valley. So you can bet they will have a trail into the mountain," Slim informed us.

I never said a word. There was no doubt that there was an old trail leading in and out of Sleeping Beauty Mountain, probably from the west coast of Vancouver Island. An ancient trail, used for centuries by the First Nations people. Could this also be an escape route for Freddie Hanson?

CHAPTER 25

Sam

The crummy ride home was quiet; not a word was spoken. We had been diverted at Camp 2, Caycuse. With the Army involved, our normal route to camp on the north side of Cowichan Lake was closed. So it would be a long ride into Lake Cowichan. Sure glad I had moved to Duncan. I had rented a room with an older couple. They fussed over me like I was one of their kids, cooking meals when I was around and entertaining me with stories when they were young and homesteading up in the Peace River area.

You could feel the tension in the crummy as we bounced along the gravel road. Usually most fellas would try and nod off on the ride home after working all day. But not today. Everyone sat staring out the windows, lost in their thoughts. My thoughts were of Sam and what he was going to do if he ran into the Army.

Lake Cowichan was bustling. There were cop cars stationed at every corner and, by the look of it, the army had taken over the area around the Riverside Hotel. They must be using the large parking lot as a staging area.

The silence was broken when old Larson spoke up. "Looks like a fuckin' war zone."

"No shit," I said.

"Wouldn't want to be up in the tree stand now," said Vasko.

No one acknowledged that he even spoke. I didn't think it would take much for someone, including me, to kick his ass.

The crummy came to a stop. It looked like they had a checkpoint set up. The door opened and a guy in full army gear poked his head in. He never said a word. He had a look at who was in the crummy and slammed the door shut and stepped out of the way.

"Guess he doesn't like loggers," Tom said and started to chuckle.

"Fuck'em," said Larson.

The loader operator riding in the back hollered. "Go fuck yourselves!"

"I wonder what he would have done if any of us had brown skin?" I asked. "Chances are he was looking for Sam.

"No shit," said our old hook tender, Ron. "I would bet they know that Sam has been helping Freddie Hanson out throughout this whole ordeal. And they know that if he isn't on one of the crummies heading to town that he'll be out in the woods. I wonder what the chances are they'll go after him?"

"Good luck with that one," spoke up Tom.

"They will never catch him while he's out in the bush. Sam is more at home out in the woods than any other place," I said

"They'll catch that fuck'er," said Vasko. "And when they do I hope they throw him in the clink!"

Again, no one in the crummy acknowledged he had spoken. It was all I could do to restrain myself from not kicking his ass. Right here in the crummy! We all knew that Vasko was loosely connected to the Ivanov gang and nobody wanted anything to do with him.

The crummy stopped at the gas station in the middle of Lake Cowichan. Ollie Larson got off and Vasko took this opportunity to get off the crummy and head out. I guess he didn't like the cold shoulder he got from the rest of us.

Ollie came back, opened the door and looked in. "You take it easy, Jed. I will see all of you once this bullshit is over."

Tom gave Ollie a nod and I said. "You bet, Ollie. We all hope this ends soon."

Old Ollie turned, shut the door and buggered off. He headed in the direction of the liquor store. We all knew that he would be piss'in it up while he wasn't working. Ollie was a hell of a good logger and I'd learned a lot from him while out on the side hill. But when he was not working, he's sure to be pissed up. I had never partied with him but had heard stories about how my old hook tender liked to party. His reputation, both on and off the job, was legendary.

The crummy started to pull away and a cop car pulled up and stopped us. Two cops got out and approached the crummy.

The door to the crummy opened and a cop leaned in and looked at us. "LaSal, we would like to speak to you," the one cop asked.

Not saying a word, I got up, grabbed my packsack and stepped out of the crummy. My gut instinct told me that I might be staying with them for a while.

"Hop in, Jed. There are some people that would like to question you about Sam," the one cop informed me.

We walked over to the cop car. "Sure thing. Not sure what good it'll do but if I can help, I'm in."

The ride was short. The cops and the army had set up a staging area at the crossroads as you entered Lake Cowichan and there was a checkpoint at the turnoff to Greendale Road as well. My thoughts were about our valley and how it had changed: a roadblock on the Silver Bridge and the cops with a command center set up in Duncan. A protest treestand on Sleeping Beauty Mountain, with Freddie Hanson in it standing guard. I couldn't help but think to myself, will the Cowichan Valley ever get back to the peaceful place that it is?

"Follow me, Jed," the cop said. I followed.

I could tell by the setup here that they meant business. I wonder why? I thought.

"Hello, Jed," greeted a familiar voice. Elsie John was a comforting but unexpected sight. With her being here I knew that the fellas from the Army were going to ask me to help out. They brought in Elsie so that it would be hard for me to turn them down.

"Hello, Elsie," I greeted her back. "Do you know what's going on?"

"It's Sam. They have cornered him out in the woods but can't get him, so they have asked if someone he trusts could go and talk to him."

"Do they know where he is?" I asked with a puzzled look. "There's a lot of areas for Sam to hide out in.

Knowing him, he probably hiked through the woods and over the mountain, giving them the slip."

Sam was good in the woods. He enjoyed spending time out in the bush, wandering around, checking things out. The army personnel would have a difficult time trying to find him, let alone convince Sam to give himself up.

"Hello, Mr. LaSal," greeted a fella dressed in the usual army uniform.

Before he could say another word, I spoke. "Why in the hell do you want to capture Sam?" I asked bluntly.

"We are going to be running some patrols and operations in the area. We want to clear out any civilian personnel."

"Look. Don't bullshit me. You are looking to capture Sam and get some information from him," I snapped back.

"You are right. I won't bullshit you. We need Sam's knowledge of the trails in and around Sleeping Beauty. Our orders are clear. We must remove the tree stand and Freddie Hanson. If Sam has any information that will help, we need that information," he said.

"What makes you think I can convince Sam to come in and talk to you?"

"We have to try something. Any information may correct this situation," he said with a forlorn look on his face.

This guy knew all too well that they would never catch Sam and he was right. Sam knew this country well. He had been going there since he was a young lad. Sam told me that his old grandpa used to take him to Sleeping Beauty Mountain to maintain the ancient gravesite. They also used to hunt and fish in the area. He said that at one time, large groups of his people used to frequent the area to catch and dry deer meat. Sam said that according to the Elders, this area was and always would be a special place to go for their people. The one thing Sam never told me was how they travelled there. All I knew was they had very old trails that their ancestors used for thousands of years. And that most people would think those old trails were only game trails used by deer, elk and bears.

I looked at this military man. "I'll do it under one condition."

"What's that?" he asked.

"Let me take a crummy and go on my own."

"That's not what we want to do," he said.

"I don't give a fuck what you want. It's the only way I will help," I said with a confident look. I could tell by the look on his face he wasn't used to being talked to like that, but I stood my ground.

"Look, LaSal, I'll give you the freedom to go look for Sam and try and convince him that the right thing to do is to give himself up and come in. Let him know he's not in trouble and that we just need his help."

"If I can find him I will let him know, but he will make his own mind up. I know Sam. He will do what he thinks is best. It's late in the day but I would like to go now," I said.

"Fine. We will take you to camp and then you will be on your own. If you cross us we will arrest you too," he informed me. I just grinned at him.

The ride to camp was quiet and once we arrived the camp was quiet too. Not a civilian was around. There were, however, several cops and a bunch of army personnel and vehicles. I got out of the little army Jeep and headed for the marshalling yard. The crummies were lined up as usual, so I strolled over to a crew-cab to see if the keys were in it. I started it and checked to make sure it had gas in it and took off for the woods. I turned on the camp radio to listen if there was any chatter, but all was quiet. It seemed odd to be heading out to the woods all by myself and even odder to not see any other crummies and logging trucks on the mainline road. I could not help but wonder what the hell I had gotten myself into now.

As I turned up Branch 36 there was a herd of about twenty or so elk crossing the road. The majority were cows. Their calves tagged along behind them. There were a few small, immature bulls and a couple of larger ones. I stopped, got out and looked over the bank. I knew that the big, dominant herd bull would be lurking somewhere in the brush. I could hear the herd as they moved through the underbrush. A couple of the calves bawled for their mom's.

My eyes scanned the area and I was listening intently. I wanted to see the big boy, the large bull that was the leader of this group of elk. With no sign of him, I decided to continue on my way to try and find Sam.

Branch 36 was steep and full of switchbacks. It was also on the opposite side of the valley, with Sleeping Beauty Mountain right across from me and would be a better place to watch the goings-on around the tree stand and Freddie Hanson. As I came around this one long corner, there he was! A very large bull elk stood in the middle of the road in all his majesty. I was face to face with him. He knew he wasn't in any danger as he stood his ground in the middle of the road. Two clouds of vapour streamed out of his nostrils. It looked like he was trying to wind me as he kept breathing in deep and then snorted out through his nose. Dark in colour, his coat was slick with not a hair out of place. I counted the tangs on his thick and heavy rack. There were seven on one side and eight on the other. One of the tangs had its tip broken off. He took half a step forward and spread his back legs. Then he started to take a long piss. I couldn't help but think he was probably letting me know that he was the dominant one on the road. After he finished pissing, he held his head a bit higher, turned and disappeared over the bank and down the hill. I, too, started on my way again.

The daylight faded so I planned to find a spot high up on the mountain where I would have a vantage point to look around and call out for Sam. I knew he would move during the cover of darkness. I also knew that if I lit a fire he would see it, or at the very least, smell the smoke.

I pulled over at an old large landing. It had lots of good firewood and was logged on the low side of the road so there was no timber to block my view. Before I got out of the crummy I blew the horn. I used the same signal we used on the side-hill when we were logging and it was quitting time - a shave and a haircut. I blew it twice. If Sam heard this signal, he would know it was a logger.

I got out of the crummy and hollered, "Sam, Sam, it's me, Jed!" My voice echoed through the still of the mountains.

My next chore was to build a big fire and wait. I chopped kindling with the double-bladed rigging axe. Then I chopped up a few short chunks of fir that still had the bark on it. It wasn't long before I had a warm fire going. I carried over a block of wood to the fire and used it as a seat. All was quiet except for the crackling of the fire and a light breeze. Strangely, the breeze was coming from the west. The valley ran almost north south. And throughout the years of working in the valley, I had never seen the wind come from the west. It seemed to be coming from the direction of the ocean and right over the top of Sleeping Beauty Mountain.

I sat and enjoyed the peace of a warm fire. The breeze enveloped me in a comforting way. I felt relaxed and at ease, something I hadn't felt in a long time. The sun was setting so it was very low in the sky and almost directly behind Sleeping Beauty. The sunrays skimmed the top of the mountain, casting long shadows, which gave that side of the valley a mystical appearance. It felt as though the Bakwus' was going to appear. I thought my mind was playing tricks on me because I thought I could hear a distant aboriginal drum echoing a soothing rhythm. It was so real that I stood up and had a better look around. But as quickly as I heard it, the drumming stopped. I thought, damn, my mind was playing tricks on me. Or was it? My thoughts turned to Freddie Hanson. I couldn't see the tree-stand or him but I knew he was across the valley, vigilantly standing guard in the tree-stand. Even though I didn't like the guy, I gave him credit for standing his ground and not giving up.

Daylight faded and the fire had burned down to coals so I thought I would sleep in the crummy. There was no sign of Sam so there was no point in staying up all night. As I lay on the front seat of the crummy a thought ran through my mind about the drum I had heard and the strange breeze that came over Sleeping Beauty. I smiled to myself. I wondered if the Bakwus" would show up?

CHAPTER 26

Sleeping Beauty Shuddered

I was startled from a deep, restful sleep by a loud bang on the hood of the crummy. "LaSal! Get yer fuckin ass out of bed!" hollered a muffled voice.

I sat up immediately and recognized my workmate and friend, Sam. He had a shit eatin grin from ear to ear. "Sam, you fuckin' pecker-head!" I yelled back at him as I stepped out of the crummy. I wiped the sleep out of my eyes. "It's about time you showed up. Did you see the fire last night?"

"I did. But I was busy and it's a long hike up this mountain."

Sam munched on a piece of dried salmon and he reached into his packsack and pulled out another piece and, with an outstretched hand, offered it to me.

"Want some?" he asked.

"Yes, thanks."

I took the salmon, gripped it and bit a chunk off. "You know, the army and cops have been looking for you," I told him.

"Yes, I know. They don't have a hope in hell of catching me out here. I'm just as at home out here as I am on the rez," my friend said with a grin. Sam had a look of confidence that only came from knowing that he was right. Sam wouldn't get captured if he didn't want to.

"They asked me to help them, Sam. So I thought I'd come out, find you and find out what the hell is going on. I hope you know I would never turn on you. I just don't want them to go to the extreme and possibly hurt you, Sam."

"Thanks, Jed. I've been watching them drive up and down the valley and some of the side roads. They don't have a clue. Yesterday they drove not more than fifty feet from me. I was sitting on a stump in the slash on the high side of the road. They drove right by me. Never even looked sideways, just straight ahead down the road. I laughed like hell. I knew from that point on I was safe and that those fucker's would never catch me," Sam informed me.

"I think they are getting ready to storm the tree-stand and arrest Freddie Hanson and put an end to the protest on the mountain," I said.

Sam stood silent and contemplated what I had said. He knew that if the army attacked Freddie that he wouldn't stand a chance. If he fought back by shooting his rifle, he wouldn't live.

"Jed. I saw Nick Ivanov up the valley." He pointed up the small but prominent valley that ran up and between Sleeping Beauty Mountain and Mt. Freeman. "He never saw me. I know he's on the run from the cops but I think he will still do what it takes to get the company logging again so the log barge can be loaded and head south."

"I bet he has gotten a lot of pressure from the people he deals with, Sam."

"Yes. I bet there must be a lot of money ridin' on the drug shipment. Getting the shipment of drugs hidden on that barge and headed south must be a priority for Ivanov," Sam said.

"They will catch him. This valley, in the big scheme of things, is small. And he'll make a mistake sooner than later," I said.

"You may be right, Jed. But when I hiked in from the coast, on the ancient trail, I noticed a different boat anchored in a little cove. It just may be there to help Ivanov escape?" Sam shared his thoughts.

"Possibly. Rumour is that his gang connections are far and wide. If he goes down, he'll probably take others with him," I said.

"That could be why that boat is anchored on the coast. They will let Ivanov take care of Freddie Hanson and then make their get-a-way," Sam said.

"And then the company will start logging and the barge will be loaded and Ivanov's drugs will be headed south," I said to Sam.

Sam calmly looked me in the eyes. " The Old One had a vision. I have had a vision. Everything's going to be fine," he said.

Out of respect, I never asked Sam what his vision was. If he thought everything would be OK, then I trusted that his vision was a good one. Being an aboriginal dancer, Sam, through dance and chanting, would enter into a state of upper consciousness where he heard and saw visions. Visions have been a part of Aboriginal mystical folklore and culture forever. At times, these out of body visions scare them, comfort them and guide them. But most of all, aboriginal people believed in them, steadfast! Most people would think he was crazy. I didn't. How this would sort itself out, I didn't know. The one thing I had learned as I rambled along on this unwanted journey was that the long arm of discrimination knew no boundaries. Over the last number of months, it had raised its ugly head throughout our little valley.

We refuelled the fire and sat around it and ate dried salmon and shared day-old thermos tea. The view was awesome. It was starting to cloud up in the far distance, out over the Pacific Ocean. The cloud was unusually dark. The wind was light and came from the direction of Sleeping Beauty, straight across the valley to us. The air had an eerie feel to it and even though the wind was light, the standing timber swayed gently, almost ghostlike. You could feel the energy in the air. It was as if something strange was going to happen. I looked at Sam. He was as calm and confident as I had ever seen him. I believed Sam knew that something big was going to happen. He sat in silence.

The more the sun came up, the more pronounced the darkening sky became. The light wind in the trees picked up too. The timber now swayed gently in the steady pronounced breeze, which caused these sentinels to creak and groan, reminiscent of a ghostly gathering. We sat in silence, no need to talk, and felt the cool wind on our faces. The smoke from the fire swirled up and away from us. The air had an unusually distinct freshness to it.

The soothing but mysterious wind kept us captivated on the horizon and the ominous darkening clouds that came our way.

Suddenly, this entrancing silence was broken by the roar of a vehicle which sped around the corner and into the landing. The driver slammed on the breaks and brought the intruders to a skidding halt.

Sam instantly bolted! I stood up as the four doors of this dark green vehicle were quickly opened. Four guys dressed in army uniforms speedily ran towards where Sam had gone over the bank and down the hill. One guy hollered, "Stop! Stop! You are under arrest!" Sam stopped, turned around and gave them the bird, then disappeared silently into the standing timber.

I stood there, silent and with a smile on my face. I knew my friend wouldn't stop and I also knew these guys wouldn't have a hope in hell of catching Sam.

"LaSal!" one of them bellowed, as they walked up to me. "Why didn't you stop him from leaving?" he asked.

"Go fuck yourself," I immediately snapped back at him. "Who the fuck are you to think I could or would stop Sam. Go catch him yourself!" I hollered back at him.

"You were sent out here to find him," one sarcastic prick said.

"I was. And I did find him. But no one said that I had to hold him or stop him from taking off into the bush. If you want him that bad, he went that-a-way," I pointed.

These guys recognized that I was not going to give in or take any of their shit, so they turned and walked over to the edge of the road where Sam had disappeared over the bank. All four stood and stared down the hill in the direction Sam went. I overheard one of them say to the others that he wasn't going into the bush to chase that Indian.

Without a word or even another look in my direction, they went back to their pickup, got in, turned around and took off back down the road, headed in the direction of the camp.

I headed for the crummy that I had driven. I stopped at the fire and grabbed my thermos and the little bag of smoked salmon that my friend shared with me. I took one last look around and got in the vehicle, started it, turned it around and started to head back to camp. I no sooner rounded the corner when another green army vehicle came right towards me. So I stopped and rolled down my window in anticipation that one of those jerks would want to talk with me.

I was right. The one on the passenger's side got out and approached the vehicle. "LaSal. Turn that pickup around and head back up to that landing at the end of the road."

I never said a word and did what he asked. There was no point in arguing with these guys. Besides, they were packing guns.

They pulled their vehicle up and stopped in front of mine. They all got out and approached me. Now, this was a sight to behold. They were all dressed like they were going to war. Helmets and all! They also carried army issued rifles and one guy packed a handheld radio. I could hear the muffled chatter over the airwaves.

"What can I do for you fella's?" I asked nonchalantly.

The one guy with the most stripes on his arm walked right up to me. "You will have to stay here, Mr. LaSal," he said.

"Why?"

"The suspect, Nick Ivanov, has been spotted on the other side of the valley. You know the spot, that little valley that runs next to Sleeping Beauty Mountain. He is in the timber and we've been told to arrest him, but he is armed. For everyone's safety, we are not letting anyone in or out of the valley. Do you understand?"

"I do."

He turned to the other guys. "Two of you stay here and guard LaSal. Make sure he doesn't leave and if you have to, arrest him," he ordered.

Two of these fellas stayed behind to watch me. And the other two took off back down the hill. It was full daylight and even though it looked like a storm was brewing, we had a good vantage point to watch this capture unfold. I walked over to the fire, put another chunk on it and sat down. I noticed that one of the guys had gone over to the crummy and took out the keys.

They stepped up to the fire. "I can be trusted, fellas. I have no desire to disobey what your superior has ordered. Besides, we will have a front-row seat," I said.

They thanked me and took up a position with one next to the fire and the other just on the outside of the landing. I guess they didn't trust me or what I said to them.

I poured another cup of day-old tea and offered the guys next to me some smoked fish. He turned it down. I no sooner took a sip of my tea when we heard gunfire. It came from the general direction of where Ivanov was supposed to be hiding out.

Pop, pop, pop. More shots came from up the creek that ran down the little valley. Then all hell broke loose. Shots rang out from several different angles in a semi-circle around that valley. It looked like Ivanov was pinned down, with no way out. I could see the flames that shot out of the army rifles. Scary shit! There was no way in hell that I would want to be challenging that well-trained army personnel.

The shooting continued with more and fast rounds from the army than from Ivanov. But I could tell that Ivanov had moved further up the mountain, probably to afford him extra cover. Not one shot came from the tree stand. I began to wonder if Freddie Hanson had left the area. Maybe Sam snuck into the tree stand and got Freddie and headed out. But logic told me that Sam didn't have enough time to do that. So it left me contemplating what the hell was going on with Freddie?

More army personnel showed up. There were many army vehicles lined up along the mainline logging road that ran along the valley bottom. There was only this road that led in and out of camp, so unless Nick Ivanov climbed up and over the mountains to escape, he had no hope in hell to make his getaway.

The shooting had slowed down, with only the odd shot. The one thing I had to hand to Ivanov was he had given these trained men a run for their money and stood his ground. But I wondered for how long?

The wind had picked up and those dark clouds that rolled in from the coast were now right over Sleeping Beauty Mountain. The sight of this impending storm was both disturbing and beautiful. The bright sun-dogs shone out from under the dark menacing clouds and stabbed the ground, which illuminated round singular spots that dotted the mountain and forest like a laser gun. My two guards sat mesmerized. So much so that I could have slipped silently over the edge of the landing and into the timber and disappeared the same as Sam had done. But there was no point other than showing them that I could escape from their clutches.

The wind was now circling much like a tornado and the sun-dogs were zapping the ground with each crack of thunder. They started to change in colour to a vibrant red, green and black. And these ominous and mysterious clouds enveloped Sleeping Beauty. I looked over at the two army fella's and they were transfixed and seemed almost unable to move. They stared in awe at what was unfolding before our eyes.

The mysterious fog-like and freaky cloud enveloped the mountain and right in the middle there was what looked like a face. Was it Bakwus' or maybe Tsonokwa? I stood in silence. The ground shook with each bolt of lightning and roar of thunder.

"Maybe we should get the fuck out of here?" one of the army fellas said.

"What the hell is going on?" asked the other.

I never spoke a word. There was no need to. I knew that at any moment we would be headed for camp. Those fellas looked scared as hell!

There was an extremely loud crack of thunder that blanketed the mountain. And the ground on our side of the valley shook violently. There was definitely a face within this violent storm. It was ever-changing. One minute it looked like Bakwus' and the next it looked like Tsonokwa. These mystical aboriginal creatures had long brownish hair that hung down past their faces and flowed smoothly in the violent wind that surrounded their position in the storm. They were coloured as if someone, some ancient aboriginal person, had painstakingly painted them and then placed them in the middle of this wild storm. We could feel the excess energy in the air and even though it was in the middle of the day, it was almost dark out!

We noticed that the contingency of army vehicles and people were headed out and back towards camp. And maybe it was a good thing they made a run for cover. It started to rain as I have never seen out here. The raindrops rebounded off the gravel road and the water ran down the roads and ditches until they were a torrent.

"Let's get the fuck out of here!" I suggested.

The one guy tossed me the keys to the crummy and we wasted no time in quickly getting in and headed off down the road towards camp, too. I sped down the road, but only as fast as it was safe. Nothing in the storm had changed; it only got worse. With each crack of thunder, the road shook and we could hardly see through the windshield it was raining so hard. We hit the mainline and never hesitated or stopped to see if any other vehicles were in our way. I poured the coal to her and sped off towards camp and hopefully safety.

The noise of this magnificent storm was behind us as we pulled into camp but we could still see that the storm had intensified both in the wind and ground-shaking thunder. I parked the crummy in front of the cookhouse. It looked like every army or cop vehicle was back in camp. There were uniformed people everywhere.

We went into the cookhouse. I headed straight for the coffee pot and noticed that there was a big pot of soup right beside it. The tables were full of uniformed personnel, both RCMP and army.

Even though we were a long way from the storm that seemed to be centralized right over Sleeping Beauty, we could see and hear this mega-storm from the cookhouse. And we could feel the ground vibrate slightly, too. There was an unusually hard and loud crack of thunder. The greenish-blue lightning lit up camp and the cookhouse like a Christmas tree. And the ground rumbled and shook. It was as if we were experiencing an earthquake. The rumbling grew stronger. The cookhouse windows rattled and shook. Everyone was silent and looked around at each other to make sure we were all fine. With another mighty blast of wind and thunder, the noise from up the valley at Sleeping Beauty was unbelievable. The ground in camp shook violently.

As quick as it came, it was gone. Most of us stepped outside and looked up the valley. The dark mysterious clouds and rain were gone. All was quiet!

Sergeant Maxwell was in the cookhouse and spoke up. "I think we just had an earthquake or something."

Custy offered to jump in his pickup and go have a look around. Sergeant Maxwell ordered two of his men to go with him. They were gone for about forty-five minutes when they pulled back into camp.

We gathered around them in the marshalling yard. "You would not believe what we saw," Custy spoke up. "There has been a major slide and over half of Sleeping Beauty Mountain is gone. We could not get close to it because the slide came down and into the valley and part way up the other side. The creek and small lake at the bottom of Branch 36 are gone. They are filled in with the slide."

"I guess the tree stand, Freddie Hanson and Nick Ivanov will have perished," said Sergeant Maxwell.

"They will have been buried by half a mountain. I don't imagine they survived this event," said Custy.

"Did you see any sign of them, Custy?" I asked.

"No. Not a sign of any living thing out there, Jed. We'll have a better look around once the area is checked out to make damn sure it's safe," Custy said.

"Well, it wouldn't surprise me if they both survived," I said.

"I guess that ends the tree stand," said Sergeant Maxwell.

"I guess it ends the logging of Sleeping Beauty, too," I informed him, with a shit eatin grin.

CHAPTER 27

Prince of the Woods

I woke up early and wow did I sleep. With all the goings on the past few weeks I was due for a good nights sleep. I must have slept a solid ten hours. I decided to head down to the Green Haven Cafe and have breakfast. It is also a good place to hear what's going on around the valley.

It didn't take long for me to make my way to the popular cafe. The waitress seated me and poured a steaming hot cup of coffee, and took my usual order of beacon and eggs. She had left a copy of the local daily news paper.

The headlines said it all "The Road Block Has Ended" and the story took up the entire front page and have of the second page. And just like that our valley just may get back to normal, I hope. The accompanying story went on to inform people about how there was a giant slide that decimated almost half of Sleeping Beauty Mountain. And because of the devastation the logging company could no longer harvest the timber in that area. According to the article there was hardly anything left within that immediate area, nothing but tones and tones of slide debris. There was a very small lake at the bottom of the valley right next to the mountain, it was apparently filled in and there was no sign that a lake even existed.

The First Nations were quick to realize that with nothing to log, it would be pointless to continue with the roadblock. So as the word spread quickly about the massive slide, they dismantled the roadblock immediately. All but the turned over school bus had been removed. And even that was soon to be cleared away. Nevertheless, traffic was once again travelling over the Silver Bridge in a single lane.

When the Band Chief was asked for a quote, all he said was. "The mountain has spoken. It is our belief that it was being protected by the Bakwus' and Tsonokwa. Our ancestors can now rest peacefully. Never to be desterbed again."

When the logging company was asked about their logging plans they said that it was abundantly obvious that no logging would take place in or around Sleeping Beauty Mountain and area. They went on to say that there was plenty of timber in other areas to harvest and that the company was now gearing up to make those changes and get back to work.

My breakfast had arrived so I put the paper down, took a sip of coffee and started to eat my meal. It was nice to sit quietly and eat. And it was also nice to know that our valley will start to heal from this awful ordeal, even though there are still questions that need to be answered. Like, what happened to Freddie Hanson and Nick Ivanov? Did they perish in the slide? After all they were on the mountain when it let go. And Sam. Where the hell is Sam?

I no sooner finished my breakfast when I felt a light tap tap on my shoulder by a gentle hand. It was Genevieve. "May I sit down?" she asked.

"You most certainly may," I said with a smile.

"Jed, it will be nice to have things back to normal, won't it? This matter has really spit the people in the valley."

"Possibly. But time heals. So it won't take too long and the Cowichan Valley will once again be the laid back place we grew up in, Genevieve."

"I sure hope you are right, Jed. Has the company said when they will go back to work full time?" she asked.

"I don't know. But I would imagine as soon as possible because they have lost a lot of time over this issue and it has hurt the bottom line for the company."

"Let's head down to the Silver Bridge and have a look," Genevieve suggested.

"Yes, let's go take a look and I will also have a look at the river, maybe we could take some time to go fishing one day soon?" I said.

Genevieve smiled, which was her way of giving me her approval.

"Before we leave I have something for you," I told her.

Genevieve gave me a curious look. I reached into my pocket and pulled out a small case. I then slid out of the booth and kneeled down on one knee. I opened up the case and showed her an engagement ring. "Genevieve, will you marry me?"

Without hesitation she looked down at me. "Yes... yes I will, Jed."

I put the ring on her finger. Genevieve stood up and gave me a huge hug and a long kiss! The people in the cafe erupted with congratulations and hand clapping. It was a bit embarrassing to say the least but I had planned this for some time and was oblivious to my surroundings with the moment, that is until the cheers started.

The Silver Bridge was only a few blocks away so we decided to walk over. We crossed the railroad tracks and cut through the mall parking lot and then took one of the old fishing trails that lead to the river. I have used these since I was a kid and once on the trail I always picked up the pace in anticipation of arriving at the river. We were close and could hear someone whoop and holler.

My instincts told me the person was fishing. I was right. It was Elsie, our Elder friend.

We stood back because she had, by the look of it, a nice fish on. She glanced our way but kept playing the large fish. I turned to Genevieve. "Looks like a nice brown trout."

'It sure does, Jed," said Genevieve. We watched as Elsie played the fish expertly. The fish took off down the river, using the current to its advantage. Our Elder friend flipped her fishing rod down and sideways, which guided the large and strong brown trout out into the middle of the river and stopped its run. The fish immediately broke water and flew through the air at least three feet above the surface of the water. And with a loud ka-sploosh hit the water on its side, which sent a plume of water high into the air. The battle went on for close to fifteen minutes, with long runs both down the river, across and then back up the river. Elsie stood her ground. We could see that this elder had experience and had played fish like this many times.

"I have never caught a big brown like this one," I mentioned to my fiancé. "I have fished this river since I was a little boy. Caught many, many fish including brown trout. But none the size of this one."

We watched as Elsie played the fish out and netted it, all by herself. Then much to our surprise Elsie gently lifted the fish out of the water, took out the hook and turned to show us the fish, and then put it back. She hung onto its tail with the head pointed up stream and wiggled it. The giant brown trout regained its strength and slowly swam away. We were awestruck.

Elsie smiled and stepped towards us. "It was a female and probably full of eggs and getting ready to spawn," she said.

"Nice catch, Elsie!" Genevieve complimented her.

"I just love to come here and spend the day fishing. If I catch a nice rainbow I will keep it for supper. One of my favorited meals is baked rainbow trout. What brings you two to the river."

"We thought it would be nice to check out the river and the Silver Bridge, now that the blockade is gone," I said.

"Yes, it is nice to have the blockade gone and hopefully everything will get back to normal. We are still in shock about Peter's death. This should have never happened. Have they caught Nick Ivanov yet?"

"No, not yet. He was in the Sleeping Beauty Mountain area when the slide took most of the mountain out, so he may be buried under all the rocks and debris," I informed her.

"Is there any sign of Sam?" asked Genevieve.

Unexpectedly, Elsie said, "He is at the police station right now. And I think the logger guy, Freddie Hanson is there with him."

Gen and I were in disbelief, but not surprised. Sam knew every inch of that area and all the ancient trails too. So if anyone could make it out he could. But what about Nick Ivanov? He would not have known that there were trails that lead out to the west coast and possible freedom by escaping by boat on the open Pacific Ocean.

"We are going to move along, Elsie and leave you to your fishing. Good luck and I hope you catch your dinner. One of these fine days we'll stop by your place for a cup of tea," I said.

"Jed. The Old One had a vision about how this was going to happen. She told me that a great storm was going to take place and that the Bakwus' and Tsonokwa were going to protect the ancient ones in our old burial grounds on Sleeping Beauty Mountain."

Elsie went back to her fishing, she had her back to us but stopped and turned and looked over at Gen. "So, Genevieve. When is the big day?" She asked.

We were both surprised because we had not said a word to Elsie about our engagement. But nothing escapes Elsie. She must have notice the ring on Genevieve's finger. "We haven't set a date yet, Elise. But I will promise you that when we do you will be on the top of the list to contact and invite," said Genevieve.

"That would be wonderful. Congratulations!" Elsie said.

We both smiled at our friend, no words were needed. Genevieve and I headed down the trail towards the Silver Bridge to see for ourselves that the blockade was gone. Once we arrived we could see a tow truck there dealing with the turned over bus. There were cops everywhere but the army was gone. Genevieve was leading the way and she turned up the side trail to that lead to the sidewalk along the bridge. I noticed that Sergeant Maxwell was on the bridge directing traffic.

"I hollered and gave him a wave and he made his way over to us. "Hello, Genevieve. Hello, Jed. How are you two doing?"

"I am well, Mr. Maxwell," Genevieve said.

"Me too," I said. "I hear that Sam and Freddie Hanson are at the police station?"

"They are. There are investigators taking statements from them, Jed. We flew over the entire area around Sleeping Beauty mountain in a helicopter looking for them and Nick Ivanov. The area was devastated and there was no sign of any humans so we thought they got caught in the massive slide. And then without warning those two walked right into the police station on their own. In regards to Ivanov, he probably was caught in the slide. We are going to do a few additional searches but truthfully, there is so much destruction and debris scattered everywhere, and in particular where Ivanov was, there is absolutely no way he would have escaped death."

"I would like to see Sam, and Freddie for that matter, too. Could you let them know that we will be over at the Doghouse Restaurant?"

"I will," and he turned and walked over to his cruiser. I swatched as he spoke on the radio. It didn't take long and he was on his way back to us.

"Jed, I am going to walk home and show mom and dad my new ring. By the sound of it you will be going back to work in a day or two, so I will call in the evening," Genevieve said I gave my future wife a hug and kiss and she headed towards her house.

"Jed. I was able to get a message to those fella's for you," said Sergeant Maxwell.

"Thanks," I said and headed in the direction of the restaurant. It was only a couple of blocks away.

As soon as I walked in the restaurant I noticed a women who was sitting at the long counter. She had her back to me and with one elbow resting on the top of the counter. Her huge head of red hair gave her identity away. It was Freddie Hanson's girlfriend. I turned and seated myself at a booth. I was going to have a cup of coffee and wait to see if Sam will show up. There is a good chance that Freddie will be coming here too. Especially because of his girlfriend being here.

I ordered a coffee and a piece of pie and thought I would go to the bathroom before the waitress brought my order.

As I reached out for the door handle, the door suddenly opened. And low and behold standing right there in front of me was Freddie Hanson. We momentarily stood in silence and just stared at each other. I broke the silence. "Hello Freddie," I greeted him with my hand out to shake his hand.

"LaSal. You fuck head. I thought that Ivanov's gang would have gotten you," he said, but started to chuckle and reached out with his hand. We shook hands like old lost friends. But it was probably because Freddie was stuck up in the tree stand for so long that it was nice for him to talk to and see a familiar face.

It was a bit awkward. "Good to see ya, Freddie."

"Well you can thank Sam for that. If he had don't come and insisted that we get the fuck out of the area, the slide would have buried me," Freddie said.

"Speaking of Sam, do you know if he is coming here?""

"Don't know but he got the message."

"What's your plans, Freddie?"

"When I leave here I am going to catch a plane for a camp up the coast. I need to get-out-a Dodge, if ya know what I mean. Sam will fill you in about everything, Jed. I have to get going."

I could see that Freddie was very impatient so I never pressured him for information. "I do know what you mean. The people in the valley were split over this issue and they knew that you were up in the tree stand. So, ya, its probably best for you to head outta here for a while."

Freddie stuck out his hand, again. "Well Jed. Good luck and we'll see you down the road."

We shook hands and that was it, Freddie Hanson and his girlfriend walked out of the restaurant. He to another logging camp up the coast and his girlfriend will in all likelihood stay here where she lives.

I just sat down to a hot cup of coffee and pie when Sam walked up to my table. "How's it goin LaSal?" asked my friend.

"Fancy seeing you here, Sam. I thought I was going to get a call to come and bale you out of jail. I am well, how about you?"

"Good, very good, now that the mountain has spoken. Maybe now we can get back to normal here in the valley. I was getting a little burnt out," Sam said.

"Me too, Sam. Me too. So, tell we what the hell happened out there?" I said with anticipation.

Sam ordered a coffee and a plate of fries-n-gravy. "Well, let me tell ya. It was a hell of a ride my friend. After I took off down the hill when those army boys showed up, I headed straight across the valley to the mountain. A few cops and mostly army guys were all around me but they didn't have a hope in hell of capturing me. Those ass-wholes have a hard enough time walking around on the road let alone out in the bush, so I teased them a little. I let them get a glimpse of me and the chase was on. I needed to lead them away from the trail that I use to get to the tree stand. The dumb fucks fell for it. They stepped off the road and spread out and chased me most of the way up the main creek that runs through the valley. It was the funniest thing you ever saw, Jed. I could hear them hollering, "he's over here. And several hundred years over another holler, No he's this way. I hid under a windfall and they walked right by me and continued up towards the head of the valley. I then backtracked and took the trail up through the timber to the treestand."

"Did you hear the shots or see Nick Ivanov?" I asked.

"I sure did. When the shooting started I took cover because they weren't that far away. I was standing behind a large fir tree and noticed something moving through the timber. I waited patiently and was rewarded. It was Ivanov! He was packing a rifle so I stayed hid and watched him head up the mountain. He looked like he knew where he wa going. But as it turned out that whole side of the mountain is gone because of the side.

So unless he made it through to the top of the mountain and found our ancient trail that leads out to the west coast, he's buried," Sam explicitly said.

"Did the cops and army guys clue in and turn around and come looking for you?" I asked.

"No. I could hear them yelling at each other until the weather changed. The minute the dark clouds rolled in over us and the weird lightning started all was quiet from them. Next thing I know they are in their vehicles up on the main road and headed in the direction of camp. Good thing though, considering what happened. Being high up on the mountain I had a good vantage point to watch the procession of vehicles speeding down the road. I got a good chuckle out that, Jed."

'Did you experience the same thing I did when the storm started?"

'What do you mean, Jed?"

"I saw what looked like a greenish blue fog and odd looking lightning bolts that looked like they hit the ground. And within all the chaos two faces appeared, Bakwus' and Tsonokwa."

"I don't need to answer that, Jed. I knew something was going to take place because the Old One warned me. She said now was the time to go get Freddie Hanson and get off Sleeping Beauty. So I did. He was reluctant to come with me so I said to him, fine, stay here and die, the choice is yours and I took off up the ancient trail towards the coast. It wasn't long and I heard a noise behind me. It was Freddie coming hell bent for leather, he even passed me without saying a word. And he looked scared."

"I guess it goes unsaid what sacred him, eh."

Sam lifted his head up from his plate of fries. "The Bakwus' works in mysterious ways." My good friend told me.

"Continue on Sam," I asked.

"When we reached the junction where we would vier off the main trail and make a long and dangious decent down to the sea and my waiting boat, that's been on anchor. I stopped to take one last look around, so I meandered down the main trail a little further. With the rain it was a bit muddy so I scoured the trail for any sign. And low and behold there it was, one lonely footprint! I am not sure why there was only one but whoever made that footprint was in a hurry."

"Do you think it was Nick Ivanov, Sam?"

"I can't say one way or the other, Jed. But what I do know is that it is very possible that he made his escape via the same route I have been using. If not, he's dead and buried under Sleeping Beauty mountain! We no sooner stepped onto the beach when all hell broke loose behind us and in the distance back towards Sleeping Beauty. The noise was deafening and the ground under us shook violently. I knew and Freddie knew, that something catastrophic had just happened. So we wasted no time in getting in the dingy and headed out to my fish boat and got the hell out of there, fast."

"Wow! That's scary shit, Sam. What made you to decide to go to the cop shop?"

"Both Freddie and I had nothing to hide and did nothing wrong, so we thought it was best to go and let them know what we saw and heard. We were right. The cops took our statements and said that we didn't do anything wrong, it was Ivanov they wanted."

"Without a body living or dead, it will remain a mystery," I said.

"You are right. The cops told me the file will remain active until such time that they obtain proof one way or the other."

"The rumours and gossip have already started. Some say he perished and others are saying he escaped. My gut feeling is telling me that we haven't seen or heard the last of Nick Ivanov!" I told Sam.

"I sure hope you are wrong my friend. I have to get going, thanks for the coffee and lunch, Jed. And we'll see ya in camp. I hear we are going back to work tomorrow."

"Yes, let's get out of here, Sam. I am going to try and get a good nights sleep. Tomorrow will be a good day. It will be nice to get on with life around this valley. Thanks for taking the time to let me know how it all went down out there. And yes, I will see you in camp."

Morning came fast and I found myself headed for camp on the town crummy. Everyone was in a stellar mood to be going back to work knowing that we will now have no interruptions, I hope. When we arrived in camp I wasted no time in heading to the bush crummy.

The old box style crummy was nice and warm because the woods boss starts them before we arrive at the marshaling yard in the morning. This is particularly comforting on dull, overcast rainy days. The heater was noisy, but it generated this warmth and also added to the smell of old logging gloves and rain gear that were laid or hung around it to dry. It was always nice to put on warm gloves first thing in the morning as you headed out and onto the side hill. I took my regular place by the door and started to tie my logging boots up in preparation for the day's work. They were also nice and warm and dry to start the day. I poured myself a small cup of tea to sip on until we headed out to the woods. There was a bit of idle chatter from the rest of the crew, mostly about the weather or what they had done the night before. Sometimes there would be teasing and kidding around with each other. And there was always someone ready to tell a good but often dirty joke. The crummy was not so crummy, but rather it was a safe haven on these nasty rainy days, of which we had many. I looked out the side window and noticed the Bullbucker, Old Simms. He had walked over from the fallers shack and was talking to Custy the woods foreman. After a minute or so of arm waving, head nodding and talk they turned and came our way.

The door of our crummy opened. "LaSal. The Bullbucker wants to talk with you. Grab your packsack and step out here, will ya," Custy informed me.

I did as he asked. "What up?"

The Bullbucker held in his hand a new wedge belt with a loggers tape on it and brand new falling wedges in the pouch. "How's it going, Jed?" he asked.

"Good," I said.

"The company has decided to break you in falling, Jed. Ya ready?"

You bet I am, looking forward to it," I eagerly said.

The Bullbucker reached out and handed me a small metal whistle. "Here," he said. "Put this on your suspenders. I don't think I need to tell you what this is for. And he motioned with his hand for me to follow him over to the fallers shack.

I turned to Custy. "Thanks Custy. We'll be seeing ya," I said.

Custy nodded his head of approval. He turned and started to walk away, but stopped. "Hey LaSal. Looks like you are now going to be a Prince of the woods?" he said.

I too stopped and turned to face him. "We'll see," I said. I also took the time to attach my fallers whistle to my suspenders and then slung my newly acquired wedge belt over my shoulder and proudly walked over to the fallers shack.

To be continued

Next novel

SOOSER

The Prince's of the Woods
Jed LaSal goes Falling

GLOSSARY OF LOGGING TERMS

This glossary is by no means a complete explanation of all logging terms. I have explained the very basic logging terms of a high lead logging operation within this novel.

BLOCK
A large steel pully used for guiding and diverting logging cables

BUTT RIGGING
A series of shackles and swivels that chokers are attached. The butt rigging is shackled between the mainline and haulback logging cables.

CAULK BOOTS
A logger's traditional footwear. They are heavy-duty leather boots with "caulks" or spikes on the soles to enable a logger to grip the logs or steep ground while working.

CHASER

He is the man in the landing that unhooks the chokers when the turn of logs are skidded in by the yarder or tower. His duties also are splicing logging cable, sometimes bucking logs, making sure the landing is safe, neat and tidy. He also helps with the hooking up of the logging truck's trailer. The chaser has many duties not listed here.

CHOKER

A length of steel cable with a ferrule on each end and a sliding bell fastener. One end is attached to the butt rigging. The other end is flung over and around a log and hooked into the bell. The log is now "choked" Three or four chokers are attached to the butt rigging.

CHOKERMAN

Most people start as a chokerman when entering the woods to work. A chokerman is the lowest paid and under the direction of the Hooktender or Rigging Slinger.

COOKHOUSE

A place where loggers eat their meals while in camp.

FALLER

Known as the "Princes of the Woods" they have one of the most dangerous jobs in the world, cutting down the big timber and they also buck the felled timber into log lengths. Many a faller didn't make it home after work.

GUYLINE

Is a large diameter cable used to secure the logging tower. There are six guylines on a logging tower. There are two front guylines, two square guylines and two back guylines. The two front guylines and the two back guylines are also called quarters, IE: front quarter.

HAULBACK LINE

A haul back cable was used in high-lead yarding. It was used to pull the but rigging and mainline back out into to fell and bucked timber after a turn was unhooked in the landing.

HIGH-LEAD

First used around 1911, this system became the most commonly used logging method on the BC coast. The high-lead logging systems evolved from the mast rigging used on sailing ships.

HOOKTENDER OR HOOKER

A Hooker is the undisputed boss of a logging "side." He is the most experienced and took orders only from a Woods Foreman or Camp Manager.

LANDING

The area around the tower where the logs are landed and loaded out on logging trucks.

MAINLINE

The heavy logging cable that pulls the turn of logs into the landing.

MOLLY-HOGAN

Is a strand of straw line and is weaved into a circle through two separate lengths of strawline; which joins the two lengths of straw line so they don't come unhooked. There are many other uses for molly-hogans.

RIGGING CREW ON A HIGH
LEAD LOGGING SYSTEM

Are the various jobs on the tower. Tower or Yarder Operator, Chaser, Hooker, Choker-Men, Rigging Slinger, Loader Operator.

ROAD LINE

The area in the fell and bucked where logs are hooked up and sent to the landing.

SETTING

The entire area or block of timber being logged. There may be a number of these settings in various areas within a logging camp.

SIDE

One yarding "side" or tower with a crew. There are usually several sides in a logging camp.

SNOOSE AND SNOOSER

Copenhagen is the preferred brand of chewing tobacco by all loggers on the coast of British Columbia. A logger will pull out a small round can of snoose from his back pocket, give it a slight tap on the lid with his hand and then "dip" into the chew with his finger and thumb. He will put this chew between his bottom lip and gum.

Most would spit the juice out as it accumulated in his mouth, but many didn't. I have even watched some old-timers keep a chew in while eating lunch. Snooser is an old logging term for a logger.

STAW LINE

Is a lighter utility cable used for several things in logging. IE: because it is lighter it is used to pull other heavier lines. It was also used to make "Molly-Hogans."

DAN LAFRANCE

Logger, Faller, Rancher, Cowboy, Guide Outfitter, Trapper, and Writer, Dan has lived the life, all of his life, that he writes about. Since the early 1990s, he has had articles and short stories published in various Newspapers and Magazines. Snooser, the Adventures of Logger Jed LaSal, is the start of the Snooser series. Dan and his wife Cathie continue the adventitious lifestyle they have lived since they were married. They currently live on their forty-foot sailboat, exploring the coast of British Columbia.

www.rambleology.com